MW00465534

WICKED CONJURING

CLAIMED BY GARGOYLES BOOK 1

Wicked Conjuring
Claimed by Gargoyles, Book One
Copyright © 2022 by Sarah Piper
SarahPiperBooks.com

Published by Two Gnomes Media

Cover design by Luminescence Covers

All rights reserved. With the exception of brief quotations used for promotional or review purposes, no part of this book may be recorded, reproduced, stored in a retrieval system, or transmitted in any form or by any means without the express permission of the author.

This book is a work of fiction. Names, characters, places, businesses, organizations, brands, media, and incidents are either products of the author's imagination or are used fictitiously. Any resemblance to actual events, locations, or persons, living or dead, is entirely coincidental.

v5

E-book ISBN: 978-1-948455-62-6
Paperback ISBN: 978-1-948455-63-3
Audiobook ISBN: 978-1-948455-68-8

BOOK SERIES BY SARAH PIPER

∼

M/F Romance Series

Monstrous Obsessions

Vampire Royals of New York

∼

Reverse Harem Romance Series

Claimed by Gargoyles

The Witch's Monsters

Tarot Academy

The Witch's Rebels

GET CONNECTED!

I love connecting with readers! There are a few different ways you can keep in touch:

Email: sarah@sarahpiperbooks.com

TikTok: @sarahpiperbooks

Facebook group: Sarah Piper's Sassy Witches

Twitter: @sarahpiperbooks

Newsletter: Never miss a new release or a sale! Sign up for the VIP Readers Club:
sarahpiperbooks.com/readers-club

CHAPTER ONE
JUDE

This many centuries into my cursed immortal existence, only three things have the power to remind me I'm not dead: fucking, fighting, and killing. Give me the full monty on the same night? Stuff of wet dreams, that. Bloody brilliant.

But thanks to the mortal feds crawling up our arses after a botched hit job on a crooked judge—not *my* botched hit job, mind you—Drae's got us on a real tight leash. Been a whole twenty-seven days since I broke a bone or spilled so much as a *drop* of someone else's blood, and he's still sore at me over the last bloke I put in the ground.

Human. Bastard abso-fuckin'-lutely deserved it too, but I digress.

As for my *favorite* way to pass the time?

Well.

I flick the lighter and hold the flame to the tip of the

joint, sucking in a deep drag of witchweed. Across a pitch-black, dead-end street in Brooklyn's Park Slope neighborhood, a square of golden light spills from a third-story brownstone window. A dozen crows hang out on the eves just above it, flapping and tittering like old codgers fighting over dominoes.

Those fucking birds show up here every night, same as me.

Watching. Waiting.

I'm pretty sure the little scarecrow inside knows she has an audience, too. But she's a nice girl. Too polite to shoo us all away.

Lucky for us.

A shadow moves behind the sheer curtains, and I keep a close watch in anticipation of what's to come.

She's undressing for bed—my favorite part of the show.

Stripped down to her bra and panties, she saunters past the window, shaking out that gorgeous mane. Dark waves spill over her shoulders, covering her perfect, oh-so-suckable tits.

It's the color of crow feathers, that hair. Shot through with a few silver locks that set off the brightest blue-green eyes you ever saw.

Unfortunately, I only ever got to see them up close the one time. I was heading back to the office from a late-night coffee run when I caught her feeding her crows in Madison Square Park. Some pervert was harassing her, but I chased him off real quick. After that, I chatted her up a bit.

Offered her the fancy-arse almond joy latte I'd bought for Auggie and made her laugh enough times to get the sound of it stuck in my head forever.

Before I knew it, I was half the fuck in love with her.

So a bit later, when she thanked me for the coffee and said she had to get home, I did what any self-respecting half-lovesick arsehole would do.

I followed her.

Never did get her name, but I've been showing up here like a stalker every night since, hiding out in the shadows across the way and hoping for a peek.

Yeah, I know. Who's the pervert now, right? Fuck it.

As for the shitbag who messed with her in the park... Would you believe it's been *exactly* twenty-seven days since anyone's heard from him? Poor chap. Although, there's a human skull on my desk presently serving as a paperweight that bears a striking resemblance. Coincidence?

The curtains flutter and her silhouette glides past once more. Every graceful movement makes my dick hard as stone, aching to sink inside her wet little cunt and make her beg for all the filthy things she never even knew she wanted. Needed.

And oh, I *will* make her beg.

In the end, they always do.

Her lights flick off. I hold my breath, heart slamming against my ribs.

Please come back, darling. I've got so *many naughty, delicious plans for us...*

Seconds later, the gauzy curtains part and I try not to squeal like a tween boy who's just discovered the dark side of the internet. I take another hit of the witchweed, then flick the butt into the gutter, my attention lasering in on that window. Her face fills the glass, blue-green eyes luminescent in the dark.

Searching. Always searching.

Perhaps she's looking for her white knight from the park, wondering if I've finally come to claim her.

Fearing it, as she damn well should.

The thought of making her tremble sends a dark thrill straight to my balls, and my human glamour ripples with the ancient magic holding it together. The real me is eager to come out and play.

Her neighborhood is quiet at this hour, all the happy little babies tucked into bed by their happy mums and dads, so fuck it. Keeping to the shadows, I give my surroundings a quick scan, then drop the glamour and let my true form stretch to fill the darkness.

If my little scarecrow saw me like this...

I nearly bust a gut at the idea. If the seven feet of muscle and massive leathery wings didn't scare her the fuck off, the horns and tail would certainly get the job done proper.

Gargoyles? We're not supposed to exist. Problem is, we do. What's left of us, anyway.

But my girl doesn't need to know that yet. All in due time.

These days, patience is a severely under-cultivated skill. Me? I'm old school. Reckless and impulsive most of the time, sure. But when something's worth the wait, my patience is damned legendary. Just ask any traitorous cunt who's had the pleasure of regaining consciousness after a beating, only to find himself chained up in my basement with his bodily fluids leaking onto my floor.

Death by a thousand cuts is the ultimate test of a killer's patience.

And this girl? Fuck. She's the reason patience is such a bloody virtue.

So as badly as I want to fly up there, smash through that window, and put her on her knees for me, I'll wait until she's ready. Until I'm *sure* she won't run off. Even if I have to show up here again and again, play our little game every night for another month. Six. Hell, I'd do it for a whole year if I had that much time left.

Drae doesn't think so. According to his calculations, unless we break the fucking curse, we've got about two months before it all goes to shit. And trust me when I say there are *plenty* of things worse than death for an immortal fucking monster.

Like being trapped in our statue forms for eternity— fully conscious—rather than just turning to stone while the sun's out.

Like being forced to watch the rest of our kind get pulverized into dust.

A rusty old ache stabs at my heart, but I don't have time for it.

Right now, there's only one rock-hard thing about me, and it's got *nothing* to do with some bullshit dark fae curse and *everything* to do with the girl upstairs.

Resting her forehead against the glass, my little scarecrow slides a hand down along her bare belly, hooking a thumb into the waistband of her panties. *Mmm*. White lace, this pair. Tiny pink bow at the top.

Back and forth her naughty thumb glides, driving me wild with every stroke. Her eyes drift closed as she tips her head back and sighs, one hand pressed flat against the glass, the other working its way lower, her back arching just so.

I'd give just about anything for a glimpse of her thoughts. Does she know I'm out here? Does she get off on the idea of being watched?

Does she have any idea what she's fucking doing to me?

I swear to the fucking devil I can almost *feel* her touch. Her small hand wrapped around my dick, eyes wide and scandalized as I command her to get on her knees, open her mouth, and...

Just fucking take *it*...

Pulling my wings close around me, I fist my dick with a tight grip, my gaze never leaving that window. That fucking girl.

Her eyes have haunted my dreams all month. Not even the feds or Drae's worries about the curse can break the spell this girl's got me under, and I don't want them to.

From the moment I laid eyes on her in the city, I've wanted her.

And one way or another, I'll make her mine.

Her fingers continue their quest, finally dipping inside the panties as her mouth parts on a soft little moan only a supernatural beast could hear at this distance.

Grateful for my highly attuned senses, I stroke myself harder, faster, still imagining the feel of her soft pink lips, her velvet-smooth tongue, the scrape of her teeth as she takes me all the way in...

That's it, darling. Just like that. God, you're so fucking good...

I fight the urge to close my eyes, focusing entirely on her. On the fog of her breath against the glass. The smudge of her damp handprint. The pretty way her cheeks darken with lust.

And—most enticing of all—the desperate, wet sounds her greedy little cunt makes as she fucks herself for me, faster and more frenetic with every stroke, drawing back to circle her clit before diving inside once more...

Fucking hell.

A sheen of sweat glazes her upper lip. Suddenly, I want to lick her, and my mouth fills with the imagined taste of it —a mix of sweet and salty that has my balls tightening, heat racing through my veins, heart slamming in my chest as I fight to keep breathing, and then...

"Fuck!"

When I come for her, it's hard and fast and messy, and her answering gasp of pleasure echoes right through me, connecting us on a fucking *soul* level as she trembles behind the window and rides out the waves of her pleasure.

Then, just as quickly as it all began, it's over.

With a deep sigh, she presses her forehead to the glass and closes her eyes, sliding her hand out of the panties.

Again, I imagine the taste of her. The way she'll moan my name as I wrap a clawed hand around her throat and suck those fingers clean, one by delectable one.

Such a good girl...

Still gazing up at her beautifully flushed face, I grin.

For now, I'll let her rest. But tomorrow night?

Tomorrow night, I'll bring her a ring. Hand-carved, of course. Lovingly crafted from the bone of a man who once tormented a young girl in the park and was never heard from again.

My grin stretches wider. She won't be able to resist.

I'll make sure of it.

"Until tomorrow," I whisper. "Sleep well, scarecrow."

Overhead, the old crows finally take flight, and I stretch out my wings, leap into the air, and chase them all the way back to Manhattan.

CHAPTER TWO

WESTLYN

The wedding hasn't even started yet—not for another hour —but I already hate everything about it.

My hair is twisted into braids so tight they're making my eyes water. The damn corset is crushing my will to live. And this dress? A black lace tragedy vomited straight out of a gothic romance novel about a damsel trapped in a castle on a very high cliff, desperately awaiting her avenging white knight.

He never shows, of course.

Typical, right?

There's no avenging knight in my story, either. Only a groom I've met a grand total of twice and a family eager to cast off the freaky, impotent witch-girl born without any actual powers.

Yeah. Did I mention the wedding I'm dreading is mine? Granted, the word "mine" feels like a stretch in this scenario considering the only thing they let me choose was my lipstick color—Blackberry Dream, naturally—but the fact remains.

In twenty minutes, the limo will arrive at the hotel to whisk me away to Thornwood Cathedral in lower Manhattan. Beneath its renowned gargoyle-topped spires and candlelight chandeliers, I'll take my final steps as *Miss* Westlyn Avery, twenty-two-year-old wandless witch and corvid-loving bachelorette, and magically become *Mrs.* Hunter Forsythe, wife of the heir to the shadow magic society, daughter-in-law of the two most powerful mortals this century has ever seen.

Then—perhaps just as magically—my father's gambling debt will evaporate.

Poof!

A familiar rage simmers, but I refuse to let it boil over. It's not Dad's fault my mother died giving birth to me and he got stuck with a lemon for a kid. A lemon who cost him buckets of cash wasted on private magical schools that couldn't teach me and pointless consultations with every so-called supernatural "healer" on the east coast, only to be told time and again I'd never cast a spell, break a hex, or amount to anything extraordinary in my life.

My only hope, they all agreed, was to marry well.

Quite a death sentence to hand a ten-year-old and her single dad. No wonder he started gambling.

Blowing out a breath, I cast off the lingering resentment and dig through my makeup bag. Like most parents who get in way over their heads, Dad did the best he could with the resources he had. So if all it takes to free us from the constant death threats and beatings from his "collectors" is me accepting my destiny as a piece of garden-variety arm candy for an elite mage nearly twenty years older than me... well. What choice do I have?

Besides, even if I wanted to turn my back on my blood and run, where would I go? Dad's my only living relative. I've got a high school diploma, no money of my own, no *magic* of my own, and zero connections.

I don't even have my own phone.

Pathetic, right? If my life was a Tarot card, it'd be the Eight of Swords. Tied up and trapped, no escape.

"Don't give me that look, Luce. At least I can still rock a dark matte lip like a fucking *boss*." I waggle my eyebrows at the raven perched on the bathroom vanity and apply the lipstick. Then, brandishing the tube like a tiny dagger, "They can take my freedom, they can take my hopes and dreams, but if they want my lipstick, they're gonna have to kill me first!"

Lucinda buries her head under a wing, totally unimpressed with my theatrics.

Tough crowd.

"Bright side?" I cap the lipstick and drop it back into the bag. "Getting married means I'm no longer fated to become the Brooklyn Bird Lady who wanders the streets feeding cheese sandwiches to crows and cackling at the neighborhood kids."

This gets a little caw, and I rub the spot between her wings with my thumb, making her squint in pleasure.

"It's true. Brooklyn Bird Lady is the avian-obsessed equivalent of Crazy Cat Lady, an honor already taken by Edith Zelasko and—"

"Westlyn, who on earth are you speaking to?" The shrill voice cuts through the hotel suite like an ax to the skull as my stepmother barges in to the bathroom, smashing the last of my pre-wedding peace to smithereens. Lucinda squawks and makes a beeline for the open window in the bedroom.

Not for the first time, I stare out after her and wish on every star in the sky I could follow her. Just jump out that window and sail over the East River, over Brooklyn and Long Island, all the way across the Atlantic. I wouldn't stop. Not until I got to England.

Eloise would find me, though. She always does. That's just how shadowmancers are.

Now, dressed in a blood-red mermaid style gown only slightly less macabre than mine, holding court in my hotel suite like the regal dark queen she fancies herself, she curls her lip and glares at me. Seriously glares. Like my choice in feathered friends is a personal affront to her good sensibilities.

"You and your birds." She crosses the room and slams the window shut, then the curtains, blocking out the bright moon. "I hope you said your goodbyes tonight, Westlyn. A mage like Hunter is unlikely to tolerate your idiosyncrasies.

He certainly won't coddle you the way your father and I have."

She says this as though they're a single force unified in their life's purpose to raise a Proper Young Witch. But Eloweasel, as I like to call her when I'm feeling petty, is a relatively new edition to the family. They've only been married for three years. I'm pretty sure she's got one foot out the door, anyway.

That's what happens when you marry a man for his once-prized name, only to discover his name is about as valuable as the pigeon shit you dodged on the walk over. Why she's so invested in *my* happily ever after is beyond me. As long as we make it through the ceremony, Dad's debts will be eradicated and the alliance between our two families made official—that's the deal he struck with Hunter's father, the Archmage. Whether Hunter hates my birds or my lipstick or even the sex? Completely irrelevant.

"Well?" I force an enthusiastic smile, ignoring her comments as well as the dread bubbling in my gut. "How do I look?"

She rakes her gaze over my entire body, from the braids her personal stylist created right down to the hem of the dress her personal seamstress designed, then back up again. Her answering smile doesn't reach her beady brown eyes, but I'll take the fake smile over the genuine scowl any day.

Fussing with one of my torturous hairpins, she says drily, "Aren't you a sight."

It's not quite a question and definitely not a compliment. I wait for her to elaborate. She doesn't.

"Oh!" Tearing her attention from my hair and yanking out a few strands in the process, she casts a frantic glance around the suite. "Where's the bouquet? It was supposed to be delivered at six p.m. sharp!"

"It's—"

"Incompetent fools. I'm telling you, Westlyn, if you want anything done right in this life, you have to do it yourself."

She whips out her phone and jabs at the screen. I manage to stop her mere seconds before she goes full-on Karen on some poor, unsuspecting florist.

"They delivered it earlier," I say. "But I asked the woman at the front desk to come take it away. Whatever flowers they used, I'm pretty sure I'm allergic."

"Allergic?" She presses her hand to her heart and gasps. Clearly, this news has ruined her weekend. "You don't have any allergies. You're vegan, for the love of the Morrigan."

Resisting the urge to roll my eyes and recite the long list of the allergies I've suffered with since childhood, I say, "As soon as I took a whiff, I got dizzy. The longer they sat in the room, the worse it got. I seriously felt my throat closing up. Lucinda didn't like them either—she squawked the entire time they were in here. And not her happy squawk, which is slightly more—"

"*Westlyn.*" That muscle in her jaw ticks. The one that

always tells me I've done something supremely offensive before she even says the words.

"It's not that I don't appreciate your efforts," I rush to add, turning up the wattage on my smile. "They really were beautiful. I'm sorry. Sometimes my body just... just *reacts* to things. I can't control it."

"Nonsense. That's just the jitters talking. Now, pack up your things. The limo will be here any second."

"But I—"

She cuts me off with a raised hand, already dialing the front desk.

It's not worth getting upset over. Not worth taking a stand. What's the point? Before the night is over, I'll be officially transferred from one controlling family to another, just like a car or a boat. When I wake up tomorrow, the only things that'll be different about my life are my name and the scenery.

While Eloise makes arrangements to have the flowers placed in the limo ("Carefully! Those flowers are worth more than your life!"), I pack up my toiletries and take one last look in the mirror at the girl formerly known as West Avery.

And suddenly, all I can think about is my mom. My *real* mom.

Growing up, I spent a lot of time convincing myself it was just the *idea* of a mother that I missed. After all, I never met the actual person. How could I miss someone I never even laid eyes on? Never touched?

But tonight, right now, I miss *her*. The woman whose voice I never got to hear outside the womb. Whose hugs and kisses I never got to feel. Whose turquoise eyes and slightly crooked smile and naturally silver-streaked black hair I supposedly inherited, even as her legendary magic skipped me.

My throat tightens around a knot of emotion. I never knew the woman who gave birth to me, but I *do* know this: lemon or not, she would *never* have allowed me to marry someone I didn't love. Not even to wipe out the family debt and get in good with the big guys.

Gazing at my reflection, I find no trace of the man who traded away my future happiness. No hint of his dark eyes, his blond hair, his prominent nose.

Mom gave me this beautiful face. This smile. The wanderlust that keeps me awake at night. The hope in my heart that refuses to die, even when things are at their most bleak.

The only things I inherited from my father were his mistakes. And now, I'm paying for them.

With a dull ache in my heart, I press my palm to the mirror, covering the sight of my reflection.

Eloise was wrong.

It's not the birds I need to say goodbye to tonight.

It's me.

CHAPTER THREE

DRAEGAN

"I need every assurance you miscreants will be on your best behavior tonight." I fasten my cufflinks and pour another glass of cognac—a pointless attempt at soothing my nerves after pacing the sacristy for an hour failed to do the trick. "No one leaves this room until I'm convinced you won't make a fucking nuisance of yourselves."

Rook offers a silent nod, his attention focused on the cathedral security feeds he's monitoring via his tablet. Augustine, busy arranging his artfully mussed hair in front of an antique silver mirror, ignores me altogether.

But Jude?

Fucking Jude.

Seems the bastard polished up his most menacing grin tonight, all for the special occasion of pushing my buttons. As dapper as he looks in formal attire, the sight of that unhinged smile sets my teeth on edge—a warning of trouble to come, no doubt.

"Now, Draegan," he practically coos, dark blue eyes sparkling like sapphires. "When have we *ever* been less than perfect gentlemen?"

Rook scoffs before I even get the chance. "Would you like that list divided by century, category of offense, or resultant body count? I've got spreadsheets, Jude. *With* color-coded tabs."

"That so?" Jude plucks the tablet from Rook's hands, grin stretching as he scans the screen. "What color's the tab for the time I threw your arse from the bell tower and watched your head split open like a melon on the street?"

"What? You've never—"

"I'm bored and in a mood. Best not to give me a reason, eh?" He shoves the tablet back into Rook's hands, then swings that crazy-eyed gaze my way. "Remind me again why the fuck I'm wearing a suit and giving up a perfectly fine Saturday night to attend a high-society bullshit wedding for a couple of high-society bullshit dickheads I've never even met?"

Summoning the last of my patience, I set my glass on the vestment cabinet and return his glare. "Because the Archmage of Manhattan is marrying off his only son, and he requested the presence of our esteemed company. Therefore, I thought it best if—"

"Lennon *Forsythe?*" Jude asks. "Shoulda known. You've been glued to him for months."

"I have my reasons."

"Care to share with the class?" He folds his arms across his broad chest, brow furrowing. "For decades, Forsythe was barely a blip on our radar. Then out of bloody *nowhere* you're spending all your time with him, practically sucking his cock, nary a word about your endgame... What gives?"

"Sucking his cock. Right." I nearly laugh, recalling all the exhausting efforts I've put in with the Archmage these past few months. "If only it were that simple."

"So all the late-night meetings, the dinners, the private tours of our properties—it was all because he wanted to lease Thornwood for his kid's big night?"

Our firm—Blackmoor Capital Group—owns the cathedral, along with a great many other historical buildings in the city, religious and secular alike. For the sake of historical preservation, most of our properties are closed to the public, reserved only for so-called "high-society bullshit" events.

Expensive bullshit events. Keeps us just legitimate enough in the eyes of the law, and the mystery and exclusivity surrounding our firm and its true purposes have given way to more than a few depraved rumors.

Kings of the underworld, some say. The men of shadow and stone. Only ever seen at night, well after sundown. Cold and untouchable. Deadly. And, of course, filthy rich.

Most mortals fear us, even if they don't understand why our presence makes their skin prickle, their heartbeats uncomfortably erratic.

To supernaturals and spellcasters, we appear as fae, just as our original dark fae punishers intended.

Gargoyles, after all, are a myth. One the fae would like to keep hidden in the mists of time, lest we reveal *their* secrets as well.

Everyone loves a good story. As for which parts are true? Irrelevant.

For what is truth but the story shouted by the loudest voices from the tallest rooftops?

"The Archmage isn't leasing the cathedral." I uncork the bottle of cognac and pour another glass. "The tours were my idea—Forsythe and I have a shared interest in the preservation of historical magical artifacts."

"Charming." Jude rolls his eyes. "Will you two lovebirds be picking out curtains and china patterns soon, too?"

"When he mentioned his son's wedding and the family's difficulty in finding the right venue," I continue, ignoring the dig, "the opportunity I'd been working on for months finally presented itself. I offered him the use of Thornwood, and in return, he extended us an invitation. I assured him we'd be delighted to attend."

Jude circles his face with a finger. "Does this look like my delighted-to-attend face?"

"Well, *I'm* delighted." This, from Augustine, who finally tears himself away from the mirror. Settling into one of the velvet-cushioned bishop's chairs lining the wall, he says, "I love mage weddings. Witches are hot as fuck."

"You can't rail the bride, asshole," Rook says. "Not in

front of so many witnesses."

"Do you know the best part about a hot witch bride?" Augustine offers a beatific smile, looking every bit the regal clergyman, save for the carnal hunger in his eyes. "Hot witch bridesmaids. And they're always looking for an excuse to ditch those ugly dresses."

Rook laughs and shakes his head, but Jude continues to glower, his usual fire burning brighter, aching for a target.

Of the four of us, Jude was never going to win any awards for the fine arts of discipline and restraint. It's what makes him my best torturer and most lethal killer, but also my weakest link. His impulsiveness is something I've learned to mitigate over the centuries, but lately he's become downright volatile. It's as if some restless demonic entity has taken residence inside him, setting his muscles ablaze with a constant need to break something. Anything.

Whether it's because I've forbidden him from carving up bodies until the latest mess with the feds blows over, or something else entirely, I've no idea. But if there's anything I won't—*can't*—tolerate in my organization, it's instability. We haven't the luxury of screwing up and getting noticed. Not anymore.

Still, he's not wrong to push me. There was a time when we had no secrets among us, no side projects. Yet I've told them nothing of my meetings with Forsythe. Nothing of his importance to our greater mission.

To our lives.

Not because I don't trust them—nothing could be

farther from the truth.

I simply couldn't risk getting their hopes up again. Not until I knew for certain.

I reach for the bottle and glance at each of them in turn, wishing I was a bit less sober for this conversation.

Bloody hell. Of all the things I miss about being human, the capacity to get thoroughly shitfaced on a thoroughly good bottle of booze is tops on the list. The sheer quantity of alcohol a gargoyle requires to feel even the *briefest* tingling in the extremities... Well. Our monthly liquor bill rivals the GDP of more than a few small countries.

I pour another glass anyway, ever hopeful. "Despite Jude's insistence that getting on one's knees is the pathway to a lasting friendship, offering the cathedral seemed like the more dignified alternative. Now, I realize there are a dozen things you'd rather be doing this evening, murder and mayhem chief among them, but I need you here. We've all got a part to play."

At that, I retrieve three more glasses from the vestment cabinet and pour them each a round.

"Should we be worried?" Rook finally sets aside his tablet. His amber eyes darken as he takes the offered drink. "You only share the good stuff when we've got something to celebrate or something to fear, and judging from the dour look on your face, this isn't a celebration."

"Actually, it's a bit of both." I pass out the other two drinks, then raise my glass. "Forsythe and his wife have acquired the elusive Cerridwen Codex. Cheers, then."

CHAPTER FOUR

DRAEGAN

I down the drink in one go, enjoying the burn of the liquor even if its true purpose is wasted on me. When I lower the glass, I find all three of my men watching me intently, their drinks untouched.

"Why are we just hearing of this now?" Augustine asks, the casual glimmer in his hazel eyes replaced with an intense vulnerability he rarely allows.

The sight of it makes my chest ache, and I have to turn away from him to gather my thoughts.

The curse that changed us from mortal men into immortal gargoyles—the bane that will ultimately turn us into permanent statues—is a powerful combination of dark fae and demonic magic so destructive, even the most sinister curseworkers avoid it today. Across all known magical systems, only a handful of spells exist to counteract it—to literally *unmake* a fae-made gargoyle. It's dangerous, complex magic promising all the side-effects one would expect from a dalliance with the dark arts: insanity, permanent disfigurement, magical coma, eternal damnation.

Et cetera.

For the afflicted, however, the magic represents something else.

Hope.

Originating from a dark fae grimoire so ancient it was little more than a series of carvings etched on a seaside cliff, the Codex was translated in antiquity by a coven of fae-descended Celtic witches dedicated to the goddess Cerridwen. Over the last two millennia, the translation was lost and found several times over, making its most recent reappearance in the basement archives of a nameless museum in Dublin just last week.

Among other things, it's said to contain an extremely rare dark fae Spell of Unmaking.

During our tenure among the cursed and the damned, my men and I have collected all manner of ancient grimoires and magical texts. We've become master scholars on the legends of Faerie, earth, and Hell alike. Rook, renowned spymaster and ace hacker, has gathered enough intelligence on the living witches, mages, fae, and demons of this city to fill the great Library of Alexandria twice over.

Yet in all that time, the key to our freedom—to eternal peace—continued to elude us.

Until now.

Crossing the sacristy, I crack open the heavy oak door

and peer into the nave. The guests are already gathering—a veritable cross-section of New York's magical elite. Other than us, however, the city's supernatural population is noticeably underrepresented. Witches and mages are still human, after all—an exclusive lot by nature. Forsythe's shadow magic society takes it to another level entirely.

I close the door and turn back to my men, relieved to see they've finally imbibed. "No point in mentioning it until I had more than a rumor and a hunch to go on."

"And you've got that now?" Rook shakes his head, once more reaching for the tablet—the world of bits and bytes where he feels most at home. "I've been searching for intel on the Cerridwen translations for centuries. Every new technology humans invent presents a new research opportunity, but it's all been futile. I hit so many dead ends, I wrote it off as legend years ago."

"Fortunately for us," I say, "Forsythe did not. Thanks to his connections with the magical community overseas, he finally tracked it down."

"So this is why you've been so cozy with him of late?" Jude asks. "Following a lead down the rabbit hole?"

"A couple of months ago, we got to chatting about his interest in fae lore after I showed him Graystone Manor in the Bronx," I reply. "*Dark* fae lore, specifically. He mentioned he might have a lead on the Codex and wondered if I'd ever heard of it. I was dubious, but I figured it couldn't hurt to start building a stronger bridge between our organizations."

"Fucking dark fae," Augustine sneers. "If any of these upstart mages ever went toe-to-toe with the real deal, they'd shit themselves. I don't get why they're all so obsessed."

"Unsurprising, given Forsythe's proclivities," Rook says. "Shadowmancers are notorious for hoarding dark magic, cobbling together spells from any tradition that suits them. Fae, druidcraft, witchcraft, conjure, voodoo, Catholicism. You name it, they've stolen it, consequences be damned."

"All the more reason not to trust the bastard," Jude says.

"Who said anything about trust?" I ask. "In any case, knowing my affinity for fae magical history, he was more than happy to brag about the acquisition over drinks the other night."

"So he's got it in hand?" Augustine asks.

"He and his wife traveled to Dublin last week. Bought it from a shadow mage scholar and museum curator who specializes in fae translations."

Rook's eyes light up with academic curiosity. "Have you seen it?"

"Not yet," I admit, "but he promised me a private showing the moment his people finish the authentication. I've no reason to doubt him. He was quite excited about it all."

"When do we make our move?" Rook swipes through the tablet so fast his fingers nearly blur. "Is it being stored at his primary residence or one of his other properties? Whichever location, I'll need access to the original blueprints for the building, which shouldn't be too hard to get.

As for security, I'm sure he's got tech *and* magic locking it down, which means I'll have to—"

"We're attempting a diplomatic approach for once," I say. "As far as the shadow mages are concerned, our interest is solely rooted in our passion for historical preservation. We'll raise fewer questions that way."

Augustine laughs. "Plus, the minute someone realizes they've got something your life literally depends on... Let the exploitation commence."

"That too," I agree.

Jude sighs and shoves a hand through his coal-black hair. "So why the monkey suits? Just wait until he gets the green light on the authentication, then let me go in and do him proper."

"Murdering the Archmage of Manhattan is neither proper *nor* diplomatic." Ignoring the ravenous hunger in Jude's eyes at the mention of murder, I collect their empty glasses and rinse them in the sacrarium, doubtlessly angering more than a few dead priests. "Assassination is out of the question. And unless we can figure out a way to steal it without igniting a war with the entire east coast magical community, we've got little choice but to play the dutiful guests. The sooner we can prove our loyalty, the sooner I can convince him to part with the precious text amicably. He's quite proud of it—he won't sell it to just anyone."

"And if it turns out the bloke's not willing to sell it at all?" Jude asks.

"*Then* we steal it, of course." I clap a hand over his

shoulder and smile, attempting to ease his restlessness. "It won't come to that. Every man has a price, Jude. We'll find his."

"It's one thing to *find* the price," he presses. "Another to actually afford it."

"One way or the other, the Archmage of Manhattan *will* give up the Codex. It's practically our legacy."

Jude laughs. "And he gives a fuck about legacies because he's such a good man, that it?"

A surge of red-hot fury burns through my chest at the very *thought* of screwing up this deal—of letting my men down again. "Because mortal or mage or the fucking monster of your worst nightmares, *no* one can resist an opportunity to put the men of shadow and stone in their debt."

For once, Jude doesn't argue. No one does. No point in it.

Because *that's* a lesson we've learned better than most:

In a world where all things have a cost, the debt of a powerful man is the most valuable currency there is.

"So what's the game plan?" Augustine returns to the mirror, still fussing with his hair. "Schmooze and booze, dance with the ladies, compliment the old man on the lovely ceremony so he invites us over for the post-wedding brunch?"

"I need you to work your usual charms on Forsythe's female relations," I say. "Get them to like you and open up to you. Dance if you must."

"I must," he says with a smile, meeting my eyes in the mirror. "Anything specific we're fishing for tonight?"

"The usual salacious details," I reply. "If the diplomatic approach doesn't pan out, we'll need all the leverage we can get." Then, turning to Rook, "Keep an eye on those security feeds. I want the names and magical lineages of every guest who walks through the door, along with a full report on their activities this evening—who's talking to whom, who's sneaking off for a clandestine romp in the coat closet, who's stealing the votives, who's gossiping about the bride-to-be. Later, we'll scrutinize the footage for anything we can use."

Rook gives me an enthusiastic nod, clearly in his element.

"What about me?" Jude's crazy grin is back in place, his ire fading in the wake of a new assignment. Running a thumb along his lower lip, he says, "Shall I help Auggie charm the pants off the old birds?"

"No. But if any of the so-called old birds need eviscerating, you'll be the first one I call."

This actually gets a real laugh. "I appreciate that, Drae."

"In the meantime," I continue, "I need you to watch my back tonight, Jude. Just because we're invited guests doesn't mean we're not walking into a trap. A few months of glad-handing and private tours doesn't make him a trusted ally."

"No?" Still laughing, Jude claps me on the back. "Shoulda gone with the blowjob, mate. Fosters a bit more loyalty in my experience."

"Thank you, Jude, for your astute assessment. I'll bear it

in mind next time the opportunity presents itself." I take a step back and look them over, a surge of pride welling inside. My men. My brothers in battle, if not by blood. The smile that stretches across my face is unplanned, but wholly genuine. "We really do clean up well these days, don't we?"

"I've always cleaned up well," Augustine says, puffing out his chest. "And it only took, what, a millennium and a half for the rest of you to get there? Nice work." He reaches into his breast pocket and procures a tin of mints, taking two before passing it to me. "Can't very well congratulate the blushing bride smelling like frat boys."

"I don't give a rat's arse about the bride *or* her blush," I grumble, but I take the offered mints anyway. I can't imagine the Archmage would look too keenly on the fact that his esteemed "fae" guests have spent the hour before his son's wedding boozing it up on hallowed ground.

Even if it is *our* hallowed ground.

As the pungent mints dissolve on my tongue, I glance around the sacristy one more time, my attention homing in on one of the massive oil paintings decorating the walls. It was commissioned by the parishioners two hundred years ago when the cathedral still held services—a moody rendition of the building's breathtaking exterior. Bathed in moonlight, a dozen gargoyles perch upon the spires, each one captured in exquisite detail.

It's a painful reminder of what we've already lost. What we stand to lose again if we can't get our hands on that Codex.

Behind me, the men are silent, waiting for my command.

I turn to meet each of their gazes once more.

It doesn't need to be said, but I say it anyway, a whisper that echoes with finality across the marble floors and straight into our immortal, fae-cursed hearts.

"Gentlemen, we *cannot* fuck this up."

CHAPTER FIVE

WESTLYN

A storm is closing in fast, casting the gargoyles of Thornwood Cathedral in sinister black shadows. The full moon that shone so brightly through my hotel windows is now completely obscured.

Tendrils of fear curl around my heart.

This is really happening...

The stars have vanished too, but as I climb the cathedral's ancient stone steps and gaze up at the looming spires, a wish flutters through my mind anyway—a wish that the gargoyles are more than just statues. That somehow, one of them will hear my silent plea, sweep me into his strong embrace, and fly me far, far away from this city.

"Westlyn, keep moving," Eloise huffs. Cradling her killer bouquet like a precious newborn baby, she barges past me and races for the heavy stained-glass door at the top. "Hurry! Before the rain starts!"

I follow her into the narthex, disappointment settling heavy in my gut.

Not only did my gargoyle fail to materialize, but so did my father.

It's the wedding of his only daughter—his only *child*, for the love of bats—and my father is nowhere to be found.

Nowhere *I* can find him, anyway. I'm sure he's making the rounds inside, air-kissing the same mages who were happy to kick him while he was down. Beyond the carved doors that lead into the nave, the whole place echoes with their fake laughter and overblown congratulations.

Frauds. At least half the people on the guest list turned down his requests for loans, cold-shouldering us when we begged for protection against the thugs who kept showing up at the brownstone.

But now that our family is aligned with the all-powerful Archmage, I guess we're all besties again.

Ahh, the politics of high-society magical life—a game no one ever taught me how to play.

Why would they? Pawns like me aren't expected to make the big power moves. We simply go where we're told and let the rest of the pieces fall into place around us.

"Take these." Eloise shoves the bouquet into my arms and restarts the tedious process of pecking at my hair and dress. I try to hold my breath and turn away from the offensive flowers, but it's no use. The damn things are on a mission to kill me, and if my watering eyes and scratchy throat are any indication, their victory is close at hand.

"For goddess' sake, Westlyn." Eloise glowers, her frown lines deepening. "How is Hunter supposed to feel when he sees his bride-to-be walking down the aisle with that sourpuss?"

Not as bad as he'll feel if I have to be carried *down the aisle in a stretcher on account of these flowers...*

Wiggling my nose to stave off a sneeze, I plaster on a sweet-puss to counteract the sour.

"Should you text Dad?" I ask, my voice overly bright. "It's almost time."

"No need. We've got the front pew reserved." *Swat-swat-swat*, goes her hand against my dress, obliterating invisible dust motes. "I'm sure he'll be taking his seat momentarily—he wouldn't miss this."

"But... Isn't he going to walk me down the aisle?"

Swat-swat. "You're not a child anymore, Westlyn. The sooner you accept that, the happier you'll be." Certain she's beaten my dress into submission, she rises to her full height and grips my chin, red-lacquered nails digging into my face.

I brace for the lecture to come, but before she can utter another word, the tingling in my nose erupts, and I blast her with a gale-force sneeze at the same time the first crack of thunder booms across the skies.

Seconds later, the deluge outside begins, soaking the streets and muting the traffic to a din.

Fire burns in her dark irises, but she doesn't scold me, doesn't make a mad dash for the ladies' room. Just shakes her head, like, *could this stepchild* be *any more ridiculous?*, and digs into her handbag for the tissues.

"You've got about ten minutes before the ceremony starts," she says, raising her voice above the hissing downpour. "I need to go check in with the High Priest. Your father and I will be right up front, watching the whole thing."

Making sure you don't screw it up.

She doesn't say that last part, but she's definitely thinking it.

Because if I can't keep it together tonight, the deal will be off and my father will end up on the streets—or worse.

And where would that leave his doting little wife?

As Eloise furiously blots her face with a tissue, I turn and glance out the stained-glass door, searching the storm-soaked streets of lower Manhattan for...

What, exactly?

Not a what, *girl,* I remind myself. *A* whom.

A strong, protective *whom* who's name I don't even know. A stranger whose cobalt-blue eyes and devilish grin have haunted my dreams for weeks.

My stomach fizzes at the thought of him, at the memory of his black-pepper-and-candle-flame scent. At the memory of all those nights I spent in front of my window, pretending the fingers trailing over my bare skin were his.

Wishing my soft moans would float out on the night breeze and find their way to him.

Wishing he was out there in the darkness, watching me. Waiting for me.

I know I said my story doesn't have an avenging knight, but if it did? Well. He would definitely get the part, no audition necessary. I only met him once—he chased off some creep trying to get a little too up-close-and-personal with me last month in Madison Square Park—but it felt like I'd already known him a lifetime.

Also? He gave me his latte.

Yeah, I know. A latte. Big deal, right? As pathetic as it sounds, it was the kindest thing anyone's done for me in years.

But despite the butterflies he unleashed inside me, I didn't stick around long enough to catch his name. Just long enough for a little chit-chat and a few laughs. I told him I liked his accent—London, rough around the edges, just enough bad-boy charm to make a girl swoon. Then I thanked him for the coffee and the save, made my excuses, and headed back home to Dad and Eloise.

I knew he wanted me to stay. *I* wanted me to stay. But I left him anyway, because I also knew if I lingered even one more minute, I'd do something incredibly stupid and mortifying. Something like... barnacle myself around his legs and beg him to save me from my own ridiculous life.

A fantasy. That's all it was. All it ever *could* be.

Since our Magical Midnight Meet-Cute, as I've come to call it, I've been trying to forget the man who showed me that small kindness and convince myself that Hunter

Forsythe will be kind, too. That just because I don't love him now doesn't mean I never will. That just because his family *bought* me doesn't mean they won't treat me with respect.

That my father, for all his obvious failings, would *never* hand me over to a monster, no matter how much cash and political clout his parents offered up in return.

But all that self-talk never works. Because no matter what our magical customs dictate or what backroom deals our family members strike, I keep circling back to the same question:

What the hell kind of a man allows his parents to buy his bride?

"Eloise?" I turn back toward her, my eyes glazed with tears that have nothing to do with the flowers.

She sighs and waits for me to speak, and the useless self-talk kicks in once more.

I tell myself her pinched brow is out of concern for me. I tell myself that underneath the gruff exterior, Eloise is a decent person. A woman who knows a thing or two about living in the shadow of powerful men, and might offer an encouraging word on her stepdaughter's wedding night.

Lightning flickers, bringing the shadows between us into sharp relief.

Blinking back the tears, I whisper, "I drew a Tarot card tonight."

"Oh?" Her brows lift. No witch can resist the pull of the Tarot. Not even a witch who believes she's already got all of life's mysteries figured out.

"The Moon," I confess, and the furrow between her brows deepens. Forcing a laugh, I say, "I know it sounds nuts. Paranoid, even. But I can't help but feel something's not right. I don't mean the arrangement part. Marrying Hunter like this... I know it's what's best for the family."

"And that's the most important thing. Westlyn, your father has worked *very* hard to build this alliance."

I nod, as if the simple act of agreeing with her can soothe my fraying nerves.

It doesn't.

"It's just... What if the cards are trying to tell me something?" I press. "I've always associated the Moon card with deception. A warning to dig a little deeper, you know?"

At my words, the storm clouds shift, briefly revealing the moon. It shines through the stained glass, illuminating the narthex in a jewel-toned rainbow.

It feels like another warning.

"Oh, Westlyn." Eloise tugs on one of my braids and smiles, a gesture so motherly it makes my heart soar with renewed hope, despite the alarms blaring inside it. "You can't pin your entire future—this *family's* future—on one little Tarot card."

"No?" I wait for her to tell me it's just my subconscious projecting my fears about marrying a total stranger.

I wait for her to tell me I'll wake up in Hunter's bed tomorrow, eager to start my new life as the wife of a prominent shadowmancer.

I wait for her to tell me my father loves me and wants

what's best for me, and no Tarot card could ever change any of that.

But all too soon, the clouds scud back over the moon, and Eloise's smile turns to ice, her grip on my hair tightening. With a sneer that chills me to the marrow, she says, "Your Tarot interpretations are as trite and meaningless as your whining. You're not even a real witch—it's a damn miracle we found a mage family willing to take you in at all."

"But... but I—"

"This is *precisely* why I insisted your father steer clear of you tonight. Your childish antics would only upset him, and goddess knows he's got enough to deal with."

Shame burns my cheeks. "I'm... I'm sorry. I didn't mean—"

"This wedding is *happening*, Westlyn. This alliance is happening. Maybe Hunter isn't your first choice in husbands, but honestly..." A cold laugh escapes as she rakes her gaze down my body. "Were *you* your father's first choice in daughters? A witch with no power? A witch who killed her own mother for the privilege of being born?"

My nerves are on fire, everything inside me desperate to flee. To smash the flowers into her smug face, bolt out the door, and let the storm wash me away. But Eloise's words are too sharp, too precise. Every one of them strikes home, stealing my voice and paralyzing me where I stand.

"Like it or not, this marriage is the sacrifice you must make for your family—for the man who sacrificed his entire *life* just to take care of you. Anyone else in his position would've abandoned you to the wolves without a second thought. So no, Westlyn, you will not be reading Tarot cards or complaining of allergies or coming up with any other excuses to delay the inevitable."

I lower my eyes, unable to bear the weight of her icy glare.

"You've got five minutes to pull yourself together," she hisses. "The *minute* you hear the organ, you will march into the cathedral with your head held high, your smile bright, and your ungrateful attitude checked at the door. If you can't manage that simple task after all we've done for you, the only *deeper digging* you'll need to worry about tonight is your grave."

CHAPTER SIX

AUGUSTINE

Mastering the fine art of blackmail really just comes down to acknowledging two fundamental laws.

Law number one? Women are the guardians of the world's secrets. They've always got a few juicy little tidbits swimming around on the surface, just waiting for an opportunity to bubble out. Probe a bit deeper, though, and you'll find the whole cache. We're talking towering, rodent-infested, hoarders-level collections of scandals, confessions, and gossip so salacious it would put the tabloids to shame.

And here's the second law. The keys to the castle, if you will. To the whole fucking treasury.

The only thing standing between all those precious secrets and the man whose mission it is to obtain them... is a thoroughly good dicking.

Hell, it doesn't even have to be *good*. Doesn't even have to progress beyond shameless flirting, if you know what you're doing. As long as she's into you and believes she's got a shot at warming your bed? Let the oversharing commence.

Call me a sexist prick if you must—it's a badge I'll wear proudly, and one I'll continue to earn.

Yes, I'm just *that* good at what I do.

"Seventy?" I press a hand to my chest, mouth dropping in mock indignation. "I refuse to believe you're a day over forty, Mrs. Deveroux."

"That's *Ms.* Deveroux, young man. Are all fae so brazen? And that dimple... goodness!" The old hag flashes a lipstick-smudged grin and sidles closer to me on the pew, pressing against me from knee to hip. Resting a bony hand on my thigh—*high* on my thigh—she coos, "I didn't realize the Archmage associated with such shameless flirts."

"I've got plenty of shame, believe me. But don't blame the Archmage for not warning you. We're relatively new acquaintances." I slide my arm across the top of the pew behind her, fingers trailing across her shoulder. "How about you? Do you know the family well?"

The hand clamped around my thigh is as wrinkled as an old paper bag, and she's getting dangerously close to home with that grip of hers, but it doesn't dim my smile a bit.

Right now, the old antique thinks she's got me wrapped around her gnarled little finger, and I've no intentions of dissuading her.

"Oh, yes," she says, rubbing me a bit higher. "Lennon and Celine are old friends—we all grew up together in Colorado. Went to college together, too."

"The Forsythes aren't native New Yorkers?" I make a mental note to run that by Rook. Could be insignificant, but archmages are regional positions elected by the local covens. I always assumed the highest ranking spellcaster in the city had deeper roots.

"No, but we've been here forty years now. We all moved out east a few days after the adoption." Her eyes turn misty. "I can't believe Hunter is getting married tonight. Married! I was there when the agency brought him over. Poor kid was so scared! Couldn't blame him, though. He was only two at the time."

"Huh. I had no idea Hunter was adopted." Another possibly insignificant tidbit, but still worth mentioning to our spymaster. Now that we're under orders to get snuggly with Forsythe, I'm sure Rook will want to start a full dossier on the man—if he hasn't already.

"Oh, he was the sweetest little mage you ever saw, too." The old lady beams. "I took so many pictures of him that day! I couldn't help it."

"Really? I'd love to see them. Portraiture is actually a hobby of mine." This, at least, is genuine. When I'm not canvasing the streets of New York for someone to bury—metaphorically, of course—I'm out there with my old Nikon, escaping into a better world through the lens.

"They're gone." She leans in close, wetting her lips to share the next tasty morsel. "Lennon made me destroy them and swear a blood oath I'd never tell anyone in New York about the adoption."

I raise a brow, my flirtatious grin growing wider. "If this is your idea of keeping oaths, I best mind my pillow talk tonight, lest I unintentionally reveal any state secrets."

A wheezy laugh escapes her lips. "At my age, I've stopped worrying about old oaths. I can't even tell you how many I've made. It's all a blur when you're on the downward slide."

"Forty is hardly the downward slide."

"Now you're just trying to get into my pants!"

"Ahh, but you're wearing a dress, my love," I tease, still stroking her shoulder. Then, steering us back on track, "Why didn't Lennon want pictures of Hunter? Seems odd for a new father, no?"

"He doesn't want anyone to know his son's adopted."

Now *that* sounds like something a bit more significant. In fact, it sounds like a secret worthy of spilling.

"Why ever not?"

"He's always had ambitions to be Archmage," she says. "For him and his son both. And you know how mages are about their bloodlines. He thinks if people know Hunter isn't actually a pureblood Forsythe, the upper echelons of the shadow magic society will shun him. Something like that could reflect badly on the whole family."

I offer a sympathetic nod. "That sounds unbearable."

"It sounds like a load of horseshit, because it is. Want to know what *I* think?"

Her fingers graze the edge of my balls as she leans in closer, and I swallow my revulsion, hoping like hell I don't have to make good on that dicking after all. Sure, I've been known to lower the bar a time or two in service of uncovering the best dirt on a target, but this? This is next-level. I'm not sure the woman even has her own teeth.

But she's clearly got the scoop, and a job's a job, so...

Brushing my lips against her ear, I drop my voice to a sultry whisper and say, "I would *very* much like to know what you think, Ms. Deveroux."

She casts a furtive glance around the nave. Satisfied no one's eavesdropping, she blurts out, "Lennon doesn't want anyone to know he can't get it up. Never could."

"He... I... excuse me?"

"Oh, yes. He's always had issues in that area."

"And you know this because...?"

"Who do you think kept him company before he started shacking up with Celine?" At this, her voice goes from bombshell to bitter in a single breath. "The little slut screwed everything up. It should be *me* sitting in that front pew, not her. Hunter should've been mine. Lennon and I always talked about adopting one day."

"I see." With a deep sigh, I remove my arm from around her shoulder, my hopes unceremoniously dashed.

For all her inappropriate groping, Ms. Deveroux has nothing to offer in return but the idle gossip of a woman scorned.

Damn it.

"Anyway," the old woman says, returning to her ball-grazing with renewed vigor. "It all worked out for the best. Now I'm sexy, single, and ready to—"

"Don't... finish that sentence." I press a fingertip to her lips and offer an apologetic smile, trying not to sigh in relief as Jude slides into the pew on her other side.

Thank the fucking devil.

Time to cut my losses, extricate myself from this relentless fondling, and find a new target. Preferably a younger one who's—what's the saying? Sexy, single, and ready to help a brazen fae drown his sorrows in pussy?

"I'm terribly sorry, Ms. Deveroux. This is a bit embarrassing, but my..." I glance at Jude, searching for an excuse. "My doctor! Yes, my doctor has just arrived with the results of my STD screening. It's never good news when they deliver the news in person, is it?"

Jude doesn't miss a beat. "We haven't seen a rash like that in decades. I'm surprised you can still piss standing up."

And just like that, the lust dims from her eyes and—with little more than a rushed excuse about seeing a long-lost University of Colorado alumnus across the aisle—she's gone.

"I could fucking kiss you." I grab Jude's face and give him a good shake.

He shoves me away. "Not with that rash, you don't."

"I swear that woman was about fifteen seconds from laying her head in my lap and going to town."

"I hope she was planning to remove the dentures first. *There's* a lesson you don't want to learn more than once."

"I... I don't even know what to say to that, so I'll just thank you for the save and move on."

"Don't thank me, mate. Had I known you were about to be gummed in church, I'd have left the old broad to it. God's work, that." He turns away from me and sighs, his knee bouncing. "I'm going stir crazy in here, Augs. I don't favor cathedrals. They make me feel like a sinner."

"You *are* a sinner."

He glares. "Yeah, and I don't need a bunch of saints and statues to rub my nose in it, do I?"

"Still in a mood, I see."

"Worse now."

"Let me guess. You asked a bridesmaid to meet you in the men's room for a quickie? How long were you waiting before you realized she stood you up?"

"You see any bridesmaids around here, arsehole?"

"I just assumed they were all in hiding, avoiding your advances. Oh! I hear Ms. Deveroux is on the prowl. Would you like me to make an introduction?"

"Not bloody likely." Jude grabs the knot of his tie and yanks it loose. "I fucking hate weddings too, you know? Same as cathedrals. All designed to make the rest of us feel like shit."

"You hate *everything* when you're not getting laid."

"Isn't that the whole point of a wedding? I'm not here for the cake and family reunions. In fact, I really shouldn't be here at all." He flips a small object back and forth across his knuckles—some sort of ring. Probably one of his creepy creations.

"Aren't you supposed to be looking out for Drae?"

"He's worried over nothing. I've already worked my way through half the crowd—just a bunch of stuck-up spellcasters who can't be bothered to give anyone else the time. They're not here to cause trouble tonight. All they care about is making an appearance." He shakes his head, then slides the ring onto his pinky and stands. "Tell Drae I had to run out. I'll see you at home later."

"Run out *where*, exactly?"

"Brooklyn." He smacks me on the cheek twice and flashes his crazy grin—the one that says he's about to stir up some shit and there's nothing we can do to stop him. "Don't wait up, love."

"I don't plan on it, dickhead," I reply, but fucking Jude's already gone.

CHAPTER SEVEN

AUGUSTINE

Fucking Jude. That's his official name now—Fucking Jude. At least it *should* be, for all the shit he's putting us through lately.

It's the same thing every night. Bailing earlier and earlier, staying out until the wee hours doing devil knows what. One of these nights he's not going to make it back by sunrise and then we're *all* going to be fucked.

No, not in the fun way.

I can see the headlines now:

Mysterious stone gargoyle found brooding on Central Park jogging path...

Unexplained appearance of ancient gargoyle in children's sandbox baffles parents and sends kids to therapy...

Woman struggles to explain to husband how she tripped and fell on sexy statue's cock...

Scoffing, I exit the pew and glance around the packed

cathedral, eager to find that more suitable—not to mention more informative—one-night-stand. Preferably one whose teeth don't need to be removed before the main event.

Ah, and there she is. Twelve o'clock, champagne-colored dress, legs for days...

Hello, gorgeous. What have you got for me?

Drae said we had to be on our best behavior tonight? No problem. It just so happens I'm at my best when I'm balls deep. There's just something about being between a woman's thighs that turns me into a model fucking citizen.

After she spills her secrets, of course.

I'm about to head over and make my opening move when a firm hand clamps around my shoulder. I know who it is before I turn to face him.

"Have you seen Jude?" Drae asks. "Rook's been making the rounds, but he hasn't heard from him since we left the sacristy. I'm a bit worried, truth be told."

Guilt churns inside as the familiar war wages.

Do I cover for Jude again? Or finally admit how worried I really am?

For now, I'm spared the torture of making the choice. The pipe organ strikes a chord, and a hush falls over the cathedral.

Drae and I slide into the nearest pew and turn to face the narthex along with the rest of the guests. The music continues in earnest and the doors swing open, revealing a bride in black lace clutching a bouquet the size of a golden retriever.

Limned in moonlight, she's all alone at the end of the aisle, no daddy dearest giving her away. Witches and mages aren't exactly known for upholding the traditions of their former oppressors, but still. Something about the scene twists me up inside.

The bride takes a few tentative steps, her head swiveling from side to side as if she's searching out the one friendly face in a crowd of monsters.

The narthex doors swing shut behind her, the moonlight fading away.

And suddenly, there she is. Warm and sparkling beneath the candlelit chandeliers. Long black hair threaded with silver. Eyes the color of a tropical bay. Dark red lips that have my heart rate kicking into high gear as I imagine stealing a kiss...

She takes a few more steps, stopping just a few rows from ours.

The entire cathedral fades into a gray haze.

Right now, right here, there's only her.

Westlyn Avery, soon to be Westlyn Forsythe. She's a fucking vision. Not in the way all brides are beautiful, but in a way that punches a hole right through my chest and grabs hold of my heart, damn near liquifying it.

I grip the edge of the pew to steady myself. Her presence is overwhelming, washing over me in dark, heavy waves. I'm drowning in it, but coming up for air is the furthest thought from my mind.

She takes another step. Then another. She reaches our

pew and suddenly, she stops. Turns toward us. Glances up, those turquoise eyes sparkling with life.

Her gaze locks onto mine and her mouth rounds into a little "o" of surprise, and I swear I feel a jolt, like whatever wrapped itself around my heart decided to give it a good yank. I'm stumbling out into the aisle before I even realize what's happening, no control over my steps, no way to fight the current pulling me toward her. I'm desperate to turn around and look at Drae—to see if he's as hypnotized as I am—but the idea of tearing my attention from her for even one *second* is unbearable.

A tremor rolls through her body, making the flower petals quake, and I reach for her, so close my fingertips brush the lace covering her arm—

"*Augustine*." Drae's grip around my wrist is painfully strong, jerking my attention away from the girl.

The spell shatters. Westlyn gasps and lowers her eyes, quickly resuming her march toward the altar.

Toward the groom awaiting his bride.

The haze lifts, that crushing force finally releasing its grip on my heart, but a strange feeling lingers.

"I... I miss her." I press a hand to my chest and turn to Drae, shocked by the strangeness of my words. By the hollow emptiness sweeping through me where only seconds ago there was... something else.

"Drae? Did you feel the... Did you see..." I trail off at the sight of his tightly clenched jaw. At the deadly cold warning in his eyes.

Something is wrong. *Very* wrong.

"Stay here," he whispers urgently. "I'll return as soon as I can."

"But where are—"

"*Augustine*." He grips my shoulder once more, his tone almost desperate now. "Whatever happens, do *not* let that girl out of your sight."

CHAPTER EIGHT
WESTLYN

What. In the name of the triple goddess. Was *that*?

Those men... As soon as I felt their eyes on me, I swear my heart stopped. Time stopped. *I* stopped. For those few breathless moments, I wasn't even in control of my body. It was like fate decided to take the wheel and bump me out of my own driver's seat.

I've been waiting for you...

Sounds crazy, but those were the exact words that came into my mind when the man with the hazel eyes reached for me. I almost said them out loud too, but right before I found find my voice, the strange, mystical tether so firmly connecting us snapped.

The whole thing was over in a handful of heartbeats, but now, even as I pass the aisle and continue my death march to the end, I still feel the heat of their intense gazes.

Somehow, it feels familiar. Safe. Like a slightly more intense version of the inexplicable connection I felt with the man in the park.

My nerves tingle at the reminder of him, my avenging knight...

No. No, no, no.

Goddess, what is *wrong* with me? I'm about to be married to another man. A prominent shadow mage whose family has the power to ensure no harm comes to me or my father ever again. A shadow mage who can provide for me and keep me safe, whether or not love is ever part of the equation.

It's the best I can hope for, just like everyone always said. And Eloise was right, too—I'm *not* a child. There's no room in my life for pointless fantasies.

Resisting the urge to turn back for another look, I take a deep breath, readjust my bouquet, and recommit myself to my family. My duty.

Head held high, happy face locked and loaded, I quicken my pace toward the altar.

But after just a few more steps, I'm nearly breathless again, my throat closing against the cloying scent of the flowers. The distraction with the guys gave my highly-sensitive senses a momentary reprieve from the assault, but now my eyes are watering so badly, I can't see straight. The cathedral's legendary beauty is totally lost on me. If Dad and Eloise are in the front pew, I can't pick them out of the lineup. My groom is no more than a smudge in a tux peering down at me from the altar, the High Priest equally dark and shapeless.

By the time I reach the end, all I want to do is lie down on the floor, press my cheek to the cool stone, and fall into a deep sleep.

Wake me when it's over.

It's not until the pipe organ fades and I hear the sharp clearing of a throat that I realize I just said that last part out loud.

Wow. This night's off to a great *start!*

Dressed in a black ceremonial robe trimmed in red and gold, the High Priest spreads his hands before me and smiles—a gesture that might be welcoming if not for the cold steel in his eyes.

"Is there a problem, Miss Avery?" he asks.

"No, sir." I hold my breath, stifling another sneeze.

"If you'd like to greet your groom before we begin," he says quietly, never breaking that smile, "now would be a good time."

The sneeze escapes, but I manage to contain it to the flowers and not, thankfully, the priest's face.

"My what?" I ask, sniffling.

He jerks his head toward the man standing next to me. "Your groom?"

"Oh! Right." *Goddess,* I'm about to pledge myself to the man till death do us part, and I haven't even looked him in the eyes. "Sorry, I'm a little foggy. These flowers are... You know what, let me just..." I lean forward and set the bouquet on the stone altar behind the priest, careful not to knock over the tall black candles flaming on either side of it.

When I step back, the air immediately clears, the scent of candle wax and stone and old things coming to life around me.

Feeling marginally more human, I finally turn to my groom. My future husband. The mage I'll be honoring and obeying for the rest of my life.

I take in his appearance—shaggy brown hair, a bit on the oily side, desperately in need of a trim. Bland face with no real defining features. A patchy beard he hasn't quite committed to. An expensive custom-made tux and crisp white shirt that seem completely wasted on such an otherwise shabby man.

Again, I try to draw on my deep capacity for self-delusion and convince myself that he's kind. That he's not just doing this as a political maneuver. That he'll put in the effort to get to know me just like I'll get to know him, and together we'll find a way to be happy. Or at least not *unhappy*.

"Hello, Hunter." I smile politely, searching his eyes for a spark of warmth, but they're as flat and lifeless as they were on the other two occasions we met—a Samhain feast a couple of years back and a family dinner last month after my father and Eloise accepted Lennon's offer for the marriage. We barely spoke at either event.

"Westin," he says, his tone bored.

"*Lyn*," I say, forcing my smile to stay in place. "Westlyn."

Hunter nods a brief acknowledgment, but his return smile doesn't reach his eyes.

"Shall we begin?" the priest asks.

Hunter's bored gaze skims down the front of my dress and back up, and I swear he bites back a snort before turning his attention to the priest. "Let's get it over with."

Get it over with? Really?

Anger heats my cheeks. Does he find me lacking? Does he think this sham of a marriage was my idea? That he's doing me a favor? That he's such a fucking catch he can scoff at his bride-to-be and forget her name and still have me worshipping at his feet like all the other sycophants in this cathedral?

I may not have magic or an investment portfolio, but I have *plenty* of other good qualities. Qualities another man would be tripping over himself for a chance to experience.

I open my mouth to tell him just that, but then I remember Eloise's warning.

If you can't manage that simple task after all we've done for you, the only deeper digging you'll need to worry about tonight is your grave...

I glance over my shoulder, finding my father and Eloise seated in the front pew, right where she said they'd be. My father's watching me, but the moment our eyes meet, his gaze drops into his lap.

Ignoring the sting of tears behind my eyes, I turn my attention back to the priest and nod. "Yes, let's get it over with. Please."

CHAPTER NINE

WESTLYN

For the next half hour, I shove my feelings way down deep, do my best to avoid Hunter's dead eyes, and focus on the monotonous recitation of the ceremony. It's an ancient one witches and mages have used for millennia, no different from any I've attended with my father over the years. Probably not even that much different from the Christian ceremonies once held in this very cathedral before Blackmoor Capital Group bought it and turned it into a private architectural marvel.

But there *is* one thing that sets tonight's ritual apart. A big one. And after the High Priest sets aside his ritual grimoire and the organ plays another appropriately macabre tune, that one thing—the moment I've been dreading even more than the post-ceremony wedding night in Hunter's bed—is finally upon us.

The priest retrieves a jewel-handled athame from the

stone altar and presents it to Hunter. Candlelight glints along the polished blade.

"Kneel, Westlyn," the priest commands.

I close my eyes and swallow the bile rising in my throat.

Most modern spellcasters who follow the old wedding traditions have eliminated the blood binding ritual, and with good reason. It's demeaning and disgusting, not to mention dangerous.

The shadow magic society has no such hangups. They're patriarchs to the core, and nothing brings them more joy than putting a woman on her knees before a man wielding a weapon.

Ignoring the churn in my stomach, I kneel at Hunter's feet and bow my head.

What's that whooshing sound? Oh, just the last of my dignity swirling down the drain...

"Westlyn, repeat after me," the priest says. "I, Westlyn Patricia Avery, willingly bind myself to Hunter Forsythe on this night in the presence of friends and family and the gods and goddesses whose blessings we now call upon."

I recite the words, each one stealing a little more of my soul.

"I hereby submit to Hunter's will," he continues, "and vow to honor, obey, and serve him in all things magical and mundane, from this night until we are parted by death."

Again, I glance over my shoulder, seeking my father.

Again, I find no love. No sign of sorrow or regret. Just a

worn-out mage undoubtedly relieved to finally shed the burden of a magic-less daughter and a mountain of debt.

I return my gaze to Hunter's shoes. The priest's words are a faint echo as I recite them without feeling, my heart as dead as my soon-to-be-husband's eyes.

"Raise your hands," he commands, and I do as I'm told. Hunter grips my left wrist, and I brace for the pain I know is coming next.

"I, Westlyn Avery, offer my blood as a symbol of my commitment to you," the priest says.

I take a deep breath, forcing the tremor from my voice. "I, Westlyn Avery, offer my blood as a—"

"Hold *still*." Hunter jerks my wrist and cuts a quick, deep gash across my palm with the athame, making me gasp. Even the priest seems caught off guard by his abruptness, but when Hunter begins speaking his part without prompting, the priest doesn't intercede.

"I offer my blood as a symbol of my power and strength," Hunter says, releasing my wrist and making the same cut across his own palm. "Through my sacrifice, I bind you to me."

He tosses the athame to the floor and grabs my hand again, smashing our palms together.

The instant my blood mingles with his, I feel it—a sharp, painful tingling that chews through the wound and straight up my arm. I cry out as it sears across my chest, quickly spreading to the other arm and throughout the rest of my body.

In a matter of seconds, it feels like my veins are burning, like some inexplicable dark fire is consuming me from the inside out.

"Let go!" I cry out, struggling against his hold. "Let me go!"

Hunter only clamps down harder. Too strong, too relentless.

I try to stand, but Hunter wraps his other hand around my throat, a vise grip that has me seeing stars.

No one in the cathedral moves to help me. No one says a word.

"Something's wrong," I choke out, my eyes imploring the High Priest to intervene. "It's not supposed to—"

"Finish it, old man," Hunter grinds out. "Bind her!"

Ignoring my pleas, the priest lifts his arms and calls out, "By the bonds of blood and magic, with the blessing of the old gods and the new, so shall this oath be... be..." He trails off, the final proclamation unfinished, his gaze shifting to the eves. "Morrigan be damned," he whispers.

My blood is boiling, my vision turning gray at the edges, but I manage to follow his line of sight.

There, perched in the eves above, are my ravens. Silent but for the gentle fluttering of wings, they don't so much arrive as *appear*, as if they've been hiding in the shadows all along.

Lucinda's here, along with her brothers, Jean-Pierre and Huxley, and so many more I can't even count them.

A murmur ripples through the nave as the guests finally begin to notice what's drawn our attention.

When I lower my gaze from the eves, I find one of those guests watching me intently.

The man from before. The one with the hazel eyes and the dimple in his left cheek. His eyes are glazed, his hand lifting as if he might reach for me again.

For a brief instant, the burning fades from my limbs and chest, replaced with a warm tugging sensation that has me lifting my hand and—

"*Finish* it!" Hunter shouts again, and that torturous pain rushes right back, making me sway on my knees. Hunter doesn't let me fall, though. Just grips me tighter, closing his fingers around my throat, his other hand still locked on mine.

The High Priest shakes himself out of his stupor and lifts his arms again, but before he can complete the rite, Lucinda swoops down onto the altar and knocks over one of the black candles. It lands on my bouquet, the flame catching on the silk ribbon tied around the stems and crackling to life.

It burns through the flowers like kerosine-soaked kindling, and then—just as quickly as it began—the fire sputters out.

Black smoke rises from the charred petals, and for the first time since Eloise thrust those flowers into my arms, a clarity washes over me.

Hunter releases my throat and fists my hair, yanking my head back and forcing me to look up into his face. Rage twists his features, his lips curled in a snarl, and as he continues to glare at me, his eyes shift from their usual dull brown to a deep, endless black. A black that speaks of terrible, ancient things. A black that bleeds out from the irises and drowns out the whites until I'm left staring into two empty pits.

Zorakkov. The unfamiliar word clamors through my skull, every syllable scraping across my mind like claws.

"Zorakkov," I whisper, and I know at once it's not a word at all, but a name.

His name.

The High Priest glowers at me like I'm a puppy who just got into the trash.

He knows...

A chill skitters down my spine.

Hunter is not a mage. Not a man.

He's a demon.

And the High Priest was about to bind me to him.

Run run run...

Everything inside me is screaming at me to flee, but I can't break free of Hunter's—Zorakkov's—grip.

I frantically turn to my father again, hoping against hope there's been a terrible mistake. He may not be up for any parent of the year awards, but surely he wouldn't sell me off to Hell...

Would he?

My stepmother shoots daggers at me from the front

pew, making a frantic "get on with it" gesture with her hands. But my father? The man I'm giving up my future to save?

He's got his chin tucked firmly against his chest, eyes nearly burning a hole in the ground.

My heart turns to stone and drops into my stomach. And in that moment, I know.

Aside from the ravens, the ritual is happening exactly as planned.

My father and stepmother sold me out. Not just to a mage whose wealthy family offered to make their financial problems disappear.

But to Hell.

Cowards. Fucking cowards.

Zorakkov sends another bolt of pain sizzling down my arm, and the priest lifts his arms once more.

"By the bonds of blood and magic," he begins, and I know if he gets the rest of the words out, if he finishes the rite, I'm done.

"...with the blessing of the old gods and the new," he continues, and the demon grips me tighter, so certain of his victory, of his power.

"...so shall this oath be—"

"Bullshit," a voice interrupts, strong and clear. Familiar.

Mine.

And with a surge of adrenaline, I—the witch who never stands up for herself, the witch who has no power, the witch who never had a fucking choice—grab the discarded athame off the floor, rocket up to my feet, and shove that blade right through the demon's throat.

I'm stumbling down the altar steps before the blood even reaches the collar of his fine white shirt.

And without so much as a glance toward the monsters who sold me out, I bolt.

CHAPTER TEN

DRAEGAN

I've always enjoyed the view from the open bell tower. It's quiet up here—far enough removed from the hustle and bustle of the streets below to grant me a moment's peace, but not so distant it makes a man forget what tethers him to the world.

It also gives me a chance to visit the gargoyles perched on the corners of the balustrade. Even in their stone forms, my oldest friends can see, hear, and feel everything that goes on around them, just like Rook, Jude, Augustine, and I can. But *unlike* the four of us, these gargoyles can't shift out of their stone forms at night.

Or ever.

None of the city's gargoyles can. That is a privilege—a burden, too—reserved only for us.

I place a palm on a familiar stone wing, noticing a new chip at its crest. Probably hail damage.

"I'm sorry, Miguel," I whisper, but of course he can't reply. Can't tell me if he's cold or in pain. If he remembers my name or even how such a cruel curse ever befell him.

My heart sinks under the weight of regrets too ancient to name, but I didn't leave the wedding ceremony to fly up here and sulk about the long list of things I cannot change.

Help her, Draegan... She'll need you before the night is through...

The strange, otherworldly voice echoes through my mind once more, just like it did in the nave when Westlyn Avery appeared. I don't know where the command originated, but the moment I heard it, there was no doubt in my mind I'd obey.

Augustine's odd behavior at the girl's arrival only cemented it for me; he was entranced. Perhaps I would've been as well, but the whispers in my mind were accompanied by a vision.

I'm not sure how or why, but Westlyn Avery is going to jump to her death from this tower tonight. And unlike the curse that trapped my friends in eternal stone, that girl's death is a tragedy I can actually prevent.

Whoever the girl is, whatever fate has in store for her... somehow, our paths are connected. I may not understand it, but I learned long ago to neither question nor ignore the mysterious whisperings of fate.

So here we are. Waiting for what? I've no idea. But I'll know it when I see it.

I always do.

The rain that'd been battering us on and off for the last few hours finally lets up again, dark clouds shifting to offer a glimpse of the full moon. I use the opportunity to pace the perimeter of the small tower balcony, checking on each of the gargoyles and making notes about any new damages. Rook might have some ideas for extending the tower roof to offer the gargoyles a bit more protection from the elements.

I text him my notes and ask about security on the main level—seems all is well. I'm curious as to how the ceremony's progressing, but I don't dare distract Augustine from the all-important task of keeping watch over the girl.

Several minutes later, I'm about to text Rook again to see if he's had any luck tracking down our missing Jude, but a sudden commotion on the ground level interrupts me. Peering over the balustrade, I catch a wave of confused wedding guests pouring out of the main entrance and onto the street, chased by what appears to be a flock of...

Ravens?

My phone buzzes—Augustine. But frantic footsteps on the tower staircase leave me no time to answer. I quickly shift into my stone form, clinging to the balustrade as if I'm part of the architecture.

Convenient bit of camouflage, that.

The small door leading into the bell chamber bursts open, and a girl barrels through it. Panting from the effort, she slams the door shut behind her and leans back against it, eyes wide with fright.

Westlyn. The scent of her raw terror is unmistakable.

Whoever she's running from isn't far behind. I hear their arguments below.

"Where the fuck did she run off to?" an angry male booms.

"Don't let her escape!" another demands—sounds like the Archmage. "The blood binding must be completed!"

"I would rather *die* than bind myself to that monster," she whispers, and all at once, my earlier vision crashes through my mind again in full, technicolor detail.

Westlyn, hiking up her lace dress and climbing out onto the balustrade. A lone shoe tumbling to the ground. A deep, shaky breath drawn and held tight. And then...

She pushes off the door and crosses the chamber, then climbs out onto the narrow balcony.

Trembling beside me, she grabs my stone arm, steadying herself as she peers down at the street.

"Damn it," she hisses. Tears streak her delicate face. "*Damn it!*"

Down below, guests continue to pour out of the cathedral in droves, desperately swatting the air as the birds swoop and dive.

A gust of wind buffets us, and the clouds creep back over the moon, throwing us into shadow. Still gripping my arm, the girl takes a step backward, her head swiveling from the chamber door to the street, then back again, uncertainty tightening her face.

Bits and pieces of panicked conversation reach my ears

from the crowd below.

Westlyn! Westlyn Patricia Avery!

She can't have just vanished!

Where did these dreadful birds come from?

Find her, or it's your ass on the line...

Heavy footfalls on the tower stairs. More bickering. More demands.

Westlyn releases my arm and takes a deep breath. "Fuck this."

And then, without another word, she's hiking up her dress and throwing a leg over the rail, a shoe slipping off her foot.

A precursor of what's to come.

"I wouldn't," I say softly.

She gasps and whips around to face me.

I shift into my human glamour before her eyes. "In case your undoubtedly mad dash up the stairs didn't give it away, we're a good ways up. Not even a witch as clever as you could survive that jump."

She backs away from the edge, her eyes wide as she takes me in—fully clothed, smiling—and I wait for the barrage of questions.

But all she says is, "It's you. You're... you're real."

"I am," I admit.

And then, wonder of wonders, a smile graces her lips, and in the depths of those bright turquoise eyes, shock and terror mingle with relief.

"I wished for you," she says softly, the earnestness in her

voice calling to some innate protective instinct inside me.

Suddenly, I want nothing more than to save this girl from whatever cruelties fate has bestowed upon her.

No, I won't let her jump. And no, I won't let the Archmage have her, either.

The door bangs open again.

The girl grabs my arm, a new ferocity in her eyes. "Help me. *Please.*"

Augustine bursts into the chamber. "Drae! Get her out of here. They're coming."

Fuck.

"Hold tight and don't look down." It's all the warning I can offer before I grab her and leap from the balustrade. She opens her mouth to scream, but before the sound escapes, I drop my human glamour and reveal my true form, a massive winged beast come to life before her eyes. My wings catch the current and we sail upward, higher and higher until we finally punch through the cloud cover and level off.

Augustine is right on my tail.

"Were you seen?" I ask.

"No. I jumped right before they breached the tower."

"The guests below?"

"Too busy with the birds."

"Good. Rook?"

"He'll meet us en route."

"Don't be afraid," I tell the girl. But when I try to look into her eyes, I find she's already passed out cold.

CHAPTER ELEVEN
JUDE

The boys still aren't home, and despite the copious amounts of witchweed I've polluted my lungs with tonight, I'm a right fucking mess. My hands won't stop shaking, my heart's fluttering like a cracked-out hummingbird, and I'm pretty sure I'm pacing a trench in the hardwood floors of Blackmoor Manor. I don't even have the strength to bother with my human glamour. My talons are probably gouging the fuck out of the finish, but I've got bigger problems to worry about than Draegan's lectures on the cost of his endless restoration projects.

Fuck.

Her window was black tonight, is the thing.

The entire fucking brownstone was black. I waited out there with the gift I made just for her—waited for a bloody *eternity*—but my little scarecrow was a no-show.

She's never done that before. Not once. Every night for

the entire fucking month that I've been visiting her, playing our little game, she's been right there waiting for me. Fucking clockwork—even more reliable than the D train.

Until tonight.

No girl. No fucking crows. Nothing. I did a flyby over her neighborhood, block by block. I went back to the park where we first met. Back to the brownstone after that, but no dice.

She's just fucking gone, and I can't stop thinking something terrible has happened and I can't even distract myself with a good bludgeoning anymore without Drae getting his balls in a twist and I swear to the fucking *devil* I'm about five seconds from—

"Still unconscious," someone says just outside the front door. "Likely in shock."

I stalk back across the foyer and wrench the door open.

And my jaw damn near hits the floor at the sight.

Auggie. Rook. Drae. All of them in gargoyle form, their wings dripping with rain.

And there, limp as a rag doll in Drae's arms, is my girl. The hem of her black dress is in torn, makeup smeared across her face. One shoe dangles precariously from a toe, its mate already gone, and her left hand is wrapped in a torn shirtsleeve soaked with blood.

The sight of it has my vision swimming with the same shade of red.

Clutching Drae's arm, I grind out, "What did you *do* to her?"

He shoots me an icy glare, his voice turning as cold as his eyes. "Out of my way before you do or say something you'll regret."

"Not until you—"

"Fucking *Jude*!" he snaps, his composure finally shattering. "Wait for me in the study. I'll deal with you after I deal with her."

"The fuck you will." Ignoring his demands, I follow him upstairs to one of the guest rooms. "You lot were supposed to be at a wedding downtown. Explain to me how this girl ended up bleeding and passed out in your arms."

In a low, menacing voice, he says, "I'm cold, I'm wet, I'm pissed off because one of my men abandoned me tonight with neither explanation nor cause. And now, as you've so astutely pointed out, I've got an injured woman passed out in my arms. So you can either calm yourself and help me tend to her, or get the fuck out of my sight."

My hands curl into fists, claws stabbing my palms, but before I can tear out his throat and bathe in a spray of his blood, my little scarecrow whimpers.

Doesn't open her eyes, though.

Drae lets out a heavy sigh, and I nod, my anger draining away.

I draw back the sheets and help him get her situated in bed, her hair fanning out across the pillow. It's done up in braids tonight, but there's no mistaking those black-and-silver locks.

A fierce wave of protectiveness grips my heart, the force of it nearly stealing my breath.

What the hell happened to you, scarecrow?

"There should be a First-Aid kit in the guest bathroom," Drae says softly, lifting her wounded hand and unwrapping the makeshift bandage. "Find it and bring it here, please."

I do as he asks, then watch as he cleans and dresses a nasty gash on her hand. I'm damn near crawling out of my skin with worry and rage, but I leave him to it. I can't distract him now. I won't. Not while he's taking care of her.

He tapes a clean bandage into place, then sets her hand on her chest, pulling the blankets up to her chin.

She looks so young and vulnerable and... *fuck*. It's all I can do not to explode.

"Drae."

Nothing.

"*Draegan.*"

Still standing at her bedside, he finally glances over at me.

I take a deep breath. Swallow hard. "What. The *fuck*. Happened?"

Drae stalks toward me, his jaw clenched tight. "Where were you tonight? I asked you to—"

"For fuck's sake! I know this fucking girl, okay? I know her!"

His eyes widen a fraction, the only hint of surprise he shows.

"Downstairs." He jerks his head toward the door. "Now."

"I'm not going anywhere until you tell me what—"

"Jude. The poor girl's been through enough tonight." He wraps a hand around the back of my neck, steering me out the door. "She doesn't need to witness a gargoyle death match. Agreed?"

He gives my neck a squeeze—a peace offering—and I nod.

He's right. Fuck, he's always right. Always the fucking voice of reason that manages to break through my bullshit and defuse the bomb just before it detonates.

I'm reluctant to leave, but I don't want to upset her. Not when she's so weak. Besides, I can't bloody think straight when she's so close to me.

But she is *close to me,* I remind myself. So, so close. I spent half the night going out of my mind believing she'd slipped through my fingers, and then my fallen scarecrow appeared —quite literally—on my doorstep. A fucking gift, that.

And now that she's under my roof, I'm not letting her leave.

Drae closes her door and locks her in—can't risk our new houseguest wandering about and uncovering all our secrets—and we head down to the study. Auggie's sprawled out on the leather sofa with his feet propped up against the fire grate, glass of whiskey in hand, flames licking his talons. Behind him, Rook's half sitting on the back of the couch, his tablet screen reflecting in two white squares on his glasses.

Drae heads right for the bar.

"Explain," he says, his back to me as he seeks out his favorite bottle from the stash. It's only now that I realize his fucking hands are shaking, his normally dark gray gargoyle coloring pale. "You said you know her. How?"

"You *know* her?" Auggie asks. "Westlyn Avery?"

Westlyn Avery... The name whispers through my mind like a sweet caress, stirring something to life inside me. Something I thought died centuries ago.

"We're sort of..." I shove a hand through my hair and drop onto the sofa next to him, stretching my wings out behind us. "Look. It's not a big deal, all right? I met her in the park on my way back from Stella's Café about a month ago. Caught some arsehole fucking with her—same arsehole I threw out of Stella's not ten minutes earlier for harassing the barista. I was practically obligated to take care of it."

"So you chased him down and what?" Auggie laughs. "Decapitated him right there on the street?"

"Don't be daft—I did no such thing." Absently, I twist the ring that used to be part of his femur around my pinky. "Not out in the open, leastways."

Drae whirls around and nails me with another look, like, *are you fucking kidding me?*

"To be fair," I tell him, "this happened *before* you instituted the no bloodshed rule."

"Jude, you can't just—"

"What's done is done, leave the past in the past, et cetera, et cetera." I wave away his concern before he gets on another of his infamous tears. "Right, then. I met her in the park last month. Helped her out of a jam, gave her an almond joy latte, and—"

"Wait. *My* almond joy latte?" Auggie laughs, a new sparkle in his eyes, the fucking sap. "I remember that night. It was your turn to do the coffee run, but you came back to the office empty-handed. You told us Stella's closed early." He smacks the back of my head. "Had I known you'd exchanged my drink for a roll in the—"

"We didn't *roll*," I say. "We chatted, enjoyed a few laughs, then said our goodbyes."

"That's it?" Drae asks, and I nod, thinking it's probably not the ideal moment to share the whole, I've-been-stalking-her-and-jerking-off-outside-her-window bit for now. Not sure they'd *quite* understand our special connection.

"Fuck," he says into his glass. "We know nothing about this girl. We're treading on dangerous ground even bringing her here."

"What the hell happened, anyway?" I ask. "I thought you were all at the circle-jerk mage wedding of the century."

"We were." Drae tosses back the rest of his drink and closes his eyes, cursing under his breath. By the time he looks at me again, I swear the old man's aged another century. "Westlyn Avery's the bride, Jude."

"The fucking *bride*?" The very word unleashes a jealous

fire that burns through my guts, pushing me back onto my feet. "But she's barely old enough to—"

"*Was* the bride," Auggie says, the sparkle in his eyes replaced with some new heat I can't quite get a read on. "She left the bastard at the altar."

"Left him at the altar?" I try not to show my absolute thrill at the news.

"*Left* is a bit of understatement." Rook finally tears his attention away from the tablet and sits down in the chair beside us. "She called off the final rites, stabbed him in the throat with a ceremonial athame, *then* left him at the altar."

"Fucking hell," I reply, more than a little impressed. "Maybe I should've let *her* decapitate the guy in the park."

"Pretty sure demon-slaying is a new pastime for your damsel," Auggie says.

"Wait... *demon?*"

Auggie sighs and passes his glass behind him for a refill. Drae tops him off, and for the next several minutes, the three of them take turns filling me in on the disastrous evening—the botched blood ritual, the mysterious ravens, the grand leap from the bell tower—but honestly, I'm barely following. My heart is pounding in my ears, I'm pacing again, and the longer they talk, the more the whole fucking story sounds like an episode of that show with the hot monster-hunting brothers.

The difference is—this episode isn't getting wrapped up in a neat little bow.

In fact, I'm pretty sure the flaming shite is about to hit the fan.

Tune in next week for the terrifying conclusion...

"So the girl who was supposed to marry Forsythe's demon son," I say to Drae, "is now a shadow mage fugitive? One we're harboring in our home?"

"Not to put too fine a point on it," he says. "Yes."

"What about Forsythe? The Cerridwen Codex?"

He shakes his head, wings slumping. "This certainly complicates matters in that regard."

"So what's our move, then?" Panic rises inside me once more, chasing away all rational thoughts. "You brought her here, Drae. Tell me you've got a plan. Tell me you've got a *fucking* plan that doesn't involve ransoming her for that *fucking* Codex or I swear to the devil I'll—"

"Rook," Drae says, keeping his eyes locked on mine, "I need you to find out everything you can about the families. Her parents, any known siblings, the Archmage, his wife and son, any known connections to demons. Are the Thornwood cameras still recording?"

Rook nods. "Two dozen cameras, and they're all still live. I've got the feeds backing up to three different servers at five-minute intervals, all of it encrypted."

"Good. I want those feeds left running for the next week at least. I'm putting additional security on the premises and closing the cathedral to events until further notice. If anyone shows up uninvited—including more birds—I want to know about it."

"Got it." Rook gives the crest of my wing an affectionate squeeze, then heads to the other side of the manor, locking himself inside the lair where he spends the majority of his waking hours cuddling with his various computers, inventing technological breakthroughs that would put Nobel laureates to shame, and playing enough video games to rot the brains of a dozen mortals.

The rest of us make for the kitchen. No one's eaten yet tonight, and it's clear we've got a lot of work ahead of us before the sun rises and turns us all to stone.

Glancing at his watch, Drae says, "We've got about four hours until sunrise. I'm going to help Rook with his research—see what we might dig up about shadow mages and demons. Augustine, you stay with the girl for now. The last thing we need is for her to wake up and—"

"Oh, I think the fuck *not*." I shake my head, my blood simmering at the thought. "No one but me is going anywhere *near* her again tonight. You two just... I don't know. Keep doing whatever you need to do to figure out what the fuck happened to her, who the fuck's to blame, and how the fuck soon I can hunt them down, bleed 'em dry, and make a necklace out of their teeth."

"*Jude*," Drae warns. "No one is making necklaces out of teeth. We need—"

"If you're not keen on the necklace idea, fine." I bang around the cupboards in search of the sugar, coconut oil, and almond extract. "Bracelets are also an option. Belly chains have fallen a bit out of fashion, but I'm happy to do a custom order if you ask nicely. For fuck's sake, Auggie. Where the *fuck* is the almond extract?"

"Um, Jude?" He reaches past me and retrieves the small brown bottle. "Far be it from me to question a raging psychopath who's clearly in the middle of a raging psychotic break, but... what exactly are you doing?"

I snatch the bastard bottle from his stupid bastard hand and snarl at him. "You can't make an almond joy latte without almond extract, Auggie. I figured you'd know that, considering it's your signature drink. Keep up."

"I appreciate the gesture, but the only drink I'm interested in tonight rhymes with dickskey and burns on the way down."

"It's not for *you*, you bloody heathen. It's for *her*." My human glamour flickers back to life, and I grab the almond milk from the fridge and get to work setting up the cappuccino machine, a beast of a thing I only know how to work on account of the barista at Stella's, and you can bet your arse I'll be sending her a thank-you card as soon as this is over.

"You're... making Westlyn a latte?" Auggie gives me his patented what-the-fuck look. "Why?"

"She likes them, you dickhead. Now fuck off and let me do this proper before the poor girl wakes up and decides to stab *you* in the throat, too. I'm still in a mood and not entirely sure I'd stop her."

CHAPTER TWELVE

WESTLYN

Soft breath ghosting across my lips.

The weight and warmth of another body lying beside me.

The scent of sweet almond and chocolate on the air, and —just beneath it—a hint of candle flame and black pepper.

All of this coalesces in my mind, slowly teasing me back to consciousness, and I finally open my eyes. I'm lying on my side, the space illuminated only by the moonlight. It feels like... like a bed, but—

Suddenly, a lamp clicks on, washing the room in a golden glow.

And there, mere inches from my face, two striking cobalt-blue eyes stare straight at me.

"Fuck!" I yelp, bolting upright. My heart leaps into my throat as I rapidly take in the unfamiliar scene—pale blue bedroom, bed covered in expensive white linens, pillowcases smudged with makeup. *My* makeup, I realize. How long have I been here? I lift the sheets and peek underneath, relieved to find I'm still fully clothed.

"It's all right," a soothing voice murmurs. "I'm not going to hurt you."

The accent... Rough-and-tumble British bad boy. Sexy. Dark. Something about the cadence of it tugs at my memory, but my head is throbbing and everything's fuzzy, and trying to remember where I've heard that voice before is like walking uphill through molasses.

I close my eyes and rub my temples, trying to grasp at something in my mind that feels just out of reach. "Where... where am I? Who are you?"

"You're in my home in the Catskills, about an hour northwest of Kingston. As for who I am... Surely you haven't forgotten me already?"

He sits up beside me, his arm brushing against mine. A spark of awareness skitters from my shoulder down to my fingertips.

"My head's kind of fuzzy tonight. I'm..." I turn to look at my bedside companion, my words falling away at the sight of him. The shocking blue eyes watching me intently. Black hair falling into his face, longer on the top and shaved on the sides. A familiar, intoxicating scent that lingers in my memory from another time, another place.

"I... I *know* you." I'm reaching for his face before I even realize what I'm doing, fingertips brushing his hair and gently trailing down to his perfectly stubbled jaw.

"Hello, scarecrow." A crooked, mischievous grin curves his mouth, and he turns and presses the softest kiss to my palm. "Miss me, darling?"

I close my fingers over the heat spreading across my palm.

Scarecrow...

For the second time tonight, my heart stops.

It's him. My avenging knight.

"You... you saved me?" I whisper, but the moment the words are out, I know they're not true. It wasn't *him* in the bell tower, but...

Bell tower...

Memories flash through my mind, snapshots of a night gone horribly wrong. The black lace dress. Eloise and her flowers. The men watching me from the pews.

The demon.

The ravens and crows.

The athame and the blood.

Running up to the bell tower and... Did I fall? No, that's not right. I was climbing onto the ledge and there was someone else close by... He grabbed me. We leaped off the tower and I was so sure we'd hit the ground, but...

Damn it. Everything in my mind is a murky gray mist. The harder I try to remember, the foggier things get.

How the hell did I end up here?

Fear crashes over me in a hot wave, sending my heart into overdrive. I try to kick off the bedding, but my lungs seize up and suddenly I can't get enough air, can't get free from the sheets determined to hold me captive. "I have to go. Let me go! Let me *go*!"

"Calm down," he says, raising his hands and giving me a little space, but not much. "I'm not going to hurt you."

"How did I get here?"

"It was your wedding night. You were running from your demon groom. You were injured. You asked my associate to help you, so he did. He brought you here. Patched up your hand, too."

I stare at the clean bandage wrapped around my hand, remembering the cruel slice of that athame. "Your associate... Where is he now? And who the hell are *you*?"

"I'm Jude, and I'll answer all your other questions in due time, but first you need to breathe." He turns toward the nightstand and grabs a mug of something hot and frothy. "Drink this."

I take the mug and give it a good sniff. The rich, creamy scent calms my racing heart—the chocolate and almonds I smelled earlier. "What is it?"

"An almond joy latte. As I recall, you're a fan."

My heart softens at the gesture, and I bring the mug to my lips, dying for a sip. But then I hesitate.

"Bloody hell, girl. If I wanted to kill you, I would've done it while you slept. It's a lot easier that way—trust me." He covers my hand with his and guides the mug to his lips, making a show of taking a deep drink.

"See?" He draws back, flashing a grin. "Nothing to worry about."

Foam coats his upper lip, and once again I reach for him without thinking. I slide my thumb across his mouth, stopping to linger at the center of his soft lips.

His eyes blaze, and he grabs my wrist and pushes my thumb into his mouth. Without breaking that intense gaze, he bites down, his tongue skating across the tip.

Something hot and dangerous uncurls in my stomach.

I snatch my thumb back and wrap my hands around the mug, forcing myself to take a sip. It's perfect—sweet and creamy, even better than the café stuff.

Finally convinced he's not trying to poison me, I say, "You said this is your house?"

"Partly. I share it with three others."

"How did you find me tonight?"

"We were at the wedding. I had no idea you were betrothed—seems you left out a few details during our little get-to-know-you chat in the park."

He keeps his tone light, but something dark crosses his teasing gaze.

Is he... jealous?

"But I *don't* know you, Jude," I say, even though it feels like a lie. Like I've known him forever and we're just now reuniting after a long, inexplicable separation. "Until two minutes ago, I didn't even know your name. We're total strangers."

"Ouch. You wound me." He presses a hand to his heart. "After all this time, I think we're a bit more than strangers."

I wait for him to bring it up. To shatter the illusion it

was all just a fantasy. To admit he really *was* standing outside my window all those nights, just as I wanted to believe.

Watching me.

Stalking me.

Obsessed with me.

My heartbeat kicks into high gear again. *A bit more than strangers...* The very idea should terrify me. It would mean he really *did* follow me home from the park that night. That he kept coming back for me, night after night, watching me as I stood in front of the window and cried out for the man with the cobalt-blue eyes and the sinfully hot accent. The man I never thought I'd see again...

I take a shuddering breath, but no, it's not terror that's got me trembling now.

It's desire.

Heat gathers in my core, and an image flashes through my mind unbidden: Jude gripping my thighs and shoving them apart, lowering his mouth to my needy flesh and—

"Is everything okay, darling?" he asks. "Suddenly you seem a bit... *feverish*."

Goddess, it's like the man can read my mind.

"I'm fine. Why did you come to my wedding?"

"My associates and I were invited guests."

Great.

"Lennon's or Eloise's?"

"Lennon's." He raises his hands in surrender at my immediate scowl. "But he's no friend, believe me. We're

more... business acquaintances. *New* business acquaintances, at that."

Lennon's. He must know I'm a witch. Which makes him
a... what? Lennon doesn't waste his time with mundane
humans.

"Are you a mage?" I ask. "Shifter?" A fresh bolt of alarm
shoots through me. "Oh, goddess... Please tell me you're not
a vampire trying to sweeten up my blood for the big bite."

Jude laughs, then cocks his head, his eyes narrowing.
"You don't know what I am? I thought most witches could
tell?"

"I'm not most witches. I'm... I was born without magic."
Heat crawls across my neck, making me itchy. No matter
how many times I've had to say it out loud, it never gets any
easier. "It's kind of a long story."

Jude lies back down again, crossing his ankles at the foot
of the bed. From his jeans pocket, he removes a small
wooden ring carved with some sort of leaf motif.

"Start at the beginning," he says, flipping the ring across
his knuckles. "And make it a good yarn, scarecrow.
Succumbing to boredom is *really* not good for my temper."

CHAPTER THIRTEEN

WESTLYN

I swallow hard, still trying to process what happened tonight. To remember. To get a read on the man who seems to have fallen straight out of my fantasies and right into my bed.

Well, *his* bed, technically. But still.

I take another sip of the latte and sneak a peek at him from the corner of my eye. There's definitely something dark and dangerous about him, an undercurrent humming along beneath the surface. But for whatever reason, I don't feel threatened by him.

In fact, I feel safer than I've felt in a long time.

"I'm what's called an augmenter," I say. "A witch with no active powers. I can read Tarot cards, connect with certain animals, things like that. Once in a blue moon, I'll get vibes off an object—like, I might be able to tell you something about the last person it belonged to. But I can't cast spells, can't heal, can't conjure or curse, can't manipulate shadows. Just about the only thing I'm good for—magically speaking, anyway—is amplifying the power of other witches and mages."

"Amplifying? But how does that even work? If you've got no power of your own, how can you boost someone else's?"

"I'm still a pureblood witch, which means I'm a magical being, even if I can't harness that magic myself. Any part of me—hair, fingernails, and especially my blood—can be used in other people's spells and rituals. And because I've never cast any magic on my own—never dipped into the well, so to speak—I'm considered untainted."

"You're a virgin," he teases.

My cheeks flame. "A *magical* virgin. Not the same thing."

"Good to know." That wicked grin slashes across his face, sending another pulse of heat to my core. "So how does a magical virgin end up betrothed to the demonic son of the all-powerful Archmage of Man-fucking-hattan?"

I drain the last of the latte and lower the mug to my lap, blowing out a breath. "My father used to be a powerful mage, too. His name opened a lot of doors in the community, but... he also has a gambling problem. Over the years, he lost all his allies, all his dignity, and racked up a lot of debt with the kind of people who aren't big on extended payment plans. I really thought they were going to kill him, too. But then out of nowhere, the Archmage made him an offer he couldn't refuse."

He stops flipping the ring, his face turning serious. "He sold you. Your own father sold you to pay off his debts."

"And to secure an alliance with the Archmage." I tighten my grip on the mug. "He'd have no standing in the community without it."

"And Mum was okay with this?"

"Stepmom, yes. My real mom died giving birth to me."

A flicker of sympathy passes over his features, but then it's gone and he goes back to twirling his ring. "So daddy gets a check and clean slate. Stepmum reaps the benefits. But what's in it for Forsythe? No offense, scarecrow—I'm sure you'd make a lovely daughter-in-law. But so would a lot of other witches in this city. Why you?"

"That's the question of the hour, isn't it?" A chill races down my spine, and I burrow deeper under the sheets. "I thought they just wanted an augmenter for their son. A witch they could control—one they knew would obey orders and be a good, submissive little wife. But that was before I knew about the demon."

"You never saw him before?"

"I only met Hunter twice before tonight, and both times he *looked* like a mage, but what do I know? He looked like a mage tonight, too. It wasn't until our blood mixed that I knew something was wrong. As soon as we touched, it felt like fire shooting up my veins, straight into my heart. I could hear his name in my head—Zorakkov." I shiver again at the memory. "Goddess, I really thought he was going to cook me alive."

"I heard you gave him the business end of a blade." Jude laughs, but I'm already shaking my head.

"I stunned him. Bought myself just enough time to run. But an injury like that wouldn't even kill a low-level demon, let alone one with the backing of the Archmage. All I did was put an even bigger target on my back." I close my eyes and tip my head back against the headboard. "Stupid, stupid girl."

"Hey, give yourself some credit, scarecrow. You escaped a demon. Fled from your own family. That takes some serious lady balls."

"It's not over yet, Jude. Not even close." I glance out the floor-to-ceiling window that spans the far wall. Beyond our reflection, I can just make out a forest of dark evergreens rising in the distance, their branches brushed with silver moonlight. "I need to get out of New York."

"You don't think a demon can track you across state lines?"

"At this point, I'm more worried about my family tracking me. It's clear my father and stepmother knew about the demon. They wouldn't have made a deal like that unless they had something major to gain."

"Or to lose."

"Either way, now that I've cut and run, the deal's off unless they can bring me back. They're not going to give me up without a fight. And who knows what the Forsythes stood to gain from all this. You're right—what the hell does a powerful mage family need with a magicless witch? And what does a demon want with me? There's something bigger going on here. I just... I have no idea. All I know is I've seriously pissed off the most powerful dark mages in the city and alienated myself from my family. I'm completely on my own."

It hits me then, all at once, just how alone I really am.

And I'm lying here in the bed of a total stranger, stuck in the middle of nowhere.

Jude opens his mouth to ask another question—ten more. A hundred. It doesn't matter, because the whole night is suddenly crashing down on me, and I need answers. If I can't get them from my family or the Archmage, I have to at least try to solve *one* mystery tonight.

I hold up my hand to cut him off. "Look, Jude. Earlier tonight, I was preparing to spend the rest of my life enslaved to a mage I barely know. Not long after that, I was pretty sure the night would end with me in a shallow grave or enslaved to a demon. So I totally appreciate the save, and I don't want you to take this the wrong way, but... who *are* you? Really?"

He sits up beside me again and shakes my good hand. "Jude Hendrix. Real estate developer, historical conservationist, artisan latte maker, man about town."

"I think we're well past the Tinder profiles, Jude." I reclaim my hand and stick it under the sheet. "We met by chance in the park a month ago. Then you attended my not-wedding. And now I'm here in your house drinking your latte and sleeping in your bed... That's a few too many coincidences for my liking."

"Doesn't mean they're *not* coincidences."

"You won't even tell me what you are. A mage? A demon?"

"You don't really want to know. Trust me on that."

A fresh rage flames to life inside me. "No. You know what? I've spent my whole life not knowing things, either because everyone around me lied to me or because I chose to keep my head buried in the sand. I'm tired of not knowing. Tired of living in the dark while everyone around me makes secret plans and moves me around like a pawn on a chessboard. So when I ask you who you are, Jude Hendrix, I want a fucking answer."

Jude's eyes glitter, his smile twisting into a terrifying grin that has me wishing I still had that trusty athame.

Leaning in close, he fingers one of my braids and says, "They call me the bone collector, darling, and if you really must know, I'm your worst fucking nightmare, which is saying something considering what you went through tonight. Now give me back your hand."

"What?"

"Give me back your hand, unless you'd like me to cut it off."

Cold fear chases away my anger, and I do as he asks.

He grips my wrist and drops the ring he's been toying with into my palm. The carvings aren't leaves like I first thought, but tiny ravens.

And it's not made of wood, but...

"Holy shit," I whisper. "Is this... bone? *Human* bone?"

"I made it special for you," he says, dodging the question. "Put it on."

My hand trembles, my wrist still locked in his grip. "I'm not putting this thing on my body. Take it back."

"Put. It. *On*," he whispers, and somehow that's even more terrifying than if he were shouting at the top of his lungs.

He releases me, and I do as he asks, but the ring's too big for my finger.

"You're a bit more delicate than I thought," he says. "Try the thumb."

It's a perfect fit—a thing that seems to delight him to no end.

He rises from the bed, collects the mug from my lap, and leans down to brush a soft kiss to my forehead. "Rest up, little scarecrow. You need to conserve your strength."

He's out of the room before I can catch my breath enough to speak.

The bedroom door shuts with a soft snick, followed by the unmistakable sounds of an electronic lock clicking into place and two long beeps that can only be an alarm. I bolt out of bed and crash against the door, frantically yanking on the knob, but it's no use.

I'm trapped. No escape.

Eight of Swords strikes again.

But here's the thing about the Eight of Swords. Sure, the

card features a bound, blindfolded woman surrounded by a cage of swords, but it's not *really* about the imprisonment. It's about the path forward. A reminder that there's *always* a way out, if only we're willing to open our eyes and see it.

For so long, I refused to see anything but the cage.

But after tonight?

I'm tearing off the blindfold, busting out of this cage, and finding my own damn path forward.

CHAPTER FOURTEEN

JUDE

I light the cigarette and take a few good pulls, but not even the finest witchweed can calm me down tonight.

Gathered before the fireplace again, all three of them are staring at me, waiting for some big proclamation that will solve all the mysteries.

Sorry, boys. Not this time.

Exhaling a thick plume, I say, "The girl doesn't know anything."

"For fuck's sake, Jude," Drae says. "You were in there over an hour. What did you talk about?"

"You fuck her?" Auggie wants to know. Cheeky bastard's got that gleam in his eyes like he's waiting for me to say no so he can have a go instead.

"Piss off before I bend you over and use your arsehole for a fucking ashtray." Another drag, then I tell them about the augmenter thing and her shite-for-brains parents.

"Do you believe her?" Drae asks.

"She didn't know what I was, Drae. Asked me if I was a mage—got all grumpy with me when I wouldn't tell her."

"*No one* knows what we are," he says.

"Yeah, but they all *believe* we're fae. That's how the curse works, right? But not with this girl. She couldn't get a read —not even the false one she was supposed to get."

Drae nods, and I continue the story with the bit about the blood ritual and the demon.

"She says his name is Zorakkov." I nearly choke on the word, on the memory of the fear I saw in her eyes when she told me about him. At the moment, it's taking every bit of restraint I've got left not to go hunt down the bastard myself, saw off his demon dick with a rusty butter knife, stick a candle in the end, and serve it to him like a piece of birthday cake.

"Are you getting all of this, Rook?" Drae asks.

"Checking on it now." Rook sets his tablet aside and reaches for his laptop.

"Is her reaction typical for a witch coming into contact with demon blood?" Auggie asks him.

"Not that I'm aware of." Our resident genius bangs away on the keyboard, then pushes his glasses up his nose, squinting through the lenses. "All right, I'm getting some hits on our boy, Zorakkov. Let's see... fantasy name generators, demon romance fan fiction, an old D&D module... This is useless."

"The demon romance fanfic might be worth exploring," Auggie says, peering over Rook's shoulder. "Click on that."

"*You* click on that." Rook snaps the laptop shut and gets to his feet. "I need to hack into the seminary school database for this. Give me fifteen minutes—I'll be back."

"There's something about this girl," I say, watching Rook retreat down the hall. "I'm telling you, Drae. I sensed it that very first night in the park. And now that she's here in our home? Fuck. I can't explain it." I suck in another drag, everything inside me still buzzing. "All I know is I haven't been able to get her out of my fucking head for a minute, and every time I get close to her, I feel like I'm either about to burn up or throw up. Or both."

Auggie rolls his eyes. "And this is different from your reaction to every woman you've ever had a hard-on for in the millennium and a half we've known you... How, exactly?"

"Dunno. Just is."

"Did you tell her about us?" Drae asks.

"Nah, not yet. She can't even remember how she got here tonight. Says it's all a blur after she ran up to the bell tower."

"That will last until the shock finally wears off," Drae says, pacing. "And when it does, she'll remember begging me for help. She'll remember watching me turn from a statue into a human, and then from a human into a living, breathing monster. She'll remember Augustine telling me to get her out of there, and how quickly I threw her off that tower. And then she'll remember passing out from intense fear before we even reached the city limits."

His tone is heavy with regret, his dark brows drawn tight.

"She'll remember you and Auggie saved her fucking life, mate," I say. "That's the main thing."

"Yes, and in doing so, we very well started a war." The fire sizzles and pops, and Drae crouches down to add another log. "Right or wrong, she's betrothed. Bound to that family and the demon by dark magic. *Hell* magic. Forget about the Cerridwen Codex, boys. As soon as Forsythe finds out we're the ones who took his promised daughter-in-law, he'll hit us with everything he's got."

I take one last drag, then pitch the butt into the flames. "Let him bloody well try it."

"This isn't a matter of who can win in a street fight, Jude. The Forsythes run the most powerful dark mage network on the eastern seaboard. If they hatched a scheme to bind Westlyn to a demon masquerading as one of their own, I'm betting the demon is also from a powerful line, and an alliance between those two forces is just..." Drae paces to the glass-front patio doors and stares out over the apple orchard that backs up to the east side of the manor. "For fifteen hundred years, we've had one prime directive— find a way to break the curse and save our people. That hasn't changed."

"We don't need the reminder," I say.

"I mean it, Jude. We can't afford to get anywhere *near* this shadow mage bullshit."

"She's locked in the guest room upstairs, for fuck's sake," I say. "We're already near it."

Auggie smirks. "Jude's so near it, he's practically *in* it."

Drae stalks over to me, his gray eyes blazing. "You're talking about risking everything we've worked for over a woman you spent fifteen minutes drooling over in the park and somehow convinced yourself she was your fucking destiny."

"*Fucking* destiny?" Auggie says. "Or fucking *destiny*? It's all in where you put the emphasis, really. If I—"

"We can protect the girl or we can protect ourselves," Drae says. "The two objectives are mutually exclusive."

"You're talking about a girl's life," I say. "A girl who, by the looks of it, is barely out of high school. A girl who—"

"A girl I personally don't give a fuck about, and—"

I crowd into his space, my hand flat on his chest. "Say it again, Draegan. Say it again, and you won't be able to protect *yourself*. Not from me."

Drae seethes before me. "I'm not sure where this obsession stems from, Jude, but—"

"You're the one who brought her here!" I shout. "You saved her life tonight. You patched her up and put her to bed like her fucking nursemaid. Why?"

"She was wounded! She asked me for help! I didn't have time to think through the ramifications of—"

"Bullshit. You don't stick your neck out for anyone but

us. Not once in the fifteen hundred years we've been here. So you look me in the fucking eyes and tell me you're ready to toss her out on her arse to face the dark mages alone, because I'm not buying your act for a *second*."

We're chest to chest now, both panting like rabid dogs, wings tucked in tight, claws out, muscles tensing for blows...

But fuck it. It's not gonna come to that. Not with us, and we both fucking know it.

Some bonds just can't be broken.

Drae finally sighs and turns back to the orchard, and all the fight inside me blows away like the leaves skittering across the patio.

When I'm calm enough to speak again, I say, "There's a connection, Drae. Maybe you don't want to see it, but I know you can damn well feel it. Deep down, you fucking *feel* it."

"Jude's right," Auggie says softly. "I feel it too. The moment I saw her walking down the aisle, something grabbed hold of me. Something I've never felt before—not as a gargoyle and certainly not as a man. I don't know what it is, what it means... I just know we're meant to protect her."

"I know." Drae turns away from the orchard and looks me in the eyes. "You're right. Both of you. I'm sorry I was so..." He runs a hand through his salt-and-pepper hair and scratches behind one of his horns. "I didn't just help her because she asked. I did it because something inside me told me I... I simply *had* to."

"I don't know what we're supposed to do about the Forsythes or the Codex," I concede. "But we'll figure it out, Drae. That's what we always do—figure it out."

He nods and wraps a hand around the back of my neck, giving me another affectionate squeeze.

"The only question is... What the fuck do we do with her now?" Auggie rises from the sofa and heads to the bar in search of a refill. Most of the bottles are already spent, though.

"You can start by staying the fuck away from her," I say. "Both of you. I'm going to look after her for the foreseeable future."

"Aww." Auggie throws back the last swig of whiskey from one of the bottles, then grins. "You are *super* adorable when you get all soft and mushy over a mortal."

"Aww!" I return his stupid-arse smile. "And *you're* super adorable when you have no idea I've been jerking off into your bottle of fancy hair gel."

The poor bastard turns white.

I laugh. "Gives a whole new meaning to that freshly fucked look you're always striving for."

"Jude." Drae sighs. "As much as we all enjoy hearing about your colorful pranks—which is to say not at all—we *do* need to figure out what to do with the witch. We can't very well keep her locked in the bedroom."

"Uh, guys?" Rook's back, his amber eyes lit up, strands of hair popping loose from his ponytail and frizzing around his head like a halo. It's a look we all recognize.

It means the mad scientist actually found something.

He removes his glasses and fogs his breath over the lenses. "You want the bad news first, or the terrible news?"

"We want the news that's least likely to have Jude tearing up the floorboards in a psychotic rage," Auggie says.

"Turns out our little witch isn't just a witch," Rook says, methodically polishing each lens with a cloth. "She's got dark fae blood in her."

Drae drops into the chair and shakes his head. "Please tell me that was the terrible news and our night isn't about to get a whole lot worse."

"No can do." Rook slides his glasses back into place, his wings sagging. "Zorakkov's a demon, all right. An original prince of Hell."

CHAPTER FIFTEEN
ROOK

"Please bear in mind that this is just my *very* nascent opinion based on the *very* limited data I've been able to find in my *very* preliminary search," I say. It's the standard disclaimer I've been using with them ever since the invention of the internet and the collective shortening of their attention spans. "I haven't even scratched the surface yet."

"A dark fae witch and a demon prince?" Jude lights up another smoke. "Sounds like a pretty deep gash to me, Rook."

"How did you determine she's dark fae?" Drae asks. "Are you certain?"

"Let's reserve the D- and C-words for when we have more concrete evidence, shall we? But for now, here's what I can tell you." I pull up a literary analysis of fae lore on my tablet and hand it over, the relevant text already highlighted. "Westlyn's visceral reaction to coming into contact with demon blood is allegedly consistent with that of a dark fae."

Drae skims through the text. "Do non-fae witches experience it differently, then?"

"Yes," I confirm, "and we know *that* for certain because there's significantly more information about it—primary source material that describes everything from ceremonial blood binding to injection, ingestion, and blood play during ritual sex magic. Witches and demons have been commingling for eons."

This was the case even before we were cursed as gargoyles. Witches are always seeking more power, and demons are always looking for a way to hitch a ride topside. It's a win-win....

Until it isn't.

The lose-lose part comes into play when most witches realize—belatedly, of course—that they can't contain demonic power and can't control the demons who possess whatever poor human or spellcaster the witch offered up.

"Do you think it's her father?" Drae asked. "The dark fae line, I mean."

"No, he's definitely a mage." I lean in beside him to scroll to another file on the tablet. "Brian Michael Avery, born and raised in Manhattan. Married his high school sweetheart—a notable witch named Madison Strauss."

"Westlyn's biological mother," Jude says. "Died in childbirth."

"Yes, that's in the records." I scroll to another page.

"Madison had no living family. Brian's parents both died in a boating accident about a year after he and Madison got married. He had one brother, but he died in the South Tower on 9/11—that was about two years after Westlyn was born."

"When does the wicked stepmother come into the mix?" Jude asks.

"Eloise Avery," I reply, "formerly DeFoe. Born in Virginia. Family moved around a lot but eventually settled in New York, where she later attended nursing school. Both parents died of natural causes several years ago. No siblings. Nothing particularly noteworthy about her in my search so far. I'm not sure how she and Brian met, but they were only married about three years ago."

"So aside from the personal tragedies and the gambling debt," Jude says, "Brian doesn't seem all that remarkable."

"Not that I've found so far, no."

Jude takes a deep drag, filling the air with the sharp tang of witchweed. "So the dark fae blood is further back in the family tree."

"It would seem so."

"Did you find anything about the Forsythes?" Drae asks.

"Information on them has been a bit harder to come by. I'll need to do some more digging."

"Hunter was supposedly adopted," Auggie says. "I'm not sure if it's relevant, but according to a close family friend I met at the wedding, he's not a Forsythe by blood. Apparently, Lennon didn't want anyone to know about it."

"Think it's related to the demon possession?" Jude asks.

"It's very possible," I say, "which then begs the question, how long ago did the demon Zorakkov take ownership of Hunter's body?"

"And was Hunter a willing party?" Drae hands me back the tablet. "We've been studying demon lore for centuries. Why haven't we come across Zorakkov before?"

"He's *old*, Drae. Much older than most demons. According to the seminary texts I found, he's one of the four original ruling princes of Hell. They say he hasn't left the realm for several millennia, content to rule his little corner of darkness and despair for all eternity. Keep in mind the source, though—these are mortal musings about a creature most mortal theologians believe is a myth. *We* know the demon exists, but I'll need to find primary occult sources to get any decent intel on him."

"What do you suppose he wants with our little witchling?" Auggie asks. "From what she told Jude, it sounds like the most she could offer is a power boost for a few quick spells before she flames out."

"Watch it," Jude warns.

Auggie rolls his eyes. "Metaphorically speaking, of course."

"Most demons want power that gives them access to the earthly realm," I say, "either for a set period to accomplish a task, or for a longer stint, which usually requires hopping bodies, because mortals have limited lifespans. But if he's already got a body—a relatively young one—"

"Hunter Forsythe is forty-two," Jude says.

"Exactly. He's got half his life ahead of him still, maybe more."

Jude flicks his butt into the fire, sending up a line of sparks. "He's too bloody old for Westlyn."

"But not for Zorakkov." I set the tablet on the bar and pour myself a finger of brandy. "Like I said, early days, boys. I need more time. Right now, we're dealing with a magicless witch with dark fae blood somewhere in her line, an ancient demon prince of Hell, a society of shadow mages who've managed to amass a great deal of power in this city while staying mostly off the radar—mages who might've sacrificed an adopted child to demonic possession..." I down the drink, letting the alcohol calm my runaway thoughts. "Right now, I can't give you any solid answers on what it all means."

"What it means," Drae says, "is we've got two powerful entities on the hunt for our runaway bride—the demon prince and the shadow magic society. And we're also dealing with a social-climbing stepmother and a degenerate father who are doubtlessly pissing themselves over what their daughter's flight likely means for them."

"Fuck them," Jude says.

"If I thought it would help keep her safe," Drae says, "I would do just that. Unfortunately, I think we need a better plan."

"I realize the girl is our main priority," I say tentatively, keeping the couch between me and Jude in case my next comment sets him off. "But what are the chances the Cerridwen Codex is still in play?"

Jude tenses, but doesn't make a move to bite off my head.

I try not to sigh in relief.

"All part of that better plan I'm thinking about." Drae glances at me, and I can almost see the wheels turning behind his eyes. "Just as the witches and demons of old, perhaps we and the girl might come to a mutually agreeable arrangement."

Before anyone can respond, something shatters on the second floor. Something big.

"What in the devil's *bleeding* arsehole was that?" Jude asks.

"I think we can *D* determine with *C* certainty..." Drae closes his eyes, cursing under his breath. "*That* was a night-stand being thrown through the guest room window."

CHAPTER SIXTEEN
WESTLYN

The climb down from the second-story bedroom—while much less intimidating than a leap from the bell tower—is a lot harder than it looks. Doesn't help that I've only got one shoe, but there's no *way* I'm turning back now. I didn't stab a demon at the altar just to end up a captive in this house of horrors, no matter how seductive Jude may be.

Lesson one from my wedding-gone-sideways? Appearances can be quite deceiving. Like when a cute guy makes you an almond joy latte, then gives you a ring made of human bone. And fine, *yes*, I'm still wearing it, but that's only because I wanted a souvenir. A reminder of the moment I decided to strip off the blindfold.

Yeah, keep telling yourself that, girl...

I finally reach the ground, dropping into the grass with a soft thud. Ditching my useless shoe, I take off at a run in what I hope is the direction of the road, but I'm met with nothing but deep, dark forest as far as the eye can see.

Fresh blood soaks through my bandage, the cut stinging like a bitch, but I don't have time to worry about that right now. I just need to find my way to civilization. A town. A tavern. Anything.

I scan the property again, doing a full three-sixty as I take in what appears to be a sprawling estate. The main house looks like a renovated gothic mansion, complete with turrets and gargoyles not unlike the ones at the cathedral. I came out on the back side, the windows completely dark but for the bedroom I just escaped. A large barn and a few other outbuildings dot the property, and there's some kind of orchard on one side and what looks like a vegetable garden on the other, a thick patch of corn stalks swaying in the night breeze.

Beyond it, nothing but forest and mist, the trees climbing up steep hills that stretch far past the property, hemming us in.

I'm about to try my luck around the front of the house when I spot a dark smudge darting across the sky, then spiraling down before me and finally landing in the grass.

"Lucinda!" I crouch down and tap my shoulder, and she hops up, nuzzling my neck. "Goddess, I'm so happy to see you. I knew you'd find me."

Tears of relief sting my eyes, and I get to my feet, once again taking in my surroundings. The trees. The mist. The endless darkness and the—

Oh, no.

A deep dread rolls through me, making my stomach twist.

Shadows. So many of them, I can't take more than a few steps without landing in one. Now that I'm on the run, every shadow is another threat—another way for the Archmage and Eloise to get to me.

A shadow is a shadowmancer's best ally. It's how they spy, how they astral travel, how they trap their prey.

How they kill.

They can't manipulate shadow energy inside properties they don't own, but public and outdoor spaces are fair game.

"Shit," I hiss. "*Shit!*"

The only thing I've got going for me is I'm pretty sure they don't know where I am, so they don't know where to start searching. But how long will that last? What if Jude's working with them and he's already told them my location?

What if he's trying to keep me here until they arrive?

The bleak reality of my situation hits me all over again. Even if I could avoid the shadows *and* find a road *and* make my way to a town, then what? Just waltz into the local sheriff's office, explain how I'm fleeing the violent, monstrous criminals who somehow rescued me from my even more monstrous family who—by the way—just tried to sell me to a demon?

A laugh bubbles out, startling poor Lucinda into flight,

and I stand motionless in the middle of the cold, wet grass contemplating my next move.

But then those damnable shadows come to life, sweeping over me in a dark wave.

I close my eyes, biting back a scream of frustration.

I broke the cardinal rule. I hesitated. I fucking *hesitated*. I'm the horror movie girl who goes down in the first act because she insisted on heading into the basement to investigate the strange noise instead of calling the cops.

And in that brief little space of time—barely a few heartbeats—I lost.

I didn't even hear them coming. One minute I was laughing at the insanity of it all, and suddenly they were just... *on* me.

No more blindfolds...

I open my eyes and square my shoulders, preparing to face my doom head on.

But the monsters who've come to claim me aren't mages at all. They're...

Gargoyles. Fucking gargoyles.

No, not the proud, melancholic statues I wished upon at the cathedral, but something else entirely. Mythical beasts that are part man, part monster, their hulking forms dressed in nothing but loincloths, their skin the color of river stones. Every muscle ripples with power.

I stumble backward and fall on my ass as the trio of winged creatures lands in the grass before me, quickly closing ranks. Horns and sharp claws flash in the moonlight, and I swear one of them smiles, his fangs glinting like knives.

A spark of mischief alights in those mysterious cobalt eyes, and in an instant, I know.

The scream lodged in my throat doesn't even make it past my lips before two clawed hands clamp around my arms, and suddenly I'm being hefted up from the grass and tossed unceremoniously over a rock-hard shoulder, ass in the air, arms dangling helplessly over a leathery wing.

"And here I thought we were getting on so well," Jude the gargoyle says, giving my backside a pat. "Draegan's going to be very, very disappointed in you, scarecrow."

CHAPTER SEVENTEEN

DRAEGAN

Not more than five minutes after the grand escape attempt, Jude hauls the girl into the study, quite literally kicking and screaming.

Unsurprising, given the gargoyles have dropped their human glamours. Rook comes in next, and even with the scholarly wireframe glasses perched on his delicate nose, he looks downright menacing. Augustine brings up the rear, his fangs and claws sharp enough to frighten even the toughest fighter.

And despite her best attempts at swinging, this girl is no bruiser.

Jude sets her on her feet, but doesn't release her from his hold, his big hands clamped around her arms.

"Cat's out of the bag, I see." I rise from the sofa and let my own glamour fall away, grateful for an excuse to dispense with the charade. Maintaining it makes navigating the human realm easier, but it's physically exhausting.

Westlyn's eyes widen, and I know at once she recognizes me from the bell tower.

"You," she breathes. "You... you're..."

"Draegan Caldwell," I say pleasantly. "And my associates, Augustine Lamont and Rook Van Doren. You're already acquainted with Jude Hendrix, of course."

Jude presses his nose to the top of her head and inhales deeply, making her shudder. "We go way back. Don't we, darling?"

"You know what?" she snaps. "Fuck you *and* your almond joy lattes." She tries unsuccessfully to jerk free of his grasp, but she can't hide the flare of desire in her eyes.

Augustine dips his head close to hers and says, "You're only encouraging him, witchling. Nothing Jude loves more than a woman who puts up a fight."

The girl seethes in Jude's grip. "Look, I don't know who you monsters think you are, but you can't keep me locked up in this ridiculous mountain hideaway like some kind of—"

"Blackmoor Manor, it's called," I supply, "named for my home village in Britain. Well, it *used* to be in Britain, until the dark fae torched it along with every other village in the vicinity, but that's neither here nor—"

"Blackmoor?" Her eyes widen once more. "As in Black-moor Capital?"

"You've heard of us? Excellent! Yes, my associates and I—"

"Own the cathedral where the Archmage and my parents tried to bind me to a demon." Her nostrils flare, and when she jerks against his hold now, Jude finally releases her. Rubbing her arms, she scowls at me and says, "So you guys were in on it, too? *Goddess*, I should've known. I bet everyone in attendance knew. Oh, yay! Here comes the bride! Let's all raise a glass to the dumb little witch about to pledge her life to Hell! Cheers!"

"As I recall," I say, taking a step toward her, "*you* asked *me* for help. Nearly begged me for it, actually."

"Help, yes. Not a Dungeons-and-Dragons-inspired kidnapping role-play, you sicko."

Rook lifts a finger. "Technically, Dungeons and Dragons doesn't offer—"

"Was I talking to you?" she snaps, whirling on her heel to face Rook. "No? That's what I thought."

The gargoyle actually blushes.

"Your situation is neither a role-play nor a kidnapping, Miss Avery," I say, trying my best to hide my amusement at her sudden fire. Quite unexpected, that.

"Then why did these brutes just hunt me down and drag me back in here against my will? Is it ransom you're after? A new torture victim for your little gargoyle party games? A weak, helpless servant to dust your wings and polish your talons for the rest of your lives?"

"Word of advice, witchling?" Augustine sighs. "I always

find it's best to just let him talk in these situations. You don't realize this yet because you're new here, but Draegan has authority issues, and he really just needs to feel like he's got everything under control. So if you—"

"Augustine?" I give him my most polite smile.

"Yes?"

My smile vanishes. "*Leave.*"

"But I was just—"

"All of you." I glare at each of them in turn. "There are a few things I'd like to clarify with our new guest about the house rules."

With little more than a sigh and a disappointed lowering of their wings, Augustine and Rook do as they're told. Surprising no one, Jude doesn't move an inch.

"Thank you, Jude," I say, "but I've got it from here. I'll let you know if we need your input."

"I'm not leaving you alone with her. No fucking way."

I open my mouth to *strongly* suggest he reconsider, but the girl beats me to it.

"I would rather be alone with him than with you," she snaps.

Jude's face falls. "But I made you a latte!"

"*You* locked me in a room. *You* hunted me like an animal. *You* threw me over your shoulder like a..." She presses her fingertips to her temples. "You know what? I'm not having this conversation. Just go."

"I will do no such—"

"I'm a prisoner here, Jude. Apparently, we'll be seeing a lot of each other. So please just... *Goddess!* Just go!"

I head to the bar, once again stifling a chuckle.

Hell hath no fury...

Jude lingers another beat, but then turns his back and stomps away, very likely gouging up my floors in the process.

"I'd offer you a drink," I say, pouring the last of the cognac into a glass, "but I'm not sure you're even of age."

She doesn't respond.

I gesture toward the sofa. "Have a seat if you'd like. The fire will warm you up."

Still, nothing.

I try another tack. "You're not a prisoner, Miss Avery, but for reasons I will eventually explain, I cannot allow you to leave. So we can either continue to play our little 'gargoyle party games,' as you've so endearingly named them, or we can sit down and have a rational discussion about—"

"Whatever you're going to do to me," she snaps, "just get it over with."

"Get *what* over with, exactly?"

"You. This." She gestures between us. "Just... just have your way with me and be done with it."

"Is that what you think is happening here?"

"It doesn't matter what I think. Doesn't matter what I say. What I do. It never has, so why should tonight be any different? All roads lead to the same dead end." As if to prove her point, she grabs a random bottle from the bar and pitches it into the fireplace. It explodes in a white-hot fire-ball that scorches my newly installed Macassar ebony mantlepiece. "Fuck you, *monster!*"

Frustration simmers in my blood. I close my eyes and sigh.

Games it is, then.

I step toward her, backing her up against the wall and crowding in close until only a few inches remain between us. Still holding my glass, I drag a clawed finger down the center of her chest, slicing through the black lace and exposing her pale skin from throat to navel. Her breath trembles, her taut stomach concaving at my touch, then quivering, just like the rest of her.

Lowering my mouth to her ear, I whisper, "I'd *much* rather discuss how *you* like to be fucked, little mortal, since that's where you seem to think this is heading. Care to enlighten me?"

Her cheeks darken, and she lowers her eyes, unable to hold my gaze.

"Nothing left to say to the monster who's about to have his way with you?" I breathe. "If you don't tell me how you like it, how will I know which pleasures to deny you?"

Her breath hitches again. "It's... It's none of your business."

"Now, now. Don't tell me you've never been intimate with a man."

"It's not that I've never been *intimate*," she snaps, some of her earlier fire returning. "It's just that I... I've never..."

"Never what?"

An eternity passes before she answers, and when she finally speaks, her voice is as soft as her skin.

"Liked it," she whispers, finally meeting my eyes. For the briefest instant, her gaze holds more pain than any mortal should have to bear.

And then it's gone, and she's pushing me away and ducking out from under my arm, the moment shattering.

Fucking hell, my protective instincts have me seething, wishing I could hunt down whoever it is that hurt her and stretch them out on one of Jude's torture racks.

I leave her alone for a moment, then take a seat on the sofa, hoping she doesn't try to bolt again.

After another agonizingly long pause, she finally curls up on an adjacent chair, tucking her feet up under what's left of her tattered dress.

Fuck.

Glancing at my glass, I say softly, "You find yourself in quite a predicament, little mortal."

"Yeah?" A bitter laugh escapes. "That's weird. Here I thought fleeing the scene of a demon-stabbing and getting kidnapped by the men of shadow and stone would be a great adventure."

"I see. And what do you know of the men of shadow and stone?"

"I know you own half the city, but your firm is most likely a front."

"A front for what, pray tell?"

"For... for things that have nothing to do with preserving old churches and historical buildings."

"But that *is* what we do," I say. "In fact, this very manor is a historical site. We purchased it from the original builder. Every few decades, we completely refurbish it."

"Great," she says flatly. "I'm sure the editors of Architectural Digest would love to know that in addition to your restoration hobbies, you moonlight as kidnappers. Not to mention murderers and torturers and who knows what else."

I lift my brows and grin. "What else is there? Seems you've covered the whole list."

She sighs and turns away from me, staring into the flames. I wait for her to speak again, to ask me questions, to demand her release, but she sits in a kind of statuesque silence that would make any gargoyle proud.

"Sixty-two percent," I finally say.

"Huh?"

"We own sixty-two percent of the real estate holdings in the New York metro area, which is *more* than half, though most of those deals were done through various other holdings and shell companies that can't be traced. We also own *more* than half the police force, an estimated eighty percent of the reputable journalists, an estimated *hundred* percent of the shoddy ones, and a good deal of the vampires, shifters, fae, and anyone else you might think of contacting in your apparent mission to make our lives difficult. In fact, the only thing we *don't* own a controlling stake in is the community of witches and mages—they tend to be much less welcoming of outsiders. But something tells me you're not keen on ringing *them* up tonight, are you?"

Again, the girl says nothing.

"I'm sorry. Did I misread the situation?" I grab my cell and thumb through the contacts. "The Archmage and I have become rather chummy of late. Shall I call him and let him know where to send his car service? I'm sure he's eager to retrieve you."

"You win," she says with a defeated sigh, getting back to her feet. "No more games. Just... just tell me what I need to do to get out of here."

"And go where? Home to the parents who sold you to Hell? To the demon prince you stabbed at the altar?" I rise and go to her, crowding into her space once more, unable to keep my simmering irritation from bubbling over. "Or perhaps, little mortal, you'd like to take your chances on the streets of New York. Plenty of opportunities for a pretty young girl there. If you're clever and resourceful enough, you might even live to tell the tale."

She glances up at me through her dark lashes, a tear glittering on her cheek. In a whisper I wouldn't be able to hear if I wasn't a gargoyle, she says, "I thought you were a myth."

"A myth created by the ones who made us, all to keep our existence secret."

"*Made* you?"

"We were men once, Miss Avery. Cursed to this life by the dark fae with a potent mix of their own magic and the demonic magic of Hell. Now, only the most powerful fae can sense what we are beneath our human glamours, and they are forbidden to speak of it. *You* are forbidden to speak of it. The only reason we're allowing you to see us in our true form is to impress upon you just how serious this situation really is."

Whether it's the darkness in my tone or the words themselves, Westlyn nods, acceptance finally settling into her gaze.

"For whatever reason," I continue, "fate has set us on converging paths. As I've said, we cannot allow you to leave."

She slumps back against the wall and rakes her hands through that inky dark hair, loosening her tangled braids. Locks of silver shimmer against the black, and my claws curl in response, almost like I can feel those silky strands myself.

"They'll come for me," she says. "They always come for me. The shadows... it's how they travel."

The very idea has my fangs aching to sink into a shadow mage's throat. "We're not going to let them anywhere *near* you."

Her eyes brighten just a fraction. I recognize that look for what it is.

Hope.

And that won't do at all.

In a dark whisper, I say, "You belong to *us* now, little mortal. And we always protect what's ours."

"Really?" Another hollow laugh rushes out, her earlier fire returning with a vengeance as she pretends to search through her non-existent pockets. "Sorry. I seem to have left the deed and title to my body back at—"

"Back at the cathedral with the demon you nearly bound yourself to?" I snap. "Or perhaps you dropped it somewhere over the Hudson as I was flying you to safety."

"So that's it, then? You tell me we're fated to cross paths and I can't leave and I'm just... just here to do your bidding?"

"I think you'll find that *our* bidding and *your* bidding have some common ground."

"Enlighten me, then."

"What is it you most desire, Miss Avery?"

She taps her lips, pretending to give it some thought, and I brace myself for the wave of sarcasm sure to follow.

"Well, let's see," she says, her voice bright and bubbly. "I'd love the chance to go to college, maybe get a job. Maybe even make a few gal pals my age. A boyfriend would be nice too—preferably not one that wants to damn my eternal soul. Oh! And I've always dreamed of opening a bird sanctuary. Is that the common ground you're talking about? To be perfectly honest, you don't strike me as the looking-for-a-boyfriend type *or* the bird-lover type, but hey, no judgements either way."

"What I'm asking you, Miss Avery, is what you want right *now*." I lean in close again, hooking a clawed finger under her chin and tilting her delicate face toward mine.

"Because something tells me you would *very* much like to see Lennon and Celine Forsythe twitching in a pool of their own blood as the light slowly leaks from their eyes. And that, little mortal, is where I believe we might find that elusive common ground. So I'll ask you once again—no more pretense, no more games. What is it you *most* desire?"

CHAPTER EIGHTEEN
WESTLYN

Gargoyles. Living, breathing, hulking gargoyles.

Part of me wants to take credit for their very existence —to call up Eloise and rub it in her face, like, *Hey, it's me! Guess what? Earlier tonight, I wished for the Thornwood gargoyles to come to life and rescue me, and voila! Here they are! Look what my so-called trite and meaningless magic has wrought!*

But looking into Draegan's storm-gray eyes now, I know his existence has nothing to do with my wishes. He and the others have been here a long, *long* time. I sensed it before, even through their human glamours. An ancient wisdom in their eyes. Hints of a deep, dark past I can't even begin to imagine.

Objectively speaking, they really are magnificent creatures. There's no other word for it. Taller and bulkier than the average man, yet sleek and graceful like jungle cats—and probably just as deadly. Dark gray skin that has me itching to run my hands over it, wondering if the texture will be as smooth as it appears, or as rough as stone. Massive, bat-like wings and streamlined tails that don't quite touch the ground. And of course—the horns, fangs, and sharp talons that clearly mark them as monsters instead of men.

But beyond their otherworldly appearance, traces of humanity remain. Each of them retains his human eyes, hair, and facial structure. His voice and mannerisms. All the unique little things that differentiate one person—or beast —from another.

A pang of sympathy strikes, and I can't help but wonder if their human glamours were drawn from the men they once were.

Jude, with his searing blue eyes and black hair, the crooked grin that makes my stomach flip. Augustine, hazel-eyed and flirty, a dimple gracing his cheek. Rook, slightly bearded, with eyes the color of honey peering out through old-fashioned glasses, his brown shoulder-length hair drawn back in a low ponytail.

And Draegan. Older than the rest and much more distinguished-looking, with salt-and-pepper hair and gray eyes that bore right through to my soul.

Who *were* these men? How did they come to be immortal? To be cursed by dark fae?

How did four ancient, terrifying, beautiful gargoyle beasts come to converge on the path of a twenty-two-year-old witch with no magic?

What is it you most *desire?*

Draegan's words whisper through my mind again, and I close my eyes, searching my heart for the real answer.

I don't know why the gargoyles have it out for the Forsythes, or why they bothered attending the wedding in the first place, but it was clear from the deadly chill in Draegan's eyes he's eager to see them dead. Rather—twitching in a pool of their own blood as the light slowly leaks from their eyes.

And he's right—we *do* have that desire in common. I'm not a violent woman by nature, but after what I learned tonight? All bets are off. The Archmage and his family were ready to sign me away to Hell, and they probably would've sealed the deal had my ravens not shown up.

Had Draegan not saved me.

I remember it now. All of it. Seeing him and Augustine in the pews—that strange connection I felt to them. Watching a stone gargoyle turn into a man on the balustrade. Confessing that I'd wished for him to come to me. Pleading for his help as my enemies closed in. And then...

I gasp as my stomach drops into free fall, memories of the jump and the flight sweeping through me.

I open my eyes and find him watching me intently, the coldness in his gaze replaced with smoldering heat.

What is it you most *desire?*

All at once, the fury that's been simmering inside me for nearly two decades boils over. After years of treating me like a burden, of refusing to let me attend college or get a job, of filling my head with reminder after reminder that I'd never amount to anything, of marrying a woman who never had a kind word for me, of wasting the small trust fund my mother set up for me on poker and booze, my father—my own *father*! —was ready to sacrifice me to a demon who would've used and abused me for all I was worth, very likely condemning my soul to Hell. That's assuming I even had a soul left to condemn after he finished with me. And my stepmother? She all but shoved me into the demon's waiting arms.

What is it you most *desire?*

My whole body is quaking with rage, but when I finally speak, my voice is calm and steady. More than it's ever been in my life.

"I want them dead," I say.

"The Forsythe family?"

"*All* of them."

"You mean—"

"My father, Brian Avery. My stepmother, Eloise Avery. The demon—goes without saying—and Hunter too, if there's anything left of him after the demon's gone. The High Priest. Lennon and Celine Forsythe, of course, along with every single shadow mage, witch, and sycophant who conspired to help them sacrifice me tonight."

Freedom.

That's the word that comes to me now. The truest desire I have—one I'm pretty sure I've been secretly harboring since I was old enough to realize the truth about witchcraft: that in a world where something as pure and beautiful as magic can be used to manipulate, control, and abuse those who aren't lucky enough to have it, freedom is the only real power there is.

And the only way I'll ever be free is if the people who've used their magic to hurt and torment me my entire life finally disappear.

Permanently.

Draegan's brows lift, his eyes flashing with a hint of surprise, but he quickly schools his features. "All of that can be arranged."

"Rock on." I smile, my anger already cooling. "Get it? Rock? Because of the whole gargoyle—okay, never mind. What do you need from me?"

"The Archmage has something of great value to us. So you, little mortal, are going to help us figure out how to steal it. In exchange, we will feed you, clothe you, shelter you, and protect you from your enemies until such a time comes when we can eliminate those enemies altogether."

"Can I get a new room?"

"Are you going to trash that one too?"

"No. My trashing bedroom days are over. Promise."

"There are three additional guest suites in the manor— pick one that's to your liking."

"Draegan. Did anyone ever tell you you're a brilliant negotiator?"

The tiniest flicker of a smile touches his lips. "Many

times. Usually from the other end of a gun, but I'm glad that won't be required tonight."

I roll my eyes. "And the house rules you mentioned?"

"We sleep in our stone forms on the roof during the daylight hours, which means you'll need to readjust your schedule as well. If you're thinking of making another break for it while the rest of us slumber, you should know that Rook is a genius with security systems. If you take so much as a single step beyond the property line during the day, the system will electrocute you into a state of temporary paralysis, photograph you where you stand, and send a text to the Archmage with the precise GPS coordinates of your location. The paralysis should wear off just in time for their arrival, so you can enjoy the tender reunion I'm sure you're all looking forward to."

"It won't be a problem," I assure him. "I'm a night person anyway, and I have no intentions of reneging on our deal *or* electrocuting myself, as fun as that sounds."

"Excellent. I'm sure we'll all get along famously, then."

I laugh. "Maybe we can start our own TV show. Real World, Gargoyle HQ."

Draegan's smile fades, his icy demeanor locking back into place. After a long beat, he holds out his clawed hand and says, "We have a deal, then?"

The fire hisses and pops, and I stare down at those sharp claws knowing that once I accept, there's no going back.

My entire life, people have been using me. In my formative years, I was a pincushion for magical healers and quacks. All through school, people—witches and mages my own age as well as the teachers—pretended to be my friends in order to get closer to my father, only to stab me in the back when things didn't go as they'd hoped. I was bullied, tortured, and hurt in ways that still haunt my nightmares.

And worst of all, my own father—my only living relative —used me in a failed attempt to secure his own standing in a society of cruel mages who would just as soon spit on his grave as they would shake his hand.

Now, the men of shadow and stone—the *gargoyles* of shadow and stone—want to use me, too. I should hate them for it.

But there's one difference between the gargoyles and the people who've been controlling me my entire life.

The gargoyles are at least being honest about it.

The image of the Eight of Swords floats through my mind again, and this time, it's not the blindfold or the cage I see, but the castle jutting out on the rise behind her.

Sometimes, the path to freedom comes from a place you least expect.

I take Draegan's hand, ignoring the shiver that rolls through me as he tightens his grip, his claws scraping my skin.

"We have a deal, Draegan Caldwell."

CHAPTER NINETEEN

AUGUSTINE

I've been out of my stone form all of twenty minutes, and already the girl has me wishing I'd been cursed as a permanent statue instead of a guardian who comes alive the minute night falls.

"You're making this difficult on yourself, witchling," I say. "Not to mention driving me fucking crazy, and no, that's not a compliment."

"By making healthy food choices?" Perched on the countertop next to me in one of Jude's T-shirts and a pair of sweats about six sizes too big, she sets down the bottle of maple syrup and crinkles her nose. "Not all of us have our immortality to fall back on. I could actually *die* from my poor choices."

"Ah, yes." I flip the pancakes on the griddle and sigh dramatically. "I was just reading a study about the rampant increase in deaths by maple syrup. Such a travesty."

"There's nothing maple about this stuff, Augustine. It's high fructose corn syrup and caramel coloring with a dash of BPA from the plastic bottle."

"I don't know what to tell you. Use jelly."

She picks up the jelly jar and squints at the label. "It's not even made with real fruit. By the way, I'm vegan. I think I forgot to mention that."

"I don't care. I think I forgot to mention that," I say, ignoring the surge of relief that my scratch-made pancake recipe doesn't call for eggs.

It's the night after the wedding—the night after she struck a deal with Drae to help us steal the Codex—and it already feels like she's been living with us for months. Her scent is everywhere, her presence filling up all the empty spaces of the manor—spaces I never even noticed needed filling.

She's taking it remarkably well, too, all things considered. Less than twenty-four hours ago, she accused us of kidnapping her. Now, she's keeping me company in the kitchen and bossing me around like she owns the place, totally comfortable.

I suppose that just speaks to how difficult her life must've been at home. With parents like hers, who the fuck needs enemies, right?

Anyway, not that I'd ever say this out loud, because she's obviously a *total* pain in the ass, but... I kind of like having her around. Been a while since I had a reason to cook, even if it means having to sit through her lectures about all the chemicals in our food and the dangers of drinking the water straight from the tap. It's not that the boys don't appreciate a good home-cooked meal—they do. It's just that we're hardly ever here to enjoy it. We spend most of our time at our offices in Midtown conducting the expensive, under-handed, and often violent business that allows us to do what we do best: keep Manhattan's oldest and most vulnerable buildings safe from so-called progress.

If the corporate real estate vultures had their way, the entire city would be a few good demolitions away from turning into a giant condo complex. And that would *not* bode well for the gargoyles entrusted to our care. The ones who can't speak for themselves.

So yeah, we do what we have to do. Sometimes that means taking a few compromising photos or trading in secrets people would much rather keep buried—my specialty. Sometimes it means making deals and greasing the right palms—Draegan. Rook's there whenever we need to hack into someone's computer files, spy on a corporate network, or change a few bank account numbers. And the other times? The times when threats and blackmail aren't enough? Well. That's where Jude comes in.

All in all, the work keeps us busy. Sometimes we don't even make it back here to sleep, and we're forced to spend the daylight hours on the roof of our office building. Thankfully, we own the whole damn thing.

We own the whole damn block, actually, and a lot of the surrounding blocks too.

All in a good few centuries' work.

"Where's Draegan tonight, anyway?" Westlyn asks. "I thought he was my jailer-in-chief."

"He's working in the city, which is where I should be, but I'm not. Do you know why? Because I'm babysitting a nosey, vegan, allergic-to-fun, label-reading witch who's determined to drive me to an early grave."

"Who's fault is that? Perhaps you all should be more discerning about who you kidnap. You need a questionnaire or something. Pre-screening, to make sure your victims are the right fit."

"Great idea! I'll keep it in mind for our next hostage situation."

She shrugs, Jude's too-big shirt slipping down to reveal a bare shoulder. It's very cute, the whole thing. The whole Westlyn Avery *package*, if you will. I'm trying desperately not to notice.

Also trying desperately not to get hard, because it's a bit more challenging to hide the evidence when I'm in gargoyle form and the only thing I've got covering myself is a loincloth.

She's lucky I even bothered with that, but Drae made me promise to be civilized.

For now.

"What about the other guy?" she wants to know. "Glasses guy. Rook?"

"Glasses Guy Rook is in the Blackmoor library researching your demon." I point through the sliding glass door at the restored barn across the lawn. "We'll meet up with him in a bit."

"And Jude?" she asks, glancing at her fingernails and feigning nonchalance. "Will he be meeting us too?"

"Miss your loverboy already?" I snap. Comes out a bit more irritated than I mean it to.

"He's the only one who's been... well, I won't say nice. None of you are *nice*. But he's... I don't know." She lowers her gaze, suddenly fascinated with the label on the strawberry container. "These have pesticides, you know. You should really get organic. Immortality aside, we're talking about quality of life, Augustine."

"Let me get this straight. The guy making you pancakes from scratch isn't nice. The guy who saved your life last night isn't nice. But you've got a thing for fucking *Jude*? He's the worst of all of us. By *far*."

Westlyn shrugs again, and I swear that bare shoulder is going to be my complete undoing.

"*Jude*," I say, rolling my eyes as I flip a few pancakes onto a serving plate, "went to Brooklyn to collect your things."

"What? Without me?" She hops off the counter in a huff. "He can't just go to my place and—"

"And *you* can't risk running into your parents."

She crosses her arms over her chest and blows out a breath. "My father and Eloise are probably in hiding by now. If they're even still alive."

Drae told me what she asked him for last night. The

terms of the deal. I know she wants them dead, and that's her prerogative. But still. Can't be easy on her.

It's never an easy thing when you wake up one day and realize the people who were supposed to love and protect you are the ones you need protecting *from*.

She turns back to the counter and dumps the offending non-organic strawberries into a colander.

"Why did you try to run last night?" I ask softly, and I know she knows I'm not talking about the wedding. "If you and Jude are already... friends. What spooked you?"

"I don't know. I just... I freaked out, okay?" She grabs a bottle of water from the fridge and pours it over the berries, giving the colander a good shake. "He locked me in the bedroom. I don't do well with being locked in. Oh, and that was after he gave me this." She sticks up her thumb, and I recognize the ring Jude was playing with at the ceremony. "I think he made it out of real human bone."

"Affirmative," I say. "That's kind of his... art."

"Well, his art is creepy, and *he's* creepy, and I wasn't exactly thinking straight last night, and I thought I'd have a better chance on my own. But—"

"But you're still wearing the ring, and his clothes, and here you are, brightening our dark nights like the ray of sunshine we all so desperately need."

This gets a little laugh, and suddenly I feel like a god. *Look, lowly mortals, what I have created with my charm and wit! A smile where before there was only a scowl! A laugh where before there was only snark!*

"I'm sorry about the window," she says. "Oh, and the nightstand."

"And the fireplace?"

She cringes. "Drae told you about that too, huh?"

"Don't worry, witchling. I'm sure he'll come up with a suitable repayment plan. Maybe he'll—"

"Oh my goddess! Lucinda!" Abandoning the berries—and me and my godlike charm—she makes a mad dash for the glass door. Soon as she slides it open, two large ravens hop inside.

"Friends of yours?" I ask.

"The best. This is Lucinda and her brother, Huxley. They have another brother too—Jean-Pierre? But he's got social anxiety, so he only comes out on special occasions. Actually, you met them all at the wedding."

I nod, recalling the swarm of ravens that chased off the guests last night.

"Hmm. Lucinda and Huxley," I say. "You can tell them apart?"

"You can't?"

"Ah, nope."

"Well, you knew they were ravens and not crows, at least. The first time we met Jude, he called Luce a crow and I'm still not sure she's forgiven him."

"And I'm still not sure Draegan wants wildlife in the house. In case you haven't noticed, he's touchy about—"

"Good thing he's not here." Westlyn taps the countertop and the birds hop on up. She grabs one of my pancakes and tears it into small chunks, feeding her friends.

At least now I know why Jude calls her scarecrow—not that these birds are afraid of her. If anything, they seem thrilled to be in her presence.

I laugh, shaking my head. "No wonder Jude's got such a hard-on for you. You're exactly his type—hot and crazy."

"That's not his type. That's his description."

"If you say so."

"It's true. Once you get past all the fangs-and-claws business, you guys are basically like a boy band." She cups her hands around her mouth and drops her voice like an announcer. "And here on lead guitar, we've got everyone's most *lovable* psycho!"

"Jude," I clarify, flipping the last of the pancakes onto the serving plate and turning off the griddle.

"Obviously. Draegan doesn't get an instrument—he's just the grumpy band manager."

"Oh, he'll love that."

"Rook's the sexy nerd, which makes him perfect for keyboards and sound engineering. And you're—"

"I'm *what*, witchling?" I grin, waiting to receive the lead-singer nomination. It's so obvious, it almost doesn't need to be said.

"*You* are... not as charming as you think you are. Tragedy, really. Things were going so well for the band, too." She flicks the tip of my nose, grabs the serving plate, and heads over to the breakfast nook, the birds hopping along behind her.

What. The fuck?

I'm not sure what I'm more offended by. The fact that she doesn't find me charming, or the fact that I let her flick my nose without consequences.

Clearly, my balls and I need to have a conversation about them running off and hiding at inopportune moments, because this is *bullshit*.

I dump the abandoned strawberries onto the cutting board and chop them up, along with a banana for good measure, and mix it all up in a bowl with a bit of fresh-squeezed lemon juice and sugar because I want to make sure she eats a good breakfast and yes, my balls truly *have* abandoned me.

"So what's on our agenda after night-breakfast?" she asks, reaching for her fork.

Setting the fruit on the table, I shoo away the birds and say, "First, *I'm* going to make us some lattes. And *you*, witchling, are going to shut your mouth, eat your chemically enhanced pancakes and pesticide laden fruit, and tell me everything you know about your almost-but-not-quite-in-laws."

I steal her fork, spear a triangle of pancake and strawberry mix, and pop it into her mouth.

She rolls her eyes and glares at me, but she doesn't spit it out.

In fact, I'm pretty sure she likes it, and I'm starting to get that god complex all over again.

Then, flashing a grin full of food, she says, "Am I telling you before or after I shut my mouth and stuff my face full of refined sugars and processed carbs?"

Fuck. I kind of hate that she's so fucking adorable.

"Ladies' choice, witchling. Ladies' choice."

CHAPTER TWENTY

ROOK

The Blackmoor library is one of my favorite places on the estate—second only to my private quarters, my server room, and my game room. Even when I'm here hitting the books so hard I forget to eat, it still feels like an oasis.

I'm used to having the old barn to myself and wasn't looking forward to tonight's planned invasion of Auggie and our new houseguest. But the minute I catch sight of her traipsing across the grass wearing Jude's oversized clothing and an infectious smile, the tightness in my chest loosens a bit.

I have no idea what's got her smiling after last night's epic battle of wills, but I'm not going to look *that* gift horse in the mouth.

Two ravens trail her, and as she and Auggie enter my domain, the birds hop onto her shoulders and tuck in close.

"Aww, who's being shy now?" she teases, stroking a finger

over one of their dark heads. "It's okay, Huxley. We're safe here."

At her reassurances, the birds take flight, chasing each other up to the rafters.

"Familiars?" I ask Westlyn, then hold my breath, wondering if she'll bite my head off again for talking to her.

She holds my gaze a bit, but then finally smiles at me. "Not officially, but yeah, that's kind of how I think of them. They're my best friends."

"It's quite a thing for a human to gain the trust of a raven."

She beams. "I know—I'm humbled by it every day. This place is... Wow." Her eyes glimmer with awe as she tilts her head back to take it all in—wall-to-wall bookshelves towering two stories high, the old hayloft converted into a cozy reading room. The main level has a fireplace, small kitchen, bathroom, and an open plan common area with library tables and several computer nooks. Overhead, massive skylights grant us a view of the stars. "You guys built all this?"

"The old barn was original to the property," I say. "But over the centuries, we've remodeled it to suit our needs. It's been a library for the last three hundred years or so."

"You're... you're *that* old?" She presses a hand to her chest, her cheeks blushing. "Sorry, that was probably rude. I mean, I know you're immortal, obviously, but I didn't realize... Goddess. Just how long have you all been here?"

I exchange a glance with Auggie, wondering how much

Drae told her about our history. He gives a quick shake of his head.

Nothing, then.

"We're veritable antiques." I wink, leaving it at that and holding out an arm for her. "Would you like to see the reading room?"

Thankfully, she's more than happy for the tour, and while Auggie makes us a fresh round of coffee drinks, I take her up the ladder to the loft, pointing out a few of my favorite collections on the shelves.

"The library houses all the books we've amassed over the centuries," I say, "and it keeps growing. Most of it is nonfiction—well, what I consider nonfiction. The mundane among us might call it mythology and allegory, but there's a trove of information and insight to be found. We've also got a ton of scholarly work here, along with sacred texts from all the major religions and a good bit of the fringe stuff too. Children's stories are another excellent resource, if you know what to look for."

"In every myth there's a grain of truth," she says, carefully turning the pages of an old fairy tale book. "This artwork is just beautiful."

"The author was fae."

"Really?"

"A lot of the art and literature that's been attributed to human creators over the millennia was actually made by supernaturals." I run my fingertip along the spine of an old French grimoire and sigh. "Conversely, many of history's worst atrocities were also mis-attributed to humans, when so much of it is just the same supernatural wars playing out in different ways across time immemorial."

"Creation and destruction. Two sides of the same annoyingly complicated coin."

I laugh, all my earlier reservations evaporating in the light of her smile and a cloud of apple-scented air.

"Sorry to interrupt the inaugural meeting of the World's Sexiest Nerds club," Auggie calls up, "but the coffee's ready, the fire's crackling, and we've got work to do."

"The great Augustine Lamont has spoken," I whisper, giving her another wink. "Best get to it."

CHAPTER TWENTY-ONE

ROOK

"I've already pulled a few books for us to start with." I gesture to the teetering stacks spread out across two library tables. "Right now, we're simply looking for any connections between dark fae and demon princes. No detail is too small to—"

"Demon... Sorry. Did you say demon *princes?*" Westlyn's on her feet so fast, she nearly knocks over her latte. "Please tell me that's just a point of interest for you and not related in *any* way to the demon I almost married last night. And what do the dark fae have to do with it?"

Again, I glance at Auggie. "You've told her nothing?"

"I thought Drae mentioned it," he says.

"Drae *didn't* mention it," she replies. "All I know is I'm supposed to help you figure out how to steal something from the Archmage. He didn't even say what it was."

Damn it, Draegan.

I offer her what I hope is a calming smile. "No worries, Westlyn. We'll get you up to speed."

"West," she says, reclaiming her chair. "You guys can call me West. Assuming you're actually about to tell me what's going on. If your big plan involves keeping the little witch in the dark, all bets are off. I'm serious. I will do whatever I can to help you, but I have a new rule: no blindfolds."

"It's not our intention to keep you in the dark, West." I take the bench across from her, meeting her gaze over the stacks of books. "So, yes, it turns out Zorakkov is a prince of hell. We don't know much about him, or how long he's been in our realm, or what he and the Forsythes intended with the marriage and blood bond. All those things are big question marks right now, so you know about as much as we do."

She sips her latte, then blows out a breath. "And the dark fae? Drae said they cursed you guys?"

"Yes, that's where the dark fae connection starts. Our curse... We've been searching for a way to break it all along."

"No luck?"

"Every promising lead has turned into a dead end... until now."

"Seems the Archmage and his wife have made quite a hobby of tracking down and buying ancient fae objects and texts," Auggie says, handing her a copy of the list I put together of all their traceable public auction and museum purchases. "They've recently acquired something that could very well hold the key to breaking our curse."

West looks over the list. "I take it that's where the stealing part comes in?"

"Yes, but there's more to it," I say. "What do you know of your ancestry?"

"Well, my father's a pureblood mage, and Mom was supposedly a pretty badass witch in her day, but I don't actually know much about her. She died giving birth to me. Dad never liked to talk about her." She fills us in on the family tree, confirming what I found in my preliminary search last night.

"Based on your reaction to the demon's blood," I say, "we think you may have some dark fae in you."

Her eyes widen. "But... wouldn't that mean one of my parents was fae?"

"Not necessarily. Could be further back in the line. In fact, that seems the most likely scenario."

"Too bad there's not a 23andMe supernatural edition," she says. "Congrats! You're eight percent dark fae, thirteen percent vampire, and ooh! Apparently, one of your parents had an affair with Bigfoot!"

I laugh. "I'm actually working on a kit like that, but haven't perfected the testing yet."

Auggie drains the last of his latte and says to West, "Have you ever felt anything... I don't know. Different? Unexplainable?"

"Dark fae-like?" She smiles, but it passes quickly. "I

don't know that I'd recognize it if I did, but I've never felt much of anything beyond what I'm guessing a normal human feels. I don't even have witch magic. Just an occasional tingle or impression with certain objects—but again, that's random and not something I can control, and I've read about regular humans experiencing the same thing."

West falls silent, and after a beat, her raven companions return from their explorations, as if they sense her distress. They land on the table in front of her and she strokes their wings, giving each bird equal attention as she ruminates on everything we've shared.

I give her a few more moments to take it all in, then say, "Our first step here is simply trying to find the connections between the types of fae artifacts in the Forsythes' collection and the demon prince. From there, we might be able to isolate possible reasons for the marriage, then consider what it may or may not have to do with our curse and why the Forsythes wanted you so badly in the first place."

"You think our situations are related?" she asks.

"I think you were brought into our lives for a reason, and we owe it to ourselves to try and figure it out."

"I don't... I'm... Thank you," she finally manages, her eyes glazing. "Both of you. I know we've got this weird, mutually beneficial arrangement going on, but still. Most people in my life haven't exactly lined up to lend a hand, so thanks for trying to help me sort this all out."

She says it matter-of-factly, but the words strike a chord

of sympathy. What was her life like before all this mage and demon business? A witch born without powers is extremely rare. In our day, their parents used to sacrifice them to the gods and goddesses.

West may not have been offered up on the sacrificial altar, but it doesn't sound like her life was all roses-and-sunshine either. Far from it.

"Hey," Auggie says, "don't get all sentimental on us, witchling. I'm just here to make sure you don't smash any more windows or befriend any more woodland creatures."

West laughs again, the sound of it bringing us some much-needed levity.

"Besides," he continues. "Rook needed a new assignment. If not for all this demon and curse business, he'd be locked away in his lair jerking off to the busty avatars in his video games."

"They're called NPCs," I say. "Non-player characters, not avatars. And I have no control over their looks. That's up to the game designers, and unfortunately, they know their target market a little too well."

"Lonely nerds who live in their mom's basement?" West asks.

"Or lonely nerds who live on a sprawling estate in the Catskills." Auggie shrugs, his dimple flashing. "Either way."

"Isn't it a little hard to play the game and play with yourself at the same time?" she asks.

"Not when you've got the right equipment." Auggie

swishes his tail, his brows jumping suggestively. "Perhaps Rook will give you a live demo if you ask nicely."

Her eyes widen as she takes in the sight of that powerful tail—dark gray like his skin, slightly curved and ringed with stiff ridges at the tip. Her cheeks darken, and—as much as I wish I didn't notice it—the scent of her desire intensifies, too.

"I'm... I'm sure she'd rather focus on the task at hand." I shoot Auggie a warning glare. "Demons. Curses. You know the drill."

"Draegan said something about gargoyles being made by fae *and* demons," she says thoughtfully. "What's that all about?"

"Not demons," I clarify. "Demon magic."

"Why would they need demon magic? I thought fae had their own."

"They do," Auggie says. "Mostly deriving from the power of nature and the elements. But that's—for lack of a better word—good magic. Dark fae specialize in finding ways to twist that magic into something more nefarious, and demonic power is a good way to do it. Good way to *bind* a curse, too."

"Why did they curse you in the first place? I mean, people don't just go around cursing each other for no reason."

"People, maybe," he says, dodging her question. "But dark fae? They don't need a reason."

WICKED CONJURING

"Aren't they worried about blow-back? Do unto others, threefold law, Karma, all that jazz?"

"Have you ever encountered a dark fae?" he asks. "They *are* the blow-back."

She considers this, her brow furrowing, then says, "And this object the Archmage has. What is it, exactly? What does it do?"

I don't respond. Neither does Auggie.

Silence falls between us again, and the birds take flight, as if simply *mentioning* the artifact calls up the dark history associated with it.

Our dark history.

Curiosity sparkles in her eyes, and it's clear she's biting her tongue to keep from asking the wrong things—from stepping on a land mine she won't be able to walk away from. I don't want to keep her in the dark—truly. But as much as I want to open up the books on the life and times of all things gargoyle, it's just too damn painful.

Once again, the old shame and hurts rear their ugly heads inside me, and I lower my eyes, suddenly wishing I had the library to myself again.

Group projects are always a terrible idea...

"Look, guys," she says softly. "I get that we just met and you're not ready to share *all* your deep, dark supernatural secrets just yet—I can respect that. I'm not exactly ready to drag all my old ghosts up out of the basement, either. But you're asking me to help you find a needle in a haystack without telling me where the haystack is located or that it's even a needle we're looking for. Not to mention the fact that we're supposed to figure out how to steal said needle, and I have no idea whether the haystack will be warded or boobytrapped or... I don't know. You see what I'm saying, though, right?"

"I have no idea what you're saying," I admit, a smile returning to my grim face. "But I like hearing you say it nevertheless."

"Careful, Rook," Auggie teases. "You don't want our witchling to think you're flirting with her."

Heat spreads across my cheeks at his insinuation, but West doesn't seem to mind.

"It's a metaphor," she says.

I shake my head. "You're breaking and reforming an idiom, which can sometimes work as a metaphor, but in this case, it's too convoluted. Metaphors are designed to simplify communication by creating a shared symbology that's immediately recognizable to both the communicator and the intended recipient. In order for successful—"

"And the man wonders why he's eternally single," Auggie fake-whispers.

West sticks her tongue out at him. "You're just jealous Rook's an evolved being and you're a primate picking fleas off your nuts and eating them."

I crack up. "Now *that* was an excellent metaphor, West. Truly fine work."

With a cacophony of monkey noises, Auggie gets up and

lopes into the kitchen to make us another round of drinks, leaving me alone with West, all the old secrets swirling through the air like those ghosts from the basement.

"The Cerridwen Codex," I finally admit. "An ancient text believed to contain a dark fae Spell of Unmaking. That's the thing Forsythe has. Initially, Drae was hoping he'd sell it to us willingly, but—"

"But now that I've screwed up his plans for world domination by dissing the royal demon he hand-picked for me," she says with a sigh, "I'm guessing the Archmage isn't in the mood to field offers."

"We're thinking not."

Tapping her finger on the library table, she says, "So this unmaking spell... It's a real thing? You could actually break your curse?"

"That's the theory."

"What happens then? Do you go back to being men, or—"

"That's enough questions for now, curious little kitten." Auggie hands out our drinks, his smile tight, his eyes flashing me a warning. Then, taking a seat and selecting a book from the top of his stack, "Time to do some homework before Daddy Drae comes home and finds out we've been screwing around all night."

"Daddy Drae, huh?" West laughs. "Sounds ominous. Will he spank us?"

"Not in the good way, I'm afraid." Auggie sighs, then goes back to his book.

"Bummer," she says with a cute little pout.

And for the rest of the evening, two proud ravens, one *very* curious little witch, and two fully-aroused-but-desperately-pretending-not-to-be gargoyles lose themselves in a trove of dark fae lore.

CHAPTER TWENTY-TWO

WESTLYN

I spend the next few nights with my new A-team of cracker-jack supernatural sleuths alternating between eating our weight in Auggie's delicious night-breakfasts, mainlining copious amounts of creamy caffeinated goodness, and digging through the lore for the clues that will lead us to that elusive needle-that's-not-a-needle in the haystack-that's-more-like-Mount-Everest. As the resident non-magic witch and mortal with less than a quarter century under her belt, I'm not sure I'm really contributing much to the project, but honestly?

I'm *really* starting to enjoy the company of my gargoyles.

Rook and Auggie's company, anyway.

Since the night we made our deal, I've only seen Draegan a few times in passing, which is probably for the best, given his less-than-sunny disposition and my newly discovered penchant for pushing buttons—especially authority figure buttons. Daddy issues much? Yeah. Given my betrayal and abandonment issues with my father, I'm sure a therapist would have a field day with that one.

But Jude?

My heart sinks. I haven't seen him since he dragged me back into the manor after my failed escape attempt, when I basically told him to leave me with Draegan and take a hike.

I know he's been around—the other night after my shower, I returned to the bedroom to find a series of boxes stacked along the wall. My clothes, my books, toiletries, my entire collection of crystals and Tarot decks—everything I owned promptly transferred from my old home to the new. My mysterious delivery man's scent was everywhere.

But the delivery man himself was nowhere to be found.

Now, as I climb into bed just after sunrise, fresh guilt gnaws at my stomach. Maybe I was a *little* harsh on him, all things considered.

Okay, *fine*. Maybe I'm starting to miss the psychotic gargoyle.

I twist the bone ring around my thumb and drift off to sleep, hoping if I can't find him in my bed, maybe I can at least find him in my dreams.

"No. No! Please... the train... Get off! Let me *go*! *Help*!" I break free of the ropes and throw myself off the tracks just as the train rushes by, but then they're grabbing me and pinning me down again, rough hands and gleaming knives and fire and pain tearing through my skin...

Wicked Westlyn... Wicked little beast...

"Let me go!"

"Westlyn."

"*Stop!*" I struggle to break free, but their hold is too strong. Suffocating. "Please let me—"

"Westlyn! It's me. Wake up, darling. Open your eyes. That's it."

I follow the soothing cadence of a familiar voice, leaving the nightmare world behind as I slowly open my eyes and take in the sight.

Horns. Fangs glinting in the moonlight. Sharp-clawed fingers stroking my hair.

"Breathe, darling," the beast whispers. "Just breathe."

I scream and throw myself off the bed, landing on the floor with a crash and struggling to free myself from the sheets...

The light clicks on, and Jude's at my side in a flash, glaring down at me. "Still sore at me about the other night, then?"

"Jude." I press a hand to my chest as the last of the sleep delirium disappears. "What the hell are you doing? You nearly gave me a heart attack."

"I heard you screaming, woman! You were having a nightmare!"

"And you thought looming over me like a B-movie

monster and stroking me with those deadly claws would help calm my nerves?"

"They're retractable!" He holds up a hand to show me, the claws vanishing, then sits on the edge of the bed, his wings slumping. "Perhaps I didn't think it all the way through."

"Jude." I let out a breath and climb up next to him. "It's fine. I'm sorry. You just startled me, is all."

He turns to look at me, his gaze sweeping down to my mouth, then back to my eyes. "All better now, then?"

"I think so. How did you get here so fast, anyway?"

"Oh, I was already here," he says matter-of-factly. "In the closet."

"You... what?"

"I like watching you sleep, scarecrow. It calms me."

A shiver runs down my spine, and I open my mouth to tell him to take *another* hike. But the truth is, that damn shiver has *nothing* to do with the creepy antics of a psychopathic gargoyle who doesn't understand the concept of boundaries and *everything* to do with the fact that my pussy is a fucking traitor because suddenly, all I want to do is crawl into his lap, grab on to those sexy-as-hell horns, and—

"I see you've already unpacked," he says.

"Ride hard!" I blurt out.

He arches an eyebrow and brushes the black hair from his eyes—a gesture that's somehow even sexier on a gargoyle than it was the first time I saw it on his human glamour. "Ride hard?"

"What? Oh! No, I said right... right on! As in, you're right. I unpacked. Right on!" I give him the double thumbs up, wondering if it's possible to spontaneously combust from embarrassment. Hoping for it, actually, because then I could put myself out of my own misery and not have to face his teasing, all-knowing smirk.

Alas, no such luck. Guess I'll just sit here, then. Blurting out stupid shit and being mortified.

"Thanks for getting my stuff," I finally say.

His eyes twinkle and he shifts a bit closer, his biceps brushing my shoulder, a wing curling around my back. I wait for him to call me out on my filthy mind, but all he says is, "If there's anything I missed or anything else you need, just make a list. We can order it."

"No, you did great." I stare at my hands, trying to dodge his heated gaze. "Thanks for grabbing all the Tarot cards."

"Well, you're a witch. I figured you didn't want to be without them—you've got quite a collection."

"Eloise says my Tarot skills suck."

"Eloise is a fucking cunt, as we've already established. And anyway, she and Daddy Dearest hit the road—the place was a fucking mess. Looked like they packed up in a hurry. Car was gone. Rook's tracking the plates."

I nod, unsure how to feel about it all. You'd think I'd be worried about my father, or at least curious about his whereabouts—some latent pangs of loyalty and family honor—but when I dig deep, all I feel is... numb.

"Where were you, anyway?" I ask. "I haven't seen you around the last couple of nights."

"*You* missed me."

"What? No. Just thought it was pretty telling that you ditched us as soon as the hard work started."

He nudges my shoulder. "You missed me. Don't even deny it, scarecrow."

A stupid smile stretches across my stupid face, and I shrug, tucking a lock of hair behind my ear. "Maybe a little. Like, a teeny, tiny droplet of missing. Such a small amount, you'd need a microscope to see it. Anyway, don't change the subject! Where've you been?"

"Nowhere. Just had some things to take care of."

"What things?"

Instead of answering, he reaches over and drops something into my hands.

A small hand-carved raven, no bigger than my thumb. Bone, of course.

Again, that shiver rolls through me.

Again, my traitorous core throbs.

"Did you make this?" I ask.

"From the same fella your ring came from."

"Fella?"

"Oh, he won't be missed, trust me. One less bastard harassing girls in the park."

My eyes widen. "You mean—"

"Don't ask questions you don't really want the answers

to, darling. Now, do you like the gift, or do I need to take it back?"

"It's... it's actually really beautiful." And it is, too. Every feature is exquisitely detailed, from its beak to its feathers and feet.

"Boys told me you're still talking to your birds."

I set the bone raven on the nightstand, giving it a place of honor next to my favorite Tarot deck and my blue calcite dreaming stone. Maybe it should horrify me, but it actually brings me comfort, just like the ring.

"We made a pact when I was younger," I say. "The ravens and I look out for each other."

"You made a pact," he says. "With birds."

"Yes."

"You know they lock people up for that sort of thing."

"Says the man who carves up people's bones?"

"Not people's bones. *Terrible* people's bones. I have principals, you know."

"Well, it may sound weird to *you*, bone collector, but the birds are my friends. They're also the only living souls in my life who've never let me down."

"Now that's hardly fair. We haven't known each other long enough for me to let you down yet."

"Fair point." I laugh, finally turning to look at him again. *Mistake.*

His eyes are fierce, the blue so intense I feel like I'm falling right into them. His soft, full lips are curved in that mischievous grin, dark stubble shadowing his strong gargoyle jaw. My hands curl into fists in my lap, fingers itching to run through his hair, to feel the rough texture of his horns, to run along the edge of his wings and make him shudder...

"Are you all right, scarecrow?" he asks with a soft snicker. "If I'm not mistaken, you're blushing."

"I saw you," I whisper, finally giving voice to the thing we've been tiptoeing around. Rather, the thing *I've* been tiptoeing around. Jude doesn't seem like the kind of guy to let anything get under his skin. In fact, he seems to be enjoying this torture.

"Outside my window," I continue, as if he doesn't know what I'm talking about. "In Brooklyn."

"Did you?" His tone is light and teasing, his eyes sparkling.

"You followed me home from the park that night. At first, I couldn't be sure, but then I kept feeling... something. I don't know how to explain it. I just knew it was you."

"Was it?" Another tease.

"You showed up every single night, watching me like some kind of stalker."

"See, there's where you're wrong. I'm not *some kind* of anything. If a thing is worth doing, it's worth going all in on. Otherwise, what's the bloody point?"

"You're a little unhinged, aren't you?"

"Like I said. All in." Jude runs a hand through his floppy black hair and shrugs. "Does it upset you?"

"Which part? The part where you killed a guy for

harassing me and made tiny things out of his bones? The part where you followed me home? The part where you stood outside my window every night for a month? The part where you've been hiding in my closet watching me sleep?"

"I told you." He leans in close, breath stirring my hair. "All. In."

"No," I reply, my voice barely a whisper. My heart's beating so fast, I'm sure he can hear it. "It doesn't upset me, Jude. Actually, it kind of—"

"I know."

"What?"

"I know *exactly* what it does to you." He breathes in deeply, then lowers his mouth to my ear, his lips brushing the shell. In a hot, dark whisper, he says, "I can smell your delicious little cunt."

Before I can even draw another breath, he pushes me down on the bed and climbs on top, clawed hands clamped around my wrists as he pins them above my head, his hard body pressing down on me, every muscle and ridge digging into my flesh.

He drags his hot mouth down along my throat, fangs grazing my skin as I shudder beneath him. If I had any doubts about his strength and power before, all of them just shriveled up and blew away.

Jude Hendrix—and every other gargoyle in this house— is an immortal, apex predator.

I am prey.

"Are you certain you're not afraid of the monster in your closet, little scarecrow?" he whispers.

"I... I'm..."

I close my eyes and try to take a deep breath, but it's hard to breathe with him on top of me, with my heart about to burst, with my entire body on fire with a sudden, unquenchable *need*.

"*No*," I finally manage, the certainty in my voice surprising us both.

"How disappointing." Jude smiles, dark and devious and utterly captivating. Then, in a low and dangerous growl, "Let's see if we can change your mind, shall we?"

CHAPTER TWENTY-THREE

DRAEGAN

The door to Archmage Forsythe's brownstone on New York's Upper East Side is as thick and imposing as the man himself, and after I bang on the brass knocker, I'm forced to wait an annoyingly long time before one of his mage-servants finally greets me.

It's the invitation I've been working on for months, and it arrived via text earlier this evening. But I'm harboring no false notions about the nature of the request. Rook picked up the intel last night on one of his many police and federal agency scanners—Lennon Forsythe reported Westlyn as a missing person. And thanks to his money and connections —and a good bit of shadowy hocus-pocus, if my instincts are correct—the Avery case is now a top priority.

If the unmarked agency vehicle parked outside didn't give it away, the servant's constant fidgeting and inability to meet my eyes would certainly do it.

I'm being set up.

"Tea, sir?" the servant asks as he leads me into a massive marbled foyer.

"That would be lovely, thank you."

He leaves me waiting while he disappears down the hall, and I stretch out my gargoyle senses to try to get a better read on the situation.

Voices filter through my awareness from deeper inside the brownstone—two men. One of them is definitely Forsythe. The other?

"...in connection with other high-profile cases. Believe me, sir. We are quite familiar with Draegan Caldwell."

Ah, yes. My *dear* friend Grant Reedsy, cocaine aficionado, taker of bribes, unfaithful spouse, abuser of sex workers, and award-winning neanderthal. Also happens to be lead investigator among the half-dozen federal agents who've been up my arse for months, salivating for an opportunity to bag themselves one of the infamous men of shadow and stone.

So the Archmage wants to play hardball? Fair enough.

"Sugar or cream, sir?" The servant's back with my tea, the cup and saucer trembling in his hands.

"Just tea, thank you."

"The Archmage will be with you soon."

As soon as he's out of sight, I drop a tiny tablet into the teacup, waiting to ensure the liquid doesn't turn red— another of Rook's handy tricks for ferreting out assassination attempts.

Certain the tea hasn't been poisoned or spelled, I take a sip and await my host.

Moments later, he emerges into the foyer, rushing over to greet me. His face is drawn and pale, his eyes rimmed in red, his normally crisp black robe wrinkled and stained. He looks as though he hasn't slept in days.

"I see you've already got your tea." He forces a smile. "Good, good. Let's have a seat in the study, shall we?"

"Lead the way, Lennon."

I follow him into a large, oak-paneled study, unsurprised to find Reedsy sprawled out on a leather sofa with a glass of whiskey in hand—clearly not his first of the evening.

"Agent! What a pleasant surprise," I say unpleasantly.

"Caldwell." He nods toward the chair across from him. "Have a seat."

I take a seat right next to him instead, more than happy to make things awkward. Glancing up at Lennon, I say, "If I'd known this was a party, I would've brought a dish to pass."

The normally stoic and commanding Archmage wrings his hands, tongue darting out to moisten his thin lips. "I... I apologize if it seems I've brought you here under false pretenses, Draegan, but I wasn't sure you'd come otherwise."

Keeping my tone light and my smile firmly in place, I say, "What a hurtful assumption, Lennon. But now that we're all together, let's get down to brass tacks, shall we?"

Then, clamping a hand down on Reedsy's thigh, "Agent, I presume you're not here on a social call?"

He rises to his feet, then turns to peer down at me, as if the new position might intimidate me into cooperating.

"Let's skip the bullshit, Caldwell. Your name has come up in seven separate federal investigations in as many months. Extortion of public officials, multiple counts of stolen evidence, murder, missing persons. Now I've got *another* missing person on my hands—Westlyn Avery—and yet again, your name's on the list as a person of interest. Coincidence?"

"Huh." I cross one leg over the other, balancing the saucer and teacup on my knee. "You'd think in a city of nine million souls, that wouldn't happen."

"You'd be surprised."

"Perhaps you should cast a wider net?" I offer an amicable smile. "Not that I would presume to tell you how to do your job, agent. I'm sure you're quite... *competent*."

"My *competence* is not the issue. The issue is your pattern of—"

"Your division is tasked with investigating high-profile missing persons cases, yes? Considering my firm owns a great many properties that host a great many events attended by a great many high-profile individuals, it's not entirely unreasonable to assume that I would have connections to some of them—connections that have nothing to do with any of the myriad crimes committed in this city each and every day. In this particular case, I was attending

182

the Forsythe-Avery wedding as Mr. Forsythe's guest after offering him the Thornwood Cathedral for his event, a fact he's certainly already shared with you."

Forsythe, who hasn't moved from the doorway, nods. "I've shared all the relevant details."

Reedsy shoots me his best bad-cop stare-down, but the effect is somewhat undermined by the white dust caked around his nostrils.

"Where were you when the ceremony began?" he asks.

"Seated with my associate, eagerly awaiting the bride's arrival."

"So you admit to seeing her that night?"

"Indeed. Lovely girl. Stunning, actually. I would've liked a proper introduction, but I didn't get the chance. I was called away on urgent business just as the ceremony began. I stepped out before she'd even reached the altar."

"And then what happened?"

"By the time I finished my call, a commotion had erupted in the nave. I was quickly escorted outside with the other guests. I had no idea what happened—I thought perhaps a fire."

"A fire?"

"Candlelit chandeliers. Always a risk."

"Did you see any birds in the church?"

"Cathedral."

"Excuse me?"

"Technically, it's a cathedral, not a church. The terms aren't interchangeable, as many mistakenly believe. A cathedral *can* be a form of church, but it's traditionally presided over by a bishop, which is obviously not the case in all churches, hence the differentiation. Actually, dating back to—"

"The *birds*, Caldwell," he prompts, impatience tightening his jaw.

"Birds..." I bring the teacup to my lips and take a long, delicate sip, pretending to give his question the consideration he seems to think it deserves. "Now that you mention it, I did see a few ravens in the rafters. Not unusual in an old cathedral. Lots of cracks and crevices for them to slip through."

"So you didn't see Miss Avery leave the premises at any time?"

"No. But there were a lot of people milling about in the confusion. Quite chaotic. Perhaps she saw an opportunity and..." I make a starburst with my fingers. "Poof!"

"Poof?"

"She's an adult woman. I've no reason to doubt Mr. Forsythe's belief that she's gone missing under suspicious circumstances, but adult women are *notorious* for having their own minds and wills. As inconvenient as that may be for the rest of us, it's a fact nevertheless."

He paces before me, glancing between Forsythe and me as if this is the first time either of them has considered such a crazy notion. "Are you suggesting she fled of her own accord?"

"Women leave grooms at the altar every day. Perhaps

she got cold feet." Turning to Forsythe, I smack my lips together and say, "This is truly an excellent blend. Where did you say you found it?"

Irritation simmers in his red-rimmed eyes, but the Archmage knows a counter move when he sees it. He set me up tonight, no warning, and *that* is a slight I won't soon forget.

Not unlike the long, *long* list of grievances I have about his treatment of my current houseguest.

A tremor of fury rolls through me, making the teacup rattle in its saucer. Pulling myself together, I drain the last of it and say, "I'm sorry I don't have anything more helpful to share, but if I hear anything about her whereabouts, I'll be sure to give you both a ring."

"You do that." Reedsy hands his empty whiskey glass to Forsythe and heads for the exit.

"Oh, Mr. Reedsy?" I call out. "How rude of me. I didn't even ask after your family. How are Kaitlyn and the children getting on? And your mother, Vera? I hope her arthritis isn't troubling her too much these days. I know the change of seasons can be particularly... *menacing*."

His face pales, and I send another silent thank you to Rook. He dug up the details on all the agents' families as soon as they started sniffing around our arseholes, but I've been saving up the knowledge for a special occasion.

Without another word, Reedsy disappears.

"If there's nothing else, Lennon, I think I'll call it a night." I rise from the sofa and hand over my teacup.

"Again, I'm sorry for the bait-and-switch." Forsythe offers a conciliatory smile. "I hope this doesn't affect our association. I was looking forward to getting to know you and your partners a bit better. I just... I'm really at a loss as to what could've happened to her. She's so young, and her parents are worried sick..." He trails off in a dramatic sigh, and it's all I can do not to tear out his throat.

Jude and Rook already confirmed her parents left town —Jude found evidence of hastily packed bags at their Brooklyn home, and Rook's been tracking their vehicle via state traffic and toll booth cameras. At last check, they were somewhere in Oregon.

"I understand your concern for the girl," I say, forcing myself to keep my voice steady, "but the trickery was unnecessary. I would've gladly spoken to the agent if you'd simply—"

"You can't lie."

"I beg your pardon?"

"Fae can't lie. So I knew whatever you told him would be the truth, and if I was here during the questioning, I'd know it too."

You manipulative piece of shit.

"I see." I nod, clapping a friendly hand over his shoulder as we head back out.

No, fae cannot lie.

Unfortunately for him, humans and gargoyles can—and some of us are quite good at it, too.

The only thing fae about me is a curse I'm desperate to

break and a glamour designed to make the rest of the world —supernatural and mundane alike—believe a pretty little lie rather than what their own instincts are so plainly telling them.

"Don't hesitate to reach out again if I can be of any more assistance," I say as we walk back down the hall to the foyer. "Oh, and I realize the timing isn't quite right at the moment, but I do hope the invitation to see the Cerridwen Codex still stands. I'd very much like to peruse the text."

His eyes dart to the ceiling, then right back to me, so quickly I'm not even sure he realizes he did it. "Yes, maybe... maybe another time. It's still being authenticated, and I've got my hands full with Hunter's missing bride. You understand."

"Of course. Thanks again for the tea."

He forces a smile and shakes my hand, then shows me to the door, not even realizing his little tell gave me *exactly* what I came for tonight.

Confirmation.

The Codex isn't at his office downtown or in any of the coven meeting houses he's got scattered across the city. It's right here in his home, somewhere on the second or third floor.

And as soon as we have the opportunity, we're going to bloody take it from him.

CHAPTER TWENTY-FOUR

JUDE

Thing about humans—magical and mundane alike—is they've got this insane sense of self-preservation. Admirable quality, that. They don't even think about their odds of survival. First sign of a credible threat, they fight or they run.

And when all else fails, when they're down and out with no escape and no help on the way, they beg.

But this girl?

I wait for her fight-or-flight to kick in. Wait for the panic to seize her heart like an iron fist. Wait for her to realize what a right terrible idea this is and thrash and scream and claw her way to freedom.

But the little scarecrow merely watches me with those bright blue-green eyes, curious as ever.

Fascinating...

"You know, scarecrow, most people—when immobilized

beneath a clawed, fanged predator three times their size—have the good sense to freak the fuck out."

She smiles and slides her hands up my arms, curling her delicate fingers around my biceps. "Is this the part where I'm supposed to run from the monster in the closet?"

"Well, now that the monster is in your *bed*, I thought I'd at *least* get a whimper of fear out of you." I push up on my arms, hovering just above her and wondering what it would feel like to wrench apart those creamy thighs and—

"Stay," she whispers. Her hands move to my face, slowly threading into my hair. "I'm not scared, Jude. I want you to stay with me."

Goosebumps prickle across my scalp, and holy fuck... there's no *way* I'm turning down a request like that. "You're a very naughty girl, Westlyn Avery."

"Am I?" She slides her hands up to my horns, stroking them with a light scrape of her fingernails that sends shock waves of pleasure straight down to my balls. I'm rock hard between her thighs, nothing separating us but my loincloth and her panties.

The white ones with the pink bow. My favorite fucking pair.

I bring a hand up to cup her arse, dipping my thumb under the lacy edge that curves around the front of her thigh.

She parts her mouth. A soft moan slips free.

"All those nights at the window," I whisper. "Gazing out into the darkness, wondering if anyone was gazing back."

She meets my eyes and smiles, her fingernails still scraping my horns, making slow, deliberate strokes from tip to root and back again.

"I think you *liked* imagining me watching you," I whisper, sliding my thumb over her bare flesh. "Liked pretending I could see you touching yourself. Didn't you?"

"I... yes." Another soft gasp escapes, and I drag my nose up the slope of her neck, inhaling her scent. She smells like the Blackmoor apple orchard in full bloom. Like something sweet and clean and delicious and just *begging* to be bitten.

"I *was* watching you, little scarecrow," I breathe. "You were right. Every night, standing out there in the shadows while you fucked yourself for me, teasing me senseless. I could hear your moans, hear the wet sounds of your greedy little cunt, and you made me so *fucking* hard for you all I wanted to do was smash through the window, take you into my arms, and fuck you through the goddamn wall."

"Jude," she whispers, her hips undulating beneath me, fingers tightening into fists around my horns, and fuck if I don't love the shape her lips make when she's got my name in her mouth.

"Say it again," I whisper. "Say my fucking name again."

Her eyelids flutter closed, hot breath misting my skin. "Jude..."

"That's my good girl." I drag my mouth across hers so softly it makes her shiver, but I don't dare steal a kiss. Not yet. "But there's a dilemma, see? I've got you pinned beneath me, just like I've been fantasizing about since the first night we met. But I don't think I'm going to fuck you tonight, darling. Not after you teased me so relentlessly all month long."

Her eyes fly open, lust mingling with disappointment. "Why not?"

"My, my. So impatient. So demanding."

She opens her mouth for another protest, and I silence her with the tip of a claw. Her eyes widen, but it's curiosity rather than fear that has her gazing up at me now.

"The night you came to Blackmoor," I say softly, "when I threw you over my shoulder and carried you inside, I could smell you. Even through your fear and the rain and the mud, the scent of your desire was unmistakable. It was all I could do not to throw you down in front of Drae and the others, bury my face between your thighs, and *lick* you until you were writhing and begging me to stop."

I slide my tongue out from between my lips, letting it extend to its full, impressive length.

"Holy shit." A sharp gasp, and her eyes go wide once more. "It's so..."

"Mmm." I retract it and grin. Then, in a low, menacing growl, "The better to *eat* you with, darling. Now be a good girl again and open your legs for me."

She obeys without protest, and I shift down and settle myself between her thighs, shredding her panties with my claws and pushing my nose through her slick heat. *Fucking hell*, she's so wet for me, so eager. The scent of her desire makes me dizzy, like when I was a boy spinning round and round in my father's fields until I crashed.

I don't want to crash tonight, though. I just want to fucking *devour*.

"Jude," she breathes, her hands curling around my horns again, hips rocking.

"Greedy girl," I tease, gripping her thighs and unfurling my tongue. I swirl it over her clit, then slide lower and dip inside, curling the tip to hit the perfect spot, and... *fuck me*. She tastes like heaven, like the very best summers of old on the seashore, warm and pure and perfect. A deep groan rumbles through my chest, and I thrust in harder, making her gasp. She tightens her hold on my horns and I pull back, sliding out just enough to tease her clit before plunging inside again, stroking her until her thighs tremble and her back arches off the bed.

Fuck, the way she responds to my touch, my kiss... It's like she's absolutely *starved* for it, and all I want to do is keep on feeding her exactly what she wants. What she needs.

I slide my palms beneath her arse and bring her closer, burying my tongue to the hilt, tapping that soft spot inside her again and again, stroking her harder, faster, licking and tasting and fucking *owning* her until she finally shatters for me, her thighs convulsing around my face as the wave of undiluted pleasure sweeps us both out to sea, the perfect summertime place that exists only in my oldest, fondest memories.

And then, all at once, she liquifies. Her hands release my horns and she relaxes back onto the bed with a soft sigh.

I draw back slowly, pulling her T-shirt down into place and stretching out on my hip beside her.

The overwhelming evidence of her pleasure is smeared across my mouth, the taste lingering on my tongue in a way I'll be fantasizing about for a long fucking time, and when she finally meets my eyes again, she smiles, and my name is the sweetest whisper on her lips.

Something surges inside, my need to protect her so fierce it damn near burns me up. I grab her face and claim her mouth in a possessive kiss, stealing the breath from her lungs.

When I finally pull back, her lips are swollen and glazed, her eyes smoldering, and I wrap a massive hand around her delicate throat and utter the only word she needs to fucking hear right now.

"*Mine*."

CHAPTER TWENTY-FIVE

AUGUSTINE

I've just popped a tray of apple muffins into the oven when I feel it—a dark, otherworldly chill sweeping through the manor like a cold wind, raising the hairs on my arms and neck. Suddenly, my skin's crawling with the feeling of being watched, my otherwise strong stomach churning with unexplained nausea.

And then, in a red-hot rush, *panic*. It starts in my chest and quickly spreads through my limbs, tiny pinpricks that sizzle and burn and threaten to steal my breath.

I sit on the bench and put my head between my knees, forcing myself to take long, even breaths until the panic finally begins to fade.

But my stomach's still twisted up, and I can't quite shake the feeling that someone is spying on me.

All the signs I've been trying to ignore.

Fuck.

The first two times it happened, I tried to chalk it off to my sometimes overactive imagination or a stress-induced hallucination brought on by all the recent upheaval in our lives. But this is the third time I've felt it since West's arrival the other night, and tonight's was the most invasive attack yet.

I check in with Rook, but he assures me the wards are still in place and nothing's amiss on the home security network—magical or otherwise. Drae's still in flight after his meeting with the Archmage. Which leaves...

Fucking Jude.

"Jude?" I catch him upstairs, heading out of West's room. He closes the door behind him and presses a finger to his lips, shushing me.

"Where is she?" I whisper. "What's wrong?"

"Resting comfortably now, I promise." He grins at me, his mouth red and puffy.

Doesn't take a Rook-level genius to figure out what he's been up to. Bastard doesn't even bother hiding the fact that his cock's hard.

Jealousy flares in my gut, which pisses me off. I don't do jealousy. It speaks of attachment, and I *definitely* don't do that.

Through gritted teeth, I say, "I can *smell* her on you, asshole."

"Poor girl had a nightmare. Needed something to help her relax." He drags his thumb across his lower lip, letting out a soft moan. "No worries. I got her settled *right* nicely. Hey, are those muffins I smell? I'm bloody starving."

I follow him down to the kitchen. "Is she coming?"

Another grin. "Not at this *precise* moment, but I know she's eager to do it again soon."

Biting back my supreme irritation, I add, "To *breakfast*, Jude. Is she coming to breakfast?"

"I think she needs a bit more rest, but she'll be down later." He grips the edge of my wing, giving it a playful shake. "Honestly, Augs. What's got your knickers in a twist tonight? We've got muffins in the oven, a beautiful girl in our guest room, no one's tried to kill us for at least a week... Show a little gratitude for the good things, mate."

"Yeah, about that 'not trying to kill us' bit?" I slump onto the bench in the breakfast nook. "Something's here, Jude. It's not good."

"Define 'something' and 'not good.'" He sits down across from me. "Come on, Augs. Use your words."

"You know those feelings I sometimes get?"

The teasing vanishes from his eyes. He knows *exactly* what feelings I'm talking about.

"Auggie's heebie-jeebies," he whispers—the nickname he gave the phenomenon when it first started happening eons ago.

Of all of us, I've always been the one most able to sense and identify otherworldly presences. Over the centuries, we've dealt with everything from Civil War ghosts to the vengeful spirits of humans hung for witchcraft allegations, demonic entities attached to Rook's collection of dark grimoires, trickster fae wreaking havoc in the orchard, you name it. I've always been able to track it down, figure out what it needs, and send it packing.

But this? This is different. This is worse.

"Demon?" he asks. "Ghost?"

"Fae, if my gut's anything to go by. Only there's something off about this one. Almost like it's not completely... formed."

"I don't follow."

"There are stories of dark entities from the void between the fae realm and ours—not quite one or the other, trapped in a sort of dark fae purgatory without a physical body, always looking for a way to get free."

"You think that's what we're dealing with?" Jude reaches for his pack of smokes on the table and taps one out. "You saw it?"

I press a hand to my still-roiling gut. "I can *feel* it."

"How the fuck could something like that get past the wards? Doesn't Rook have safeguards for this kind of shit?"

"That's the thing—I'm not sure it *did* get past."

"Explain."

"Rook says the wards and security systems are solid. Nothing's showing up on the cams or sensors—nothing magical, nothing visual. Honestly?" I shake my head, hoping to the devil I'm wrong, but that churning in my gut has never led me astray. "It doesn't feel like something trying to get *in* from the outside. It feels like something that's already here, and it's just starting to wake up. And Jude?"

He lights the cigarette, the tip crackling as he sucks in a deep drag.

My skin prickles again with that incessant, nagging feeling that someone—*something*—is watching us.

Through the gray haze of witchweed smoke, I whisper, "Whatever it is, it's old. It's dangerous. And it's *pissed*."

CHAPTER TWENTY-SIX

WESTLYN

Mine...

The word echoes in my mind, sending aftershocks rippling through my body from the roots of my hair all the way down to my purple-painted toenails. Everything inside me is buzzing and electric, my heart banging around like a trapped bird.

I can't believe I just let a near-stranger—a *gargoyle* stranger—a gargoyle stranger with sexy horns and a tongue the size of a zucchini—go down on me.

I've never, *ever* had a man use his mouth on me. Hell, I've never even had a man make me come before.

Goddess, it felt so good.

Goddess, I hope we get to do it again soon.

And maybe next time I'll even get to return the favor. Maybe *next* time things will progress beyond mouths. If the size and skill of his tongue are any indication, whatever

Jude's got going on under that loincloth will probably put me in the hospital...

Oh, no. I'm in serious trouble. I shouldn't even be *thinking* about his loincloth. Or his loins. Or said loins wrecking me to the point of needing an ambulance.

But here I am. *Thinking* about it. Wishing for it.

And what's worse? I heard Auggie outside the door when Jude left, and now I can't stop fantasizing about what it would be like to have not one, but *two* immortal apex predators between my thighs, their hot, filthy gargoyle tongues going at it like it's all-you-can-eat dessert night at Big Al's Diner and I'm the chocolate cream pie.

Damn it!

Forcing away my depraved thoughts, I take a deep, calming breath, close my eyes, and try like hell to fall back asleep. After that stupid nightmare, I was hoping to catch at least another hour or two before heading down to eat and hit the books again.

But twenty more minutes of tossing and turning brings me no closer to dreamland.

It only makes me hotter, wetter, and way more frustrated.

My pussy is still bare on account of his claws shredding my underwear.

My clit is still throbbing on account of his relentless tongue-lashing.

And all I can think about now is begging him to rush

back in here, pin me down with those vicious talons, and do it to me all over again.

But... no. I *refuse* to beg. Jude obviously has better things to do than give me back-bending, mind-altering orgasms all night—if he didn't, he'd still be here.

With a resigned sigh, I part my thighs, muscles aching where he gripped me, and trail my fingers down between them. The barest brush over my sensitive clit has me gasping, unleashing another electric jolt as I remember his demanding mouth, the feel of those hard, rough horns against my palms...

I picture both gargoyles here now, Jude and Auggie, their powerful talons pinning me to the bed as they take turns kissing and licking and sucking, their fierce, possessive growls of pleasure vibrating across my skin as they fuck me with those deadly tongues...

My hips rock, and I dip two fingers inside, slowly drawing back to circle my clit with hot, wet strokes before sliding in deep once more, every thrust bringing me closer, the imagined feel of our tangled bodies setting my nerves ablaze as I drag my wet fingers across my clit again, then fuck myself deeper, faster...

Fuck yes... yes!

My core clenches around my fingers and I cry out into the darkness, everything inside me coming apart at the seams as the orgasm explodes—

"Westlyn!" The door bangs open, and for the second time tonight, a hulking gargoyle looms over the end of my bed, wings outstretched, fangs gleaming as he scans the room for a threat. "What happened?"

I take in the sight of his salt-and-pepper hair, the dark gray eyes flashing in the moonlight.

"D-Draegan?" I gasp, my voice breathy and strained.

"Are you hurt?"

Oh, goddess. This is bad. This is really bad.

"No, I... I had a nightmare," I blurt out.

He glances around the room once more, then folds his arms across his chest and sighs. "A nightmare. Really. You seem quite alert at the moment."

"Right, I... I meant earlier. I had a bad dream tonight, but then Jude came in and... calmed me down. So I'm totally fine now. Thanks for checking, though!"

"I'm not talking about earlier, Miss Avery. I'm talking about just now, when you were shouting as if someone had mounted an attack."

Mounted...

"Oh! That. That was just... therapy. You know, re-create your nightmare, face your inner demons head on, change the outcome. It's the, um, nocturnal reframing approach? Very effective. They've done studies. Do you have nightmares? You should totally try——"

"Miss Avery." Draegan takes a step, then another, and suddenly he's *right* by my side, his imposing presence swallowing up all the space. All the air.

His eyes are blazing.

I'm flat on my back, half naked beneath the sheet, completely helpless against his raw, masculine power. I should be terrified, just like I should've been terrified of Jude.

But all I can think is...

Daddy Drae is finally going to spank me.

"Are you *lying* to me, little mortal?" he demands, his voice low and menacing.

"Um... no?" I squeak out.

Without warning, he yanks off the sheet, grabs my hand, and brings it to his face. There's a deep inhale, and then... *holy hell...* he sucks my fingers into his mouth.

My thighs clench, fire burning between them as he licks my fingers in a slow, erotic caress with that luscious tongue, his storm-ravaged eyes never leaving mine.

This is so not helping...

A soft moan escapes my lips unbidden, and then, right as I'm about to throw myself on his mercy and beg for him to put that tongue to better use, he draws my fingers out with a wet smack of his lips and leans in close, his mouth hovering just above mine.

Oh, fuck... Is he actually going to kiss me? Or is he—

"There are many indiscretions I will tolerate, Miss Avery," he whispers, breath tickling my lips, "particularly since you're still coming to terms with the sudden and unplanned turn your life has taken. Deception, however, is *not* one of those indiscretions. Lie to me again and I assure you, the nightmares that haunt your sleep will pale in comparison to the ones I unleash upon you during your waking hours. Understand?"

I nod, too stricken to do anything else.

His grip around my wrist tightens, claws scraping my skin. "Sorry, I didn't quite catch that."

"I... I understand." I clear the tightness from my throat. "I'm sorry. It won't happen again—I swear."

"See that it doesn't." He loosens his grip around my wrist, then gently places my hand against my chest and pulls the sheet up to my chin—a tender gesture completely at odds with his cold demeanor.

When he speaks again, his voice has lost some of its edge. "I'm sorry you're having trouble sleeping. It can be hard for mortals to adjust to our schedule."

"I'll manage. Like I said, I'm already a night owl. A few more days and I'll be all synced up with the boys."

"Good. I..." He holds my gaze for another beat, but whatever he meant to say, he lets it go. "Anyway, I'll see about getting you something to help you sleep. I know a reliable potions master who's more skilled than any mortal pharmacist."

A flicker of annoyance sparks to life, chasing away the earlier heat. "*That's* your solution? Drug me?"

"We can't very well have you screaming bloody murder every night. How are we to know whether you're actually in danger? Not to mention, it's downright disruptive. You share a home with four others now, Miss Avery. Try to keep that in mind."

Goddess, the guys were right. He really *is* like a dad. A supremely irritating one.

"I'm sorry if my nightmares are inconvenient for you," I say, "but we made a deal. I share a home with you now, just like you said. Me. A mortal. And that comes with all my quirks and foibles—disruptive nightmares, hair in the shower drains, annoying dietary restrictions, avian companions, and whatever else might be on your list of things to complain about. And in exchange for putting up with me, I help you with the fae research and whatever I can tell you about the—"

"And it's not enough."

"No?" I scoff. "What else can I give you, Draegan? What do you need? Because I'm at a loss here."

"What I *need* is that Codex—a thing that's currently locked away in the Archmage's brownstone. And I can't make him an offer, because right now, there's only one thing in the whole bloody world the Archmage would be interested in acquiring, and he doesn't even know we've got it."

He shoves a hand through his hair, the muscles in his jaw ticking. When he meets my eyes again, I swear I see a flash of anguish in his gaze.

"I know," I whisper, shame heating my cheeks. It's no wonder he's so cold and distant with me.

Me. I'm the thing Forsythe wants. The thing Draegan's keeping secret.

And at what cost?

If not for me bailing at the altar, he might've already

gotten the Codex. The gargoyles might've already broken their curse.

"You wish you hadn't saved me," I say softly. It's not a question. "You wish you could go back to that night in the bell tower and just... just remain a statue and let me dash my brains on the street below. Your life would be a lot less complicated now, wouldn't it?"

I search his eyes for that anguish again, for the storm, for even the slightest hint of emotion, but there's nothing there. All of his walls are firmly back in place.

"It would," he says flatly. Then, turning on his heel and heading for the door, "I have a meeting in Kingston. You should... go eat something. I'm sure Augustine is eager for you to try his apple muffins."

CHAPTER TWENTY-SEVEN
AUGUSTINE

"Well! Look who decided to join the land of the living." I grin at the groggy-faced witch shuffling into the kitchen. "Lucinda and Huxley were starting to worry."

"Can't talk." She plunks herself down on a bench at the breakfast nook, where her birds are busily pecking away at a muffin. "Need caffeine."

"One step ahead of you, as always." I set the almond joy latte before her, and she grabs it like a ravenous fiend and downs half of it in one go.

Only then does a true smile grace her face. "Thank you, Auggie. You're a lifesaver."

"Don't let *that* get out. My reputation as a stone-cold killer can't afford the hit."

She laughs and finally looks up at me, but the moment our gazes connect, she lets out a little gasp and lowers her eyes back to the mug, her cheeks darkening.

Devil's balls, that shade of pink looks good on her...

I've got no idea what's going on in *her* mind right now, but mine? Let me break it down. I'm standing here looking at a girl sitting on a bench in her eggplant emoji boxer shorts, white knee socks pulled all the way up to mid-thigh, sky blue hoodie zipped to her chin. Her freshly washed hair is piled on her head in a wet bun, sheet marks still crease her face, and her small hands are wrapped tight around the mug of a drink I made for her—a drink we both love. Two ravens pace the table, occasionally nudging her hand for an affectionate head rub. Whole thing's a fucking photograph —a picture-perfect snapshot that's already sealed in my memory for the rest of my immortal life, no camera required.

All of this, I can clearly see. I can name it, too—as if it were already hanging in a gallery: A Girl and Her Ravens. But no matter how hard I try to focus on the girl sitting right in front of me in all her fresh-out-of-the-shower gloriousness, all I can picture is that same girl naked and feverish, her fingers curling into the sheets, back arching off the bed as Jude eats her sweet pussy and makes her cry out his name in ecstasy...

Fuck. I should *not* be fantasizing about Jude fucking this girl. I should not be fantasizing about *me* fucking this girl. The last thing we all need is to complicate an already complicated situation with a romantic entanglement.

But Jude's already done just that. And now I can't get the fucking idea out of my head.

Her stomach growls, and I jump at the chance for something else to do—*anything* else besides fueling my depraved fantasies.

"Anyway, yeah." I force a casual tone as I head to the fridge. "The guys already ate, but there's plenty of food left. I made my infamous apple muffins. Apple waffle batter, too. All vegan, of course. We've always got a shit ton of apples this time of year—I try to find different ways to use them."

This perks her right up. "I love apples! I used to get them from the farmer's market in Union Square, but I haven't been able to go this year."

"Farmer's market? *Pffft*. I picked these myself, right from our own backyard. Never spent a day of their lives on a conveyer belt or in a delivery truck sitting in traffic on the Cross Bronx."

"Even better, then." She downs the rest of her latte, still not quite looking me in the eye. "Drae told me he had a meeting in Kingston, but where are the other two brooding gargoyles this morning? Scratch that—evening? Still getting used to this extreme night-owl business."

"They're with Drae. Some of our properties need a few upgrades and we're trying to convince the state to oversee and pay for them as historical landmark improvements. They're meeting with a few building inspectors to see what we can do. They'll be back in a bit."

West nods, her stomach growling again.

"What'll it be, witchling? Muffins or waffles?"

"Waffles to start, muffins for dessert."

"Excellent choice." I plug in the waffle iron and get out the leftover batter, along with the apple compote and syrup, keeping my back to her and my mind on the task at hand. It's all going just swimmingly, too—I'm making waffles, she's chatting with her birds, no one's thinking about the feel of hot, wet mouths sliding over hot, wet body parts...

But then, just as I flip the piping hot waffle onto her plate, she decides to join me at the counter.

"Need help?" she asks. Her shoulder brushes the edge of my wing, sending a ripple of pleasure right through it.

"I'm..." I close my eyes, trying to keep my thoughts from spiraling. "No, I'm good."

"What was that?"

"What?"

"Your wings did this... fluttery thing."

"Oh, that's just... just a shiver."

"Are you cold?"

Far from it, witchling.

I shake my head, trying like hell to remember how to form words, but she's so close to me with her damp hair and her sweet face and those fucking knee socks and all I want to do is bend her over the counter and run my tongue along the tops of them until she's begging me to fuck her...

"Can I touch them?" She reaches for me, and it takes me a beat to realize she's talking about the wings.

"If it's touching you're after," I say with a laugh, if only to cover what would otherwise become an all-to-obvious groan, "I've got plenty of other things you can put your hands on."

West lowers her hand, her smile fading. "You can say no, you know. You don't have to mock me. It's not like I know all the gargoyle rules and regulations."

"Sorry. I'm not mocking you. I'm just... They're sensitive, that's all."

She nods and turns away, but I grab her hand and give her a gentle tug.

"It's okay. You can touch them—just go easy on me."

"You sure?"

I nod and turn around, crouching a little lower to give her access. She uses both hands, and with a light touch, she traces her fingertips down the center of my back, then slowly spreads outward, running along the membrane all the way to the edges, then back again.

I bite back a hiss, forcing myself to remain still even as her soft touch has my heart slamming against my ribs, my nerves on fire.

"They're so tough," she says, her tone reverent. "Leathery, almost. But thin. I guess that's how you can fold them in so easily? And lie on them without damaging them?"

"Mmm-hmm." It's all I can manage.

"And the sensitivity probably helps you with flying. Like, you need to be able to detect subtle changes in the wind speed and temperature and stuff, right?"

She's exactly right, but I can't respond. Can't do

anything but remain absolutely still and try not to fucking incinerate.

"They feel... so smooth. I like touching them," she says, her strokes becoming more deliberate, fingers drawing patterns across the membrane, her hot breath ghosting against the back of my neck, the heat of her touch radiating right down to my bones, and I can't—

"Auggie," she sighs, her hands sliding up into my hair, fingertips brushing the base of my horns.

In a flash, I spin around and grab her hips, more than ready to devour her. But then I remember why we're here— research, Codex, curse, demons—and simply lift her up and set her on the countertop.

"Only good waffle is a hot waffle," I say firmly, as if we both need the reminder. "Don't let it get cold."

She nods, letting out a shaky breath, and I can't help feeling like we both just dodged a bullet.

One I'm still aching to step in front of.

"Also," I say, trying my damndest to keep it together, "there's only one right way to eat my hot apple waffles, so I hope you like it, because anything else is blasphemy and I won't tolerate it."

She smiles. "I'm trusting you here, but okay."

I drag a pat of vegan butter across the top, making sure it gets into all the nooks and crannies. The apple compote goes on next, spiced with just a hint of cinnamon, ginger, and cardamom. Then, finally, the maple syrup.

When I set down the syrup bottle, she gasps.

"You... you got me *real* maple syrup?"

"Don't read into it, witchling. Your oh-so-helpful critique the other night made me realize we'd all gotten a bit lazy in our shopping, so I decided to make some upgrades."

"Excellent choice."

"I thought so."

"So, are you going to keep standing here staring at me? Or are you going to let me taste these hot apple waffles you've been hyping up for a million years?"

"Oh, it's not hype. This is the real deal, baby." I cut her a piece and spear it with a fork, then cup her chin, slowly sliding it into her mouth.

She closes her eyes and chews slowly, a soft moan of appreciation floating to my ears, and I take a moment to look at her again—the soft pink cheeks, the damp hair that's just starting to frizz, the boxers riding up on her thighs.

The fabric of her hoodie is thin, and judging from the pert nipples poking out against it, she's not wearing a bra...

For fuck's sake, this fucking girl and her fucking nipples and moans and—

"More," she demands. "Goddess, that's good. More!"

Laughing, I spear another bite and feed it to her, watching in abject fascination as she chews and swallows it, her throat bobbing, a dribble of maple syrup escaping.

"Wait. You've got a little..." I swipe my thumb along her lower lip, catching the runaway syrup. But before I draw back, she grabs my wrist, and her eyes flare with something that makes my heart slam against my ribs all over again.

Damn it, this woman. How the fuck she can go from sweet, innocent schoolgirl to red-hot vixen at the drop of a dime is a damn mystery, but my cock is *here* for it.

She glances down, noticing the bulge I couldn't even hide if I wanted to.

And I *don't* want to. Not anymore.

CHAPTER TWENTY-EIGHT

AUGUSTINE

West meets my eyes again and shifts closer, thighs parting to bracket my hips.

In a low growl, I say, "You're playing with fire, witchling."

"Yeah. I should *probably* be more careful, but... You know what? I don't really care." She flashes an adorably wicked grin, then closes her lips around my thumb, her tongue gliding across the tip. I can't help it—I push in deeper, then slide out, only to slip right back in again.

Her eyelids flutter closed and another soft moan vibrates from her lips. One that goes far beyond appreciating my cooking.

I push in deeper once again, then pull back, in and out and in and out until suddenly I'm straight up fucking her mouth with my thumb, and I've never felt anything so erotic in my life. The nip of small teeth, the warm velvet of her tongue, the hot mist of her breath as I plumb that soft, wet heat...

Fuck it.

I pull out of her mouth and descend on her like a storm, shoving my hands into her hair and yanking her close. Too close to fucking move, to breathe, to do anything but take it as I crash against her lips and steal the kiss I've been fantasizing about since that first night I saw her walking down the aisle.

She slides her hands into my hair and wraps her fingers around my horns, and I push my tongue deeper into her mouth, licking and teasing her, *tasting* her—fuck, she's maple and coffee and the sun I haven't felt on my skin in centuries and suddenly all I want to do is take her. Fuck her.

Own her.

I grab her by the throat and push her down on the counter, flat on her back, spilling the bottle of syrup. Her eyes darken with pure lust, mouth curving into a sexy little smirk that dares me to keep pushing.

"You good?" I ask, hoping like hell I'm reading her right, or I've got a long, painful night ahead of me.

"Yes," she breathes. "Don't stop."

I've got one hand firm around her throat, the other already reaching under my loincloth for my cock, more than ready to shove those cute little boxers and panties to the side and claim her right here in a river of maple syrup—

"Since when did night-breakfast become a full contact

sport?" Jude laughs, crashing into the moment with all the subtlety of a train wreck.

I was so caught up I didn't even hear them come in, but now he's right on the other side of the counter, leaning across to drag his tongue over West's maple-soaked thigh. "Mmm. Nothing quite like the real thing, is there?"

He glances up at me and winks, his grin as crazy as ever. *Fucking Jude.*

If he's upset about catching me with the witch he devoured last night, he doesn't show it. In fact, if I didn't know better, I'd say he's pretty damn turned on.

The others enter behind him, arms laden with grocery bags. Drae's looking dour as usual, but Rook's got a vase of bright yellow flowers that immediately cheer the place up.

"What's all this?" West hops off the counter and readjusts herself, grabbing a wet paper towel to clean off the rest of the syrup as if it's perfectly normal to have three gargoyles walk in on the fourth one about to crack your fucking spine on the kitchen counter.

"Since you're not getting much sunshine these days," Rook says, "I thought we could bring some sunshine to you. It's not the same, of course. You'll still need to spend at least a few minutes outside during the daylight hours to get your Vitamin D, but... I double-checked your list of known allergies, and these all pass the test."

"They're beautiful, Rook." She takes the vase and sets it on the table, letting her birds investigate. After a few curious pecks, they hop off the table and head for the door, and West lets them outside. "That was really thoughtful of you."

Rook blushes, but he can't hide the shit-eating grin spreading across his face.

West stretches up on her toes to kiss his cheek.

"You know, scarecrow," Jude says, sneaking around behind her and leaning in to nuzzle her neck. "I'm beginning to feel a bit left out here. Have you got a kiss for me?"

"Hell no!" Squealing, she squirms away from him. "Bring me flowers or make me waffles—then we'll talk."

"I don't want to talk," he says. "I want to—"

"So!" I blurt out, *really* not in the mood to hear their bedroom talk. Turning to Drae, I say, "How'd the meeting with the inspectors go?"

"Fine," he replies. "We've got all the renovations covered, thanks to Jude."

Jude grins. "I was quite persuasive."

"You always are," I say, wondering if he had to spill any blood. It doesn't usually come to that with building inspectors—they don't have enough of a personal stake to care one way or the other how the city or state funding gets divvied up. Negotiations like that? Most of the time, all it takes is a flash of Jude's knife, a glimpse at that crooked grin and those crazy eyes, and they're willing to give us whatever we need, no real violence required.

"Now that you're all here," Drae says, his tone even more somber than it was a minute ago, "you should know about the *other* meeting I had this evening."

"Forsythe?" I say, and he nods.

"Rook's police intel was correct—they've reported Westlyn as a missing person."

West shovels in another bite of waffle and rolls her eyes. "Of course they did. They have to make it look like a kidnapping, otherwise they'll be forced to admit a tiny, magicless witch stabbed their precious demon-boy and fled."

"Agent Reedsy was there as well," Drae says.

"Forsythe set you up?" I ask.

"He did, and he knows I'm not pleased about it, so I'm hoping he'll back off a bit for now. As for the agent, I gave him the usual runaround. They've got nothing connecting us to Westlyn and no real reason to think we had anything to do with her so-called disappearance. Reedsy's just looking for an excuse to nail us to the wall."

"I'll send him some pictures of his kids," I say. "Remind him who he's dealing with."

Drae nods. "There was *one* bit of good news to come of it, though. I'm ninety-five percent certain the Codex is being held at the brownstone, somewhere on the second or third floor. He glanced up when I mentioned it—seemed a bit uneasy about it."

"Third floor," West says firmly. "He's got a library and ritual room up there—it's where he keeps all his books and magical stuff. If it's in the brownstone, that's where it'll be."

Drae's mood brightens considerably. "You're certain?"

"I was there for a family dinner not too long ago. He

gave us the whole tour—couldn't resist the urge to brag about all his artifacts, most of them pilfered from developing countries, which is just another reminder of what an upstanding mage he is."

"Is it locked?" Drae asks. "How many square feet, would you say?"

"It takes up the entire third floor, and it's all open plan. There's a staircase that goes up—I don't remember there being a door, but it could've just been open at the time. I was a little distracted—I'd just learned about the betrothal."

"Do you think you could sketch it for us?" Rook asks. "Maybe make a few notes about what you remember? Windows, walls, bookshelves, what kinds of things he's got up there—anything you remember."

"Definitely."

"That's good news, Drae," I say. "It means we can pretty much rule out his other properties and start making a real plan to steal the damn thing."

Drae nods. "Assuming we can get access. I don't get the sense he and Celine have left the brownstone much since the wedding debacle."

"Hunter's been sequestered as well," Rook says. "We've got cameras outside his apartment in the East Village and a tracking device on his vehicle. He's had a few visitors from the shadow magic society, but he's been sticking close to home. As far as we can tell, he hasn't even seen his parents since the wedding night."

"Great," I say, cleaning up the last of the breakfast mess.

"So all we have to do is get the lay of the land from West, figure out how to lure the Forsythes out for a few hours, and make our move."

A wide, bright grin stretches across West's face, and I can tell by the mischievous gleam in her eyes I'm not going to like whatever she's about to say.

"You know what makes for an *excellent* lure?" she sing-songs, her smile undimmed. "Bait! And boys? I know *just* the right girl for the job."

CHAPTER TWENTY-NINE

WESTLYN

"Jude and I are with you every step of the way." Auggie's voice is clear and reassuring through the tiny sapphire mic-and-earpiece combo Rook designed to look like a tragus piercing. "We've got our eyes and ears on you the entire time."

"I know." I hold my hand up to my face as if I'm admiring my new ring—a nondescript cocktail piece fitted with a fake ruby that's actually a camera—and smile. "Try not to miss this face too much."

"If you get uncomfortable for any reason," Auggie says, too focused on the mission to enjoy my teasing, "just say the code phrase and we're there."

"Code phrase: hot waffles," I confirm, and a nervous laugh bubbles up at the ridiculousness of it all—me, walking down Lexington Avenue en route to meet the most powerful mage and witch in the city, parents of the asshole mage-and-or-demon I stabbed at the altar, muttering to myself about hot waffles while two sexy, dangerous gargoyles watch my back from their positions on the restaurant roof...

How is this even my life?

I'm still not entirely sure it is.

It took me a full day to convince Draegan to agree to my Westlyn-as-bait plan, and the whole rest of the week to talk Jude into letting me get anywhere *near* my enemies without a full-on army at my back. I even did three separate Tarot draws asking if this was the right call, and each time I pulled the same card: the Queen of Swords.

In other words, take no bullshit, get 'er done, you've got this, girl.

But in the end, it was Rook who helped sway the votes with his high-tech spy gear. Not just my mic and camera setup, but a fully warded, mage-proof, bulletproof car for the boys to drive me into the city, and a phone tower relay system that allowed me to call the Forsythes from the manor while making it look like the call came from an office on Wall Street.

My acting skills were definitely put to the test with that phone call. Through a mess of fake tears, I told them I made a huge mistake. That I got cold feet and freaked out, and I've been so worried about Hunter I haven't been able to sleep, and I never meant to screw things up between our families, and could we maybe meet for dinner and talk about getting back on track? Oh, and if it's not too much to ask, could Hunter sit this one out? I'm not quite ready to face him yet after my violent outburst—so uncharacteristic of me, I'm in counseling for it, I really do feel terrible, boo hoo, boo hoo.

Whether they bought my sob story or not is irrelevant. Like I told Draegan when I pitched him the idea—I didn't need to be convincing, just tempting. The Forsythes are smart and calculating, but they're also desperate to find me, and desperation makes even the most clever, cunning people do some really dumb shit.

Like venturing out to meet up with the woman who stabbed their pet demon at the altar, leaving the precious Cerridwen Codex blissfully unguarded long enough for Draegan and Rook to break in and steal it.

I'm not worried about the Forsythes trying to kill or seriously hurt me tonight. Regardless of my actions at the wedding, they still need me. An augmenter is no good to a demon prince if she's dead or bleeding out.

But there's a ninety-nine-point-nine percent chance they'll try to kidnap me, and we've planned for that. They won't get very far, of course, but still. Annoying.

"I'm here, guys," I finally say, flashing one more smile at my cocktail ring. "Here's hoping we don't have to mention the waffles."

Then I open the door to Carmine's Trattoria, call up a few distraught tears, and step inside.

CHAPTER THIRTY

WESTLYN

The Archmage and his wife are seated at a table in the back, looking supremely uncomfortable in a dark suit and an emerald-green wrap dress. I'm not used to seeing them in so-called civilian clothes; on the few occasions we've met before, they were both dressed in elaborate ceremonial robes designed to set them apart from the witchy riff-raff like me.

Several other couples and families occupy the surrounding tables, the wait staff bustling about, and I relax. The restaurant was my suggestion, and I chose it specifically because it's popular with the city's late-night dinner crowd. The Archmage may have a few tricks up his sleeve for me tonight, but the last thing he'll want is to cause a scene in front of a large group. Shadow mages aren't big on drawing attention to themselves among mundane humans—

too many questions, too many cover-ups, a big pain in everyone's collective ass.

"Mr. and Mrs. Forsythe! Thank you so much for coming," I say breathlessly, taking a seat across from them and swiping my fingers beneath my eyes to catch those crocodile tears. "I wasn't sure if you'd actually show. I know this must be really hard for you."

"We just want what's best for you and our son," Lennon says, and Celine nods, her lips curved in what I think is supposed to be a smile but looks more like she just sat on something sharp. "Anything we can do to facilitate that, we will."

"Really?" I force a grateful smile. "Goddess, that means so much to me. You have no idea."

"Lots of marriages have rocky starts, dear," Celine says. "That's no reason to give up on them."

Rocky starts? So that's what we're calling this?

"Is... is Hunter okay?" I ask, my face a mask of concern. "I just feel so terrible about what happened. Rather—what I *did*. Those were *my* actions at the wedding—my choices. I need to take responsibility for them. My counselor says that's the first step to making amends."

"It's good that you recognize that," Celine says. "Physically, Hunter is fine. Fortunately, the blade just nicked him."

Jude's laugher rings through my ear. "Nicked him, my arse! Our girl straight up shish-kabobbed that motherfucker."

"What a relief!" I say, pressing my hand to my chest to give the boys a peek at my dining companions.

"Emotionally, however..." Celine dabs her eyes with the cloth napkin, shaking her head as if she's simply too overcome to continue.

Jude snorts. "Somebody pass the old cunt a Kleenex before she ruins the nice white linens."

The waiter finally shows up to take our drink and appetizer order, but before I can even open my mouth to ask for a glass of wine, Lennon's already waving him away.

Which probably means he doesn't intend on being here long enough for a drink, let alone a multi-course Italian meal.

Shit. The guys need more time at the brownstone.

Guess I'd better stall.

"Excuse me, sir?" I call to the waiter, waving him back and squinting at his name tag. "Sorry, Randall. I'd like a Cabernet, if you don't mind. Also, how's the bruschetta here?"

"One of our house specialties, miss. Shall I..." He glances nervously between me and Lennon. "...bring an order for the table?"

Lennon clears his throat. "No, that won't be—"

"Can you do a vegan version?" I ask. "Oh, and if you've got any of those squishy little squid rings? What are those called again?"

"Calamari, miss. But those aren't vegan."

"Can't you make them without the squid? Just do up the crispy part?" Turning to the Forsythes, I wrinkle my nose apologetically. "Sorry for jumping in—I'm just really hungry. I'm staying with a friend right now and her kitchen is like a culinary graveyard. *Anyway...*"

I spend the next ten minutes confusing and baffling the waiter with all manner of inane questions about vegan options and hidden ingredients and food allergy reactions before finally settling on a few other special-order appetizers.

When he leaves, I pick up my water glass and take a deep drink, then smile at the Forsythes again. "Thank you for accommodating me. I know my dietary restrictions can be difficult sometimes."

"It's fine," Lennon says through gritted teeth. Then, tapping his finger on the tabletop, "Hunter is quite upset about what transpired. I think it will take some time for him to forgive you, if he can even get there at all."

"Oh, I'm not expecting any miracles." I press my hand to my heart, giving the boys another view. "Mr. and Mrs. Forsythe, I know our arrangement wasn't based on love or even friendship. This was about an alliance between our families—I get that. But I truly hoped Hunter and I would grow to love each other, just as you two do. I'm grateful for even the *slightest* chance to try to make amends, even if... Goddess forbid... even if he doesn't want me in the end."

Auggie chuckles through the earpiece. "Laying it on pretty thick, witchling."

"She's a natural schemer," Jude teases. "We may have to keep her around after all this, Augs."

Butterflies swirl through my stomach at the comment, and I take a sip of ice water to keep from blushing.

"And your parents?" Celine asks. "Have you heard from them at all? I understand they're on some sort of... vacation?"

Where is the waiter with that wine?

I set down the water glass and close my eyes, pretending to gather my thoughts, once again milking the moment for as long as I can. When I finally look at them again, I've got the waterworks all cued up for the performance.

"I... I haven't heard from them since the wedding night." I let the tears fall freely, my eyes wide and full of regret, poor little orphan girl that I am. Then, lowering my voice, "I don't like to speak about my father's business, but we all know about his financial troubles. I'm pretty sure that's why they left—and no, it's not a vacation. Without your family's alliance and backing, he can't pay his debts, and it's simply too dangerous for them to stay. It's just so hard for me to... to even think about, because... because *I* did that. I put them in that situation, and it's just one more thing I'm trying to come to terms with."

"I'm disappointed your father ran off in such a hurry," Lennon says. "A lot of society members are. I would've appreciated an honest conversation, mage to mage, about how we might resolve the issues. I never rescinded the offer of the alliance, but at this point..." He shakes his head. "I'm not sure how I feel about it, even with your considerable efforts tonight."

"I understand." I dash away my tears and offer a serene smile. "I'm not here to ask you to pay my father's bills. I'm here of my own accord because I really *would* like the chance to make amends with Hunter, and I'm willing to do whatever it takes to earn back your family's trust."

They both nod, faces placid and accommodating, but a calculating sharpness glints in their eyes.

"Where did you say you were staying, dear?" Celine asks.

"Oh, just with a friend." I try to flag down a different waiter since ours seems to be on perpetual break, but none of the other servers even glance our way.

"Which friend?" she presses. "I'd very much like to meet this witch. Assuming she is a witch?"

"She's... kind of shy. Likes to lie low. Hey, have you guys seen the waiter? I was really hoping to try that bruschetta."

"You know, I really don't love the idea of my future daughter-in-law living in squalor with some random stranger." Celine smiles. "I'd really prefer it if you stayed with us, Westlyn. We're family."

I wave at another passing server, but it's like she's looking straight through me.

They *all* are, I realize. It's like we're not even here.

Now that I think of it, the only server who's spoken to me since my arrival was our original guy, and he's nowhere in sight. When I first walked in, the hostess didn't even greet me. I walked right back to the table without so much as a hello from anyone.

The skin on the back of my neck prickles.

Cloaking spell. Damn it.

If I'm right, then no mundane human can see us. I'm betting our so-called waiter is a society mage and doesn't even work here.

"Thanks," I say, desperately trying to figure out my next move. There's no way Draegan and Rook are done at the brownstone yet, but how much longer can I drag this out? "But that's not necessary. I don't want to impose, and I'm still not ready to see Hunter yet."

"Oh, don't be silly." She smiles again—the smile of a shark who's just caught its prey. "We *insist*."

"You know what I *really* love?" I hop up from my seat, waving my arms like a lunatic at the entire restaurant. Not a single person even glances my way. "*Hot waffles*," I say. "Does this place have hot waffles? Because hot waffles are so good, and hot, and... waffley..."

The Forsythes merely grin.

"Sit down, Westlyn," Lennon says. "No need to make this more embarrassing on yourself."

"Sir. There's nothing embarrassing about hot waffles."

But still, no sign of my gargoyles. No words of reassurance in my ear, no crashing through the windows.

Damn it, where are they? Aren't they seeing this? Hearing it? Am I offline?

The Forsythes must've figured out I was wired and did something to scramble the tech.

"I should... Yeah. I should go." I stumble back from the table, nervously thumbing toward the exit. "My friend is waiting for me. It's my turn to do the dishes. Um... I'll be in touch? Thanks again for the—"

A massive arm wraps around me from behind, crushing my chest like a steel band as a meaty hand clamps over my mouth. I struggle to kick free, but this guy's got me in a vise grip. I can barely breathe.

"Take her back to the brownstone," Celine tells the guy, her voice cold and businesslike. "We'll be right behind you."

Lennon's already got his phone out. "Hunter? Yes, we've got her secured. Meet us there in fifteen minutes."

Panic shoots through my limbs as the guy drags me back through the kitchen, the cooks and dishwashers paying us no mind. Kicking open the emergency exit, he hauls me out into the service alley behind the restaurant, where a running car awaits.

He releases me just long enough to open the car door and shove me inside, then climbs in after me, hauling me against his chest in that crushing hold once more.

"Drive," he barks out to the guy in front.

To Randall, I realize. Our fucking absentee waiter.

Randall smashes the accelerator, but before we're even halfway out of the alley, something crashes down onto the roof of the car, buckling it.

"What the fuck?" Randall jams the car into reverse and

slams on the gas again, and something big rolls onto the hood.

Auggie. In full-out, utterly terrifying gargoyle form. He smashes his fist through the windshield and grabs Randall by the throat, hauling him out through the broken safety glass just as a someone wrenches the backdoor off its hinges.

Jude leans in and grins, a witchweed cigarette dangling from the corner of his mouth, his eyes wild. "Are these dick-heads bothering you, darling?"

Goddess, I've never been so happy to see his psychotic gargoyle face.

"Oh, you have *no* idea," I say. "Randall never even brought me my wine!"

Jude gives me an apologetic frown. "Sorry we're late, scarecrow. You cut out on us partway through—we had to improvise."

"They had a cloaking spell. They must've done something to disable the tech, too. Did you see them?"

"Just left out the front door—hopped in a cab. We've already let Drae know they're inbound."

Auggie's got Randall wrapped in a chokehold next to the dumpster, and now Jude hauls my manhandler out of the car, shoving him against the bricks next to them.

"Wh-what the fuck, man?" My guy stammers, looking a lot less intimidating with that piss stain rapidly spreading across his crotch. "What the fuck *are* you guys?"

"Wrong question, mate," Jude says, blowing a plume of

smoke into the guy's face. "What you *really* want to be asking is, what the fuck are you guys gonna do to us? And *that* is a question I'm more than happy to answer." He jerks the guy forward, then slams him into the wall again, the back of his skull cracking against the bricks.

Next to them, Randall is whimpering and babbling, his head bleeding profusely on account of his all-expenses-paid trip through the windshield.

"First," Jude says through that unnerving smile, cigarette still dangling, "I'm going to ask you to *look* at the witch you put your hands on tonight."

"I—I was just following orders. I didn't—"

"I said *look* at her!" He slams him back into the wall so hard, the bricks around him crumble.

Groaning in pain, the guy turns his head my way, his eyes wide and glassy.

"That's better," Jude says. "Now, I want you to take a good, long look at that beautiful girl, because I believe a man has a right to understand why another man might be driven to violence. Sometimes it's random, sure. But in this case? No. This is very, *very* deliberate." With one hand wrapped around the guy's throat, Jude tears the sleeve off his jacket, then shoves it into his mouth, muffling the screams I know are coming next. To me, he says, "You might not want to watch this part, scarecrow. Could get a bit messy."

I nod, but no matter how badly I want to turn away, I just can't.

Jude grabs the guy's wrist and slams it into the wall again and again, pummeling his hand against the bricks until it looks like a bloody, boneless balloon. Then he does the other hand, same deal, no doubt shattering every bone. "*No* one puts hands on her and lives. Fucking *no* one. Understand?"

Tears and snot leak down the guy's face, his whole body trembling. He barely manages a nod.

"Excellent." Jude yanks him close, then spins him around, shoving him face-first into the bricks. Leaning in, he says softly, "This is the part where I tear you a new arsehole. Literally."

A soft whimper escapes, but that's all the protest he has time for before Jude unleashes hell.

Claws shred through clothing and flesh. Bones snap. And the blood... So much blood I can smell it.

But Jude is calm and serene, a master at work, and for the first time since we met, I get a glimpse of the true darkness inside him.

A shiver creeps down my spine, but I still can't look away. Not even when he picks up the wasted carcass, throws him into the dumpster, and douses him with kerosine.

A final deep drag on his cigarette, then he flicks the butt, and the whole thing ignites in a glorious blaze.

"Oh, fuck *me*," Randall mutters, the heat of the blaze bringing him back to semi-consciousness.

Jude laughs, taking him from Auggie and tucking him against his chest in a warm embrace. Stroking his hair, he says, "Oh, you're definitely fucked, mate. Just not in the way you were hoping for." Then, to Auggie, "Would you mind fetching the car and driving our little scarecrow home? Randall and I will be taking the long way back."

CHAPTER THIRTY-ONE
ROOK

I love books. I love holding them in my hands, feeling their cracked leather covers against my palms, smelling the old musty pages. I love cataloging them in my system, then arranging them on my shelves in their proper order, admiring their stately presence when they're all lined up in the right place, just waiting for someone to select a volume, crack it open, and travel to another world.

The only time I *don't* love books, in fact, is when we're supposed to be stealing one—a very important, very old one —and it's located in a room filled with hundreds upon hundreds upon *hundreds* of other old books just like it.

And we've got no idea what the hell we're even searching for.

Standing in the middle of the Archmage's impressive third-floor ritual library with Drae, I finally realize our grievous oversight.

I assumed we'd thought of everything. Studying the brownstone's original blueprints. Hacking into the cloud-based security system and disabling the alarms. Activating a wearable device that emits electromagnetic pulses to temporarily scramble a mage's magical warding. Flying in and landing on the roof, allowing us to sneak in from the rooftop deck rather than through the front door, thereby avoiding detection by nosey neighbors. And of course, getting the occupants out of the way for a few hours—West's idea.

But now that we're here, I have no clue where to start.

Glancing around at the floor-to-ceiling bookcases, I shake my head and sigh.

Suddenly, West's convoluted haystack metaphor makes a lot more sense.

"This is... unfortunate," Drae says.

"Please tell me you've got some idea what we're looking for, Drae. Please tell me we didn't put West at risk just to get a peek at the guy's library."

"I was hoping... *Fuck*." He paces from one end of the massive space to the other, shoving a hand through his hair in frustration. "I don't bloody know! I thought we would just... sense it. Or perhaps he'd have it on a special shelf or altar we could easily identify."

"He's the Archmage of Manhattan and the leader of the shadow magic society." I pluck a fist-sized crystal ball from the shelf—polished obsidian. "*All* his shelves and altars are special."

Drae curses under his breath.

"Think, Draegan," I say. "In all your conversations with Forsythe about this book, did he ever mention any physical characteristics? Do we even know whether it's a literal book or something more like a scroll?"

"When he first told me about it, he mentioned water damage on the top right corner, so I'm assuming it's a book."

"Okay, that helps. Do we know what color the jacket is? Or what material? Leather? Some other kind of animal hide? Was it re-bound at any point?"

Drae shakes his head. "That's all I've got, Rook. That and a blind hope."

I set the obsidian ball back in its holder. "This is going to take a while."

An hour later, we've ransacked several shelves, two desks, and a stack of crates full of other books, yet we're no closer to finding the elusive Codex.

"It might not even be here, Drae," I remind him. "Maybe you read his signals wrong that night. Maybe—"

"It's here, damn it. I can feel it." He shakes out his hands. "There's a... a current or something. A connection. Not unlike what I first felt with Westlyn. The longer we're up here, the stronger it's getting. Can't you sense it?"

"I can, but that's not an unusual reaction for me with dark fae objects. There are a *lot* of old things here."

"I know." He blows out a breath and takes one more look around, and I know what he's going to say next before he even utters the words. "We're just going to have to take them all. Empty out the crates and pack up whatever dark fae works we can find. If you're not sure, go by your gut. Any tingling, any odd sensations, anything at all—we take it."

"Forsythe might've been able to overlook one missing book for a little while, but he's going to notice if all his favorite dark fae artifacts suddenly vanish from his library tonight."

"I'm no longer concerned about that. He would've connected the dots, anyway. Forsythe's well aware of my interest in the text—he's been dangling it in front of my nose like a carrot from the moment he acquired it. And as soon as he realizes it's gone, he'll very likely make the connection between the mysterious theft and his clandestine meeting with Westlyn, and then he'll know *exactly* where to find her, which puts us all at a severe disadvantage."

"Yeah." I grab a couple of dark fae lore books from the shelf and set them into the crate at my feet. "I was worried about that."

"I think our best course of action at this point is to take whatever we think may be of use, then trash the place.

Make it look like a smash-and-grab. I'm sure he's got a lot of important books here—the missing Codex might turn out to be the least of his concerns."

"That's your plan? Smash and grab?"

"Not ideal, granted, but given the options? I think it can buy us a few extra days before he realizes who fucked him in the arse and launches a counter-attack."

The thought of damaging books—even books that belong to an enemy—horrifies me to the core, but... yeah. Drae's right. A few extra days can mean the different between keeping West safe and...

No. I won't consider the alternative.

"Okay," I say. "Let's get moving, then."

We work quickly after that, trying to parse through an impressive collection of esoteric magical items, grimoires, and historical texts I'd love to have for our private collection, but there's no way we can bring everything with us. So, ignoring the pangs in my heart, I pack up the dark fae works and trash the rest, tearing out pages, smashing crystals and devotional statues, knocking over shelving.

I'm just about to bring down another bookshelf when a sharp, pained gasp from the other side of the room stops me cold.

"Drae?" I run to the spot where he's been on his knees for the past twenty minutes, flipping through books in search of that water-damaged corner. "You okay?"

He gets to his feet and turns to face me. In his hands, a

large tome bound in cracked leather emanates a faint purple glow, tiny black sparks crackling around it.

"I think," he grunts out, struggling to hold it, "we've found our Codex."

"Are you—"

"Quite certain, and quite uncomfortable, yes. A little help, if you don't mind?"

I grab a mage robe from a hook on the wall and wrap it around the book, then drop it into one of the crates.

Drae slumps against the wall, panting. "Looks like we're going to have our work cut out for us with *that* thing."

Excitement races through my veins. "I can hardly wait to—"

Drae's phone buzzes, cutting me off.

"Jude," he says, scanning the text. "Forsythes are inbound. Jude and Augustine are going to extract Westlyn. We need to go."

I glance around the room once more. We really did a number on the place, but... "I don't think this mess alone will stop him from realizing the Codex is gone, Drae. That book is... it's something else."

"You're telling me. All I had to do was pick it up, and I could literally see and feel the dark power it contains. It's... it's quite remarkable, honestly."

"And probably the first thing he'll look for when he realizes he's been robbed. There's no way—"

"I know." He paces to the windows along the far wall

overlooking the street. "Any ideas? We don't have much time."

"Only one." I heft the crate to my chest and sigh, taking one last look at the treasure trove of history around us. "Burn it. Burn it all."

CHAPTER THIRTY-TWO

JUDE

"Fun bit of trivia for you, mate." Human glamour back in place, I pull up a stool, metal scraping painfully along the concrete, and take a seat. "I used to kill people a lot more indiscriminately, but the boss has kept me leashed these past couple months."

"That's... that's good news, right?" The naked meat sack in my basement asks, his voice high and tight, though I can't tell if it's just the nerves talking or the fact that I've had him chained and strung up by his wrists on a meat hook for the last twenty-four hours, his head still bleeding from last night.

The metal cuff around his ankle ensures he won't be accessing his mage powers anytime soon, either—another of Rook's handy devices.

Drae and Auggie are busy with some bullshit in Manhattan tonight. Rook and my little scarecrow have been hard at work in the library, still trying to figure out how to open that sparkly magic book.

But me? *This* is my part to play.

And I was fucking *made* for it.

"Good news for the blokes I *didn't* kill, perhaps. Not so much for you, Randall. All this pent-up rage has made me a little..." I select a scalpel from the array of tools on the workbench beside me, then change my mind, going for the hammer instead. "...twitchy. See that?" I lift my hand, showing him my slight tremor. "Grip isn't what it used to be."

A whimper escapes his greasy lips.

"Oh, thanks for your concern," I say, "but fortunately, I'm not a surgeon. Steady hands aren't a requirement for my line of work. Even with the precision cuts, we've always got a bit of wiggle room. Oh, that reminds me... You're not a model, are you?" I laugh. "Sorry, I don't mean to make you feel self-conscious. I just like to know these things in advance so I can give you the proper disclaimer."

"Di-disclaimer?"

"Yeah, you know. Side effects and whatnot? Actually, I should stand up for this part. More official that way." I rise and kick the stool away. The meat sack flinches as it clatters to the ground.

"P-p-please," Randall stammers. "I already told you, I don't know anything. I'm just a—"

"The following procedure has *not* been approved by the FDA," I begin, tightening my grip on the hammer. "Side effects may include but are not limited to..." I smash his face, right beneath his eye. "Shattered cheekbones." Another strike, this time right in the teeth. "Poor dental health, and—" I bring the hammer down in a series of punishing blows across the collarbone. "Sudden onset inability to wear strapless gowns."

The scents of blood and piss mingle with the music of his agonizing screams in a perfect symphony—one I haven't had the pleasure of enjoying for far too long. I almost wish I could share it with my little scarecrow, but no. I'm not quite ready to wave *all* my red flags just yet—sucks the mystery right out of things.

I set the hammer aside and turn back to my tools. "Before we move on to phase two of our treatment plan, I'd like to give you another opportunity to share your thoughts on Archmage Forsythe and his family."

"I already tol' you," he slurs, his words as thick as molasses. "I barely know them."

"You mean to tell me the Archmage entrusted someone he barely knows to kidnap the witch he's been desperate to find for weeks? The witch intended to marry his degenerate son?"

"No. No, that's not—"

"No, he *doesn't* barely know you? No, he *didn't* entrust you to take her? Or no, he *hasn't* been desperate to find her?"

The meat sack falls silent, save for the *prat-prat-prat* of his blood dripping onto the floor.

"Why does he want her so badly?" I ask.

No response.

"What are his plans for the witch and his son? Why was their marriage so important to him?"

Prat-prat-prat goes the blood, but the fucker's totally stonewalling me.

Good. Gives me more time to play.

Skipping the blades and scalpels, I grab a bin full of various odds and ends and give it a good shake, trying to decide my next move. "What'll it be, what'll it be. We've got rusty knives, rusty screwdrivers, lots of forks, pliers, a metal file, and... Well! Would you look at that! I was wondering where that got off to."

I pluck the blackened nub from the bin and hand it over, folding his fingers around it. "Hold this. And you'd better not drop it—I don't want to lose track of it again."

"What... what the fuck is—"

"Thumb of the last bloke I chained up down here. Normally, I'm meticulous about cleaning up my workspace, but it just goes to show you. Practice *rarely* makes perfect, which is why we must keep practicing. Ahh, here we are! Yeah, this will be quite nice." I select the tool that caught my eye and flip it in the air, catching it right in front of his face. "Most people are afraid to get started in a career like this because they think they need to invest in specialized equipment. Surgical and dental tools, electric saws, flamethrowers. But some of the most effective instruments can be found right in your kitchen drawer. Do you know what this is?"

"Issa... sa... melon baller?" Randall slurs. Blood slides from his mouth in thick ropes.

"Excellent! And on the first guess, too. Do you know what it's for? Wait—don't answer. When it comes to learning, I find a demonstration's always better. Show, don't tell, as the saying goes." Without further ado, I push up his eyelid with my thumb and shove the baller into the socket, giving it a good twist and scooping out his eye. "Perfect! All in the wrist—that's the secret."

The sound he makes would shatter glass. Good thing I don't have any windows down here.

"Now that's lovely workmanship. Would you like to see?" I grab a handheld mirror from the workbench and hold it up. His good eye goes wide, the wailing starting up all over again.

"Yeah, you're right. Something's off there. I think I know the problem, though. It's the asymmetry of it all— that'd bug me too. Well, that's an easy fix." I grab his face, do the other eye in a jiff. "How's that? Oh, shit. Sorry. You can't see. You'll just have to take my word for it. Hey, speaking of words... Any you'd like to share with me?"

"Fuck... fuck you," he pants.

Gotta hand it to the bloke. Most of them crack before I even touch the second eye.

No matter. There's one surefire way to get him talking. The one method that's never let me down.

"You know, Randy, there's a special place in hell for men who hurt women. Since you'll be heading there soon enough, I'd like to send you off with a prequel of what's to come. Best to be prepared for a trip like that, you know? My mate Auggie's that way. Prepared for anything, that guy. Quite an admirable trait, really."

I turn on my blowtorch, adjusting it to a nice, toasty level, making sure he can smell the flame.

Then I drag it down his bare chest, just close enough to singe his chest hair.

Randall arcs away from the heat, but he can't get very far on account of the chains.

"Playtime's over, Randall. Start talking."

Nothing but babble now.

With that, I lower the torch beneath his shriveled cock and drag it right across his nutsack.

And Randall just...

Well, *that* is a scream you don't often hear from a man.

Five seconds of that, then I pull back, giving him a moment to gather his thoughts.

And then, wouldn't you know it? Fucker's singing a song of sixpence about Hunter's private adoption out west, followed by the move out east. How the Forsythes kept him under lock and key his entire childhood, hiring private mage tutors and trainers, along with various witch nannies and security guards, all from the shadow magic society. Turns out Randall here's one of Hunter's lifelong personal guards.

"Few... few months after Hunter turned nineteen," Randall pants, still holding on like a trooper, "they started letting him out more. Had me taking him to the hospital every week for some... some kinda thing. Hey, could I get some water or—"

"No. *What* kind of thing?"

"I don't know. Just... just a thing. I thought maybe he was sick or something. Once a week for three or four hours, every week like clockwork. Never missed one." He turns his head and spits out a mouthful of blood.

"And Hunter never told you about them?"

"We never talked. Wasn't allowed—only for security related business." Randall coughs, more blood splattering his chin. His breathing is getting shallower, his skin pale. Not much time left, poor bloke.

"When was the last treatment?" I ask.

"About a month ago."

"That recent?"

"Yeah. Then he just stopped."

"And you're sure you don't know what the treatments were for?"

He shakes his head, fresh stalactites of blood and spit wagging from his lips.

"Care to speculate?"

No response.

"Oh, for fuck's sake, Randy. You're holding a severed thumb. You've got no eyes, dozens of broken bones, and you're bleeding so much I'm surprised the vampires aren't circling. Death is breathing down your neck, and in your final moments, you don't even have the balls to make a few lousy guesses? I can't believe the—oh, right. That was insensitive of me, mentioning your balls. Sorry—I'm a bit out of practice. Bedside manner isn't what it used to be. I'm—"

"Jude? Are you down here?"

Westlyn. Her voice is heavenly, her sweet scent cutting through the coppery bite of the blood.

"It seems we have a spy in our midst, Randall," I whisper, then turn around and catch her descending the stairs. She stops on the bottom step, her mouth falling open in a silent gasp.

"Help me," Randall pants. "He's... he's fucking insane. Help... me...."

"Randall! She's a lady, for fuck's sake. You don't use that kind of language in front of a lady." With a heavy sigh, I grab the closest blade and slash it across his throat, putting us *all* out of his misery once and for all.

He was done singing for me, anyway.

At the sink, I scrub the evidence from my hands and arms, then hang up my apron on the hook I installed for just that purpose. Without turning around, I say, "You shouldn't be here, little scarecrow. My workshop is no place for nice girls."

She doesn't reply, but curiosity gets the better of her, footsteps echoing on the cold cement as she walks a few paces into my den of sin.

"I... I was looking for you," she says. "I missed you."

Fuck, her words have me going soft inside. I turn around and look her over. Her eyes are on me, barely even noticing the fresh corpse hanging from the ceiling. She's got her hair twisted up in her usual black-and-silver bun, her favorite blue hoodie zipped up tight, those hot little eggplant shorts peeking out the bottom.

"Come here," I command.

She obeys at once, and I fold her into my arms, pressing a kiss to the top of her head.

She's trembling.

"Are you afraid of death, darling?"

She shakes her head.

"Is it the blood?"

Another shake.

"Then what's got you so scared?" I pull back and cradle her face in my hands. Her eyes are wide, her cheeks pink.

"You don't look like you," she whispers. "Your eyes... I've never seen them so wild. Not even last night in the alley."

"Hearing a man beg for his life for hours on end does that to me—especially when it's a man who tried to hurt you. You know what else that sound does to me?"

She shakes her head again, the poor girl, and I grab her hand and press it firmly against my stone-hard cock, my glamour fading away to reveal the true monster underneath.

The sweet little gasp she makes...

Fucking hell, I nearly come right there.

Her eyes dart from side to side, first to the shelving over

my workbench, stacked high with bones of all shapes and sizes stripped clean and awaiting inspiration.

Then to the stairwell.

I dip my head close to her face—so close I can smell the apple pie she just ate. "Right about now," I whisper, "you're wondering if maybe Randall's diagnosis of me was correct."

She doesn't answer. Just blinks up at me, her body trembling like a rabbit caught in a snare.

Part of me hates that she's so fucking scared of me. I never wanted her to see this side of the business.

But part of me—that feral, untamed part that so often takes charge—is so *bloody* turned on I can't think straight.

"Everything inside me is telling me to run," she finally admits, her voice barely audible above the pounding of her heart.

"Your insides give good advice. You should listen to them. Unfortunately, it won't do you any good."

Her eyes dart to the stairwell again, and I know she's thinking of making a break for it. Pure survival instinct. Even her heart can't override that.

"Think you can outrun me?" I tease, brushing my mouth along her jaw, her soft little pink earlobe. "Give it a go then, love. I'll even give you a head start. I'm feeling rather sporting tonight."

"But I... Drae doesn't want me to leave the manor."

"Best find a good place to hide, then."

"Hide?" she squeaks, trying to take a step backward.

I follow her, crowding her against the wall, not giving

her an *inch* of space. "If you can manage to evade me for fifteen minutes, I'll take care of this *unbearable* hard-on myself and let you go about your evening in peace. But darling?"

She swallows hard, her delicate throat bobbing, pulse flickering beneath her skin. I press a kiss to the very spot, then drag my tongue up to her mouth, nipping her bottom lip.

Her breath hitches, her eyes wide with that delicious instinctual fright.

"Be a clever little witch," I warn, a dark whisper that stirs the fine hairs escaping her bun. "Because if I find you before the time is up, I'm going to drag you out of your hidey-hole, throw you against the nearest wall, and *fuck* you until my cum is dripping down your thighs and you no longer have the strength to stand up."

CHAPTER THIRTY-THREE

DRAEGAN

The man seated on the other side of my antique mahogany desk is young—mid-thirties, perhaps—which means he was very likely raised under the modern parental dogma that leaves children believing they truly *can* achieve anything they set their minds to and that unfettered ambition is an admirable quality.

If Jude were here, I'd probably let him break my no-decapitating rule just to see the man's *ambitious* smile roll across my floor.

But Jude is not here. He's home, brutally torturing one of the mages responsible for hurting Westlyn last night.

I clench my fists beneath the desk. It's with great effort that I manage to keep my glamour in place when all I want to do is let my claws burst free and slash everything in my fucking sight into bloody ribbons.

Especially the snot-nosed toddler masquerading as a real estate developer sitting across from me.

He snaps the leather folio shut and tosses it onto the desk. "Impressive presentation, Mr. Caldwell. But as I said in my email, your proposal was already rejected."

"No less than ten minutes after I sent it, Mr. Teague."

His smile doesn't dim. "Why prolong the inevitable? The Marchande Hotel had its fifteen minutes of fame over a century ago. It's—"

"Preserving this city's history is worth a bit more discussion than an email rejection." I steeple my fingers and lean back in my chair, returning his award-winning grin. "I'd love for you to take another look."

The Marchande is a decrepit hotel we're trying to buy on the city's Upper West Side—a onetime favorite of old Hollywood celebrities and a stunning example of neo-gothic architecture that's been featured in everything from postcards to travel shows.

More importantly, it's home to fourteen gargoyles under my protection. Gargoyles that—if Mr. Teague's ambition has its way—will soon be demolished, their souls cursed to an eternal purgatory.

Relocating them is not an option; the dark fae made certain of that. If they're moved, they'll instantly crumble to dust, their souls suffering the same horrific fate.

"We're prepared to go another thirty percent on the offer," I tell him, irritated it's even come to negotiating. That's another thing I despise about this latest crop of developers, city officials, federal agents, and yes, even the fire inspector I had to threaten earlier this evening to ensure faulty wiring would be the official determined cause of the Forsythe blaze.

They don't know Blackmoor Capital Group the way their fathers and grandfathers knew us.

They don't understand that in *our* city, corruption is a two-way street. We all must do our part to keep it running smoothly.

In the end, they always figure it out. But I'm growing tired of having to remind them.

Especially when I'd rather be home looking after that reckless, incorrigible little mortal...

"Thirty percent?" He sighs, his mouth sagging into a condescending frown. "I realize your firm specializes in historical preservation, and I'm typically a fan, but—"

"A fan?"

"*But*," he continues, "the Marchande was built on a weak foundation. To bring it up to code would cost millions of dollars and years of lost revenues the city simply can't afford. It's a relic, Mr. Caldwell. The land is worth more with it gone."

"More to whom? So-called *developers* who develop nothing but their profits while they suck all the color out of this city and homogenize the architecture to within an inch of its life—"

"Gregor Perrault has already—"

"Gregor *Perrault*," I practically spit. "The man wouldn't

know a good opportunity if it bit him in the pompous white arse."

"He's already purchased most of the surrounding buildings. The Marchande is the last holdout on the block."

"If thirty percent isn't enough, double it."

"It's not just the money. Perrault's firm makes a compelling case all the way around. Not just for the land, but for what his new condominium project will bring to this city. Jobs, affordable housing—"

"Since when is three million dollars for a studio apartment considered affordable housing?"

"Jobs," he says again. "Not to mention—"

"Traffic congestion, noise pollution, overcrowded schools and subways, and let's not forget the environmental impact."

He shrugs as if none of this matters. "That's just the cost of progress. Out with the old, in with the new. It's the way it's always been, Mr. Caldwell."

I glare at him, wishing I could shove all that *progress* right up his arse.

"I'm sorry," he says, clearly not. "I know this was a pet project for you, but the deal is done. The demolition is scheduled for next Thursday. You're welcome to attend if you'd like. They bring it down with controlled explosions from the inside—it's quite something."

I'm sure it is.

"There's nothing I can say to dissuade you?"

"No. You could always try to convince Perrault to restore the building and work it into his development plan, but I'm not sure the gothic style meshes with his modernistic sensibilities." He laughs. "The aesthetics would be a nightmare."

"I'm truly sorry you feel that way, Mr. Teague."

"Just business, my friend. Just business." He rises from his chair, but I lift a hand to stop him.

"Actually, there's one more matter I'd like to discuss, if you've a moment?"

His smile finally falters, and the first hint of fear shines in his eyes.

That's more like it, Mr. Teague.

"It's late," he says, "and I have a dinner to get to before—"

"No worries. This will just take a second." I buzz the intercom for Augustine, who strolls into my office with a thick manilla envelope in hand.

"You're familiar with my associate, Augustine Lamont?" I ask.

Teague clamps his mouth shut and sits back down, his face considerably paler. "We've never actually met, but—"

"But his reputation as a fine photographer precedes him," I say. "Yes, yes. You're not the first to sit in that chair and speak those very words." Then, to Augustine, "I believe Mr. Teague would like to see your portfolio. Would you mind giving him a peek?"

"My pleasure." Augustine tosses the envelope on the

desk. A stack of glossy eight-by-tens slides out across the surface, tawdry and garish against the rich mahogany.

Teague swallows audibly, tiny beads of sweat popping along his hairline, fat tongue darting out to lick his lips. "Perhaps I... I was too hasty in my rejection of your proposal."

I nod. "Perhaps."

"I'll take another look and get back to you tomorrow."

"That sounds like a fine idea." I smile, ever the polite negotiator. "Oh, and Mr. Teague? We'll be lowering our original bid by thirty percent for the trouble. I'm sure you won't have a problem making the numbers work."

"Of course not, sir." With trembling fingers, he shuffles all the photos back together and shoves them into the envelope. "Really excellent work, Mr. Lamont. Your talent with lighting is just... Do you mind if I keep these?"

Augustine grins. "Those are your copies to do with as you please. Although I'd probably think twice before sticking them on the fridge. Not sure your wife and children will have the same appreciation for my talent with lighting."

"These are... copies?" he whispers.

"Sure," Augustine says. "Always best to make multiples. Digital backups too. You know how easy it is for files to get lost these days. So many thumb drives, so many online services. Clouds upon clouds. Who even remembers where these things end up? Right, Draegan?"

"Who indeed?" I grin at a visibly shaken Teague across the desk. "I guess that's just the cost of progress, isn't it?"

The man collects his evidence and vanishes out the door without another word.

Turning to Augustine, I say, "Do we even know who was in those photos with Mr. Teague?"

"Sure as hell wasn't *Mrs.* Teague. And speaking of compromising positions... Got a call from Jude."

"Did our man talk?"

"According to Jude, he... Wait, let me get the accent right." He clears his throat and makes his eyes go wide and crazy in a scarily accurate approximation of our beloved enforcer. "You wouldn't believe it, Augs. Who doesn't like roasted nuts? I'll tell you who. This fucking twat. Five seconds under the blowtorch and he was singing like a pretty little songbird. Only not that pretty, on account of me gouging out his fucking eyes with a melon baller."

"Your impersonation is getting quite good."

He beams. "I've been practicing."

"Great. That's just what the world needs. *Two* fucking Judes." I shut down my computer and hit the lights, then we head to the window and climb out onto the ledge, dropping our human glamours. "I asked Jude to leave him alive. Any chance he obeyed?"

"You know you can't leave him unsupervised in the basement, Drae." Augustine laughs. "Kid in a fucking candy store. I'm just hoping he hasn't given poor West any more severed body parts as a token of his undying affection."

"Don't count it." I take a deep breath of crisp autumn air, glad for the chance to clear my head on the flight upstate. "Let's go."

Wings outstretched, we leap from the ledge and soar out over the city, bound for home.

CHAPTER THIRTY-FOUR

WESTLYN

I don't think. I just run.

Up the basement stairs, across the first floor from one end of the manor to the other, then back again, totally uncertain. I start to head upstairs to the bedrooms, but that's no good. Where am I supposed to hide? The closet? Under the bed? Those are the first places he'll look.

Fuck. *Fuck!*

Adrenaline and desire buzz through my nerves in alternating currents, electric tingles zipping through me from head to toe. The look in Jude's eyes was just... feral. No other word for it. I should be fucking terrified. I *am* fucking terrified.

And I've never been so turned on in my life.

But some latent sense of self-preservation has me frantically searching for a safe haven, and I finally end up in the study. There's an old cedar storage trunk behind the leather sofa, empty but for a few blankets and a bunch of Draegan's old architecture magazines.

Perfect.

As quietly as I can, I slip inside, gently closing the lid and covering myself with the blankets. Taking a deep, cedar-scented breath, I shut my eyes and—

Footsteps on the hardwoods, the unmistakable click of gargoyle talons.

Closer and closer they come, one deliberately slow step at a time.

I can hear every move he makes—pacing the perimeter of the room, stopping to toss a log on the fire, then crossing to the patio doors that look out across the orchard.

And then, silence.

I don't know how much time passes—five minutes? Ten?

I strain to listen, but there's nothing but the crackling fire.

Has he grown bored with the game? Or is he trying to—

Firelight suddenly floods my hiding spot as he wrenches open the lid and tears the blankets from my body.

"Lookie, lookie what we've got here," he says, eyes flashing. Before I can draw another breath, he hauls me out of the trunk so fast it tips onto its side, then shoves me back against the wall, one hand wrapped around my throat, the other digging into my hip.

I'm trembling in his hold, heart pounding in my chest, my core flooding with molten heat.

Jude inhales deeply, his gaze dark with a mix of predatory hunger and pure animal lust.

"I probably should've warned you the game is rigged." His grin is wicked, fangs gleaming like knives in the firelight as he lowers his mouth to mine. In a dark whisper, he says, "I can smell your sweet little cunt clear across the house."

I gasp, but there's no time to suck in another breath before he crashes into me, his mouth punishing in its relentless attack. His tongue thrusts between my lips, forcing my mouth open as he licks and bites and claims what he wants.

He tastes like smoke and sin and my darkest, wildest desires—all the ones I've been so afraid to admit, finally shoved into the light.

And I let him. I let him take, and take, and *take* until I can't fucking breathe.

And still, the monster wants more.

Lifting me up, he yanks off my shorts and panties, then shoves two massive fingers inside me, thrusting hard and deep, stretching me wider and wider until...

Oh, fuck.

His muscular tail slides between my thighs, teasing my clit before dipping inside me without warning, replacing his demanding fingers.

A shudder of pleasure ripples through my body as he drives his tail in deeper, then drags it out again, in and out, in and out, those thick, hard ridges rubbing all the right places, the curved tip brushing against my G-spot until he's got me panting and weak and out of my fucking *mind* with lust.

"Do you like that, darling?" he whispers, fangs scraping against my neck. "Fucking my tail?"

"Goddess, yes." It feels amazing, every stroke sending tingles racing across my scalp and down my spine, my core on fire for him.

"That's it, scarecrow. Use me. Show me how you get yourself off."

His words unravel me, and I rock my hips, pushing against his relentless thrusts, chasing that wave as it rises inside me, higher and higher as he plunges deeper, shifting the angle so it glides against my clit with every thrust, and then...

I gasp, and Jude seals his mouth over mine, stealing my scream as the wave finally crests and breaks and tosses me into a spiral of endless pleasure, again and again and again as my body clenches around his tail and I completely shatter.

I'm not even through the final aftershocks when he drags his tail out of me and drops his loincloth, giving me an unobstructed view of his fully nude form for the first time.

His cock is massive, the hard, dark-gray length of him sleek and beautiful in the firelight, as smooth and perfect as the rest of his muscular physique.

But when I try to imagine that sleek, beautiful thing fitting inside me...

Goddess, help me...

"What's this?" Jude teases, noticing my shocked face. "Have I finally managed to scare my little scarecrow?"

"I just wasn't expecting it to be so... so..." I trail off, unable to find the right word. Big? Huge? Soul-shattering? None of them seem to do it justice.

"I told you what would happen if I found you," he warns, his tail slowly winding around his cock, giving it a long, even stroke that has me whimpering with desire all over again. "Are you telling me you're giving up on our little game already?"

"No," I breathe. "I just... No. I'm not giving up."

As crazy as it sounds, I trust him. He's fucking unhinged, but he's also sweet and protective and thoughtful, and deep down, I know he would never hurt me.

Maybe that makes me even more insane than Jude, but I don't care. For the first time in my life, I'm not ashamed of my desires. I'm not ashamed to ask for them, to take them, to let myself feel fucking amazing, no matter how dark or twisted someone else might find them.

If that makes me crazy? Fine. Call the men in the white coats, because just like my psychotic gargoyle, I'm going all in. Maybe for the first time in my life.

I slide my hands into his hair and wrap them around his horns, holding on for dear life. Then, in a wanton whisper I barely recognize, I say, "*Fuck* me, Jude Hendrix. Make it *hurt*."

He closes a hand around my throat again, the other

hitching my thigh up around his hip. With a primal grin that sends another instinctive bolt of fear shooting down my spine, he pushes the head of his cock between my thighs, teasing my entrance. Already it's stretching to accommodate him, hot and slick and pulsing with urgent need.

"Don't say I didn't warn you, darling," he breathes.

And this is the part where I learn Jude is *truly* a gargoyle of his word.

He's not gentle.

He's not slow.

He's not sweet.

He shoves inside me so fast it leaves me gasping for breath. One hard thrust, then another until he's fully buried, and he stills, resting his forehead against mine as a shudder wracks his body.

"Fuck," he hisses. "You feel... you feel too fucking good."

"Then why are you stopping?" I pant, unable to catch my breath.

Heat flares in his eyes, and he tightens his grip on my throat, his hips rocking against me as he fucks me harder, faster, deeper than I've ever been fucked before, stretching me beyond comprehension. Tears glaze my eyes, but it's the best kind of pain, a deeply satisfying burn that quickly gives way to pleasure, hot and all-encompassing as he delivers thrust after punishing thrust, my back slamming into the wall again and again, hair tumbling loose, his body on fire with the same unquenchable hunger that's burning through mine, two twin flames surging and glowing bright, consuming each other in a wild frenzy that doesn't end until I'm clenching around his cock and crying out his name and he's exploding inside me, letting loose a fierce roar that rattles my bones and marks my very soul.

Still rock-hard inside me, he brings his mouth to my ear, breath hot on my skin.

"*Mine*," he says again, just like that first night he pinned me in bed.

And this time, I say the word I wanted to say that night. The word I've known was true from the very first moment we laid eyes on each other in the park. "Yours."

CHAPTER THIRTY-FIVE
WESTLYN

When our ragged heartbeats finally return to normal, Jude releases my throat and slowly pulls out, a hot gush spilling out after him.

He meets my eyes again, all the earlier bloodlust and rage gone from his gaze, nothing but the clearest cobalt blue remaining. Through a soft smile, he says, "You all right, scarecrow?"

I nod and smile in return, not trusting my voice.

"Stay here," he says. "I'll be right back."

I do as he asks, closing my eyes and leaning back against the wall for balance as his release continues to leak down my thighs, just like he warned me it would.

Just like he promised.

He's back a moment later, kneeling before me and gently guiding my thighs apart. "Hands on my shoulders. I've got you."

I lean on him as he slides a warm washcloth between my legs and wipes away the mess. After a few more gentle strokes, he stops and presses his lips to the apex of my thighs.

A low moan of appreciation rumbles through his chest and shoulders, straight in to my palms.

"Darling," he practically growls. "Do you know how fucking sexy you are with my cum leaking out of you?"

I try to find the words to respond, but his mouth is so hot and silky and perfect, and then he's moaning again, soft kisses turning feverish as he buries his face deeper between my thighs and...

Holy fuck, how am I already so primed up for more?

Without protest, I slide my hands into his hair and grab on to his horns, a move that has him moaning for me all over again. His long, devilish tongue swirls around my clit, his breath a teasing mist as he licks a hot path to my entrance, then slips inside, fucking me all over again as he laps up the remaining evidence.

I'm so turned on right now, I can't see straight. My hands tighten around his horns, stroking them in time with his thrusts, every one of his delicious kisses soothing the burn of his earlier attack. His tail flicks against my backside, teasing the tight entrance as he continues his deep, erotic kiss. The twin sensations quickly whip me into another white-hot frenzy, and soon I'm gasping his name again, his tongue hitting that perfect spot inside me, and once again I'm gone.

A moment later, he gets to his feet, his eyes still dark with desire, his sexy smirk unleashing a flurry of sparks in my chest.

"Don't move," he says, grabbing the spent washcloth and disappearing again. It's several long minutes before he returns, and this time he's carrying a silver tea tray complete with a steaming teapot, two teacups, and a pile of cut fruit.

"What's all this?" I ask.

"I find tea to be the perfect accompaniment to a thoroughly excellent dicking. I hope you like peppermint, and also, what the hell is so funny?"

"You look like a butler. Well, if a butler had horns and wings and a huge gargoyle dick just dangling in the breeze."

"Gargoyles aren't ashamed of nudity." He sets the tray on a side table and gestures at the hoodie I'm still zipped up in. "You shouldn't be, either."

I cross my arms over my chest and back up against the wall. "I'm not."

"Then we're in agreement." Jude stalks toward me again, one graceful step at a time. When he reaches me, he crowds in close, fingers brushing along my zipper. "Tea tastes even better when you're naked—trust me."

"No, I'm... I'm cold."

"I'll warm you." He grabs the top of the zipper, and panic floods my gut in a hot rush.

Shorts are one thing, but this? No. This stays on. Always.

Twisting away from him, I force some lightness back into my tone and say, "Tell you what. I'll make you a deal."

"What makes you think you're in a position to negotiate, scarecrow?" He gives me his crooked smile, and I know I've already won him over.

"Here's my offer. The top stays on, but I'll keep the bottoms off. For *now*."

"You drive a hard bargain, darling, but I'll accept. For *now*."

He leads me to the sofa and draws me into his lap, his wings wrapping around me like a protective blanket. Pressing his lips to the top of my head, he murmurs, "And you're sleeping in my bed from now on, too."

"On the roof?"

"In the bedroom."

I reach for my tea and take a warm, comforting sip. "But you won't even be there."

"I'll be there until sunrise. And after that, I want my bed to smell like you. Yet another reason you won't be wearing bottoms for the foreseeable future." He trails a hand up my bare thigh, drawing lazy circles with the tips of his claws. I've seen those things shred fabric like it's a wet napkin, yet his touch is so gentle, it could put me to sleep.

I'm just starting to drift into a comfortable daze when the front door opens, announcing the return of the other three gargoyles.

And I'm sitting here half-naked on the fourth gargoyle's

lap, both of us very obviously, very thoroughly, very recently fucked.

I bolt upright so fast I nearly douse Jude in tea. "Where are my shorts?"

Jude reaches behind his back and yanks out my rumpled shorts and panties, then promptly tosses them into the fire.

"Jude!"

Flashing me the psychotic grin that's never far from his lips, he says, "I'll buy you new eggplant shorts, scarecrow, but a deal is a deal."

"This is *so* not fair."

He cocks his head. "What's that? Footsteps? Sounds like they're almost here. You've got a decision to make. Storm out of here with your bare arse out for all to see—and a fine arse it is, mind you—or stay here under the privacy of my wings and keep my cock warm."

"Those are both terrible choices."

"Not for me." He draws his wings tight, pulling me in closer.

"Fine." With a resigned sigh, I say, "But *don't* get any sicko ideas."

"When it comes to you, I've *always* got sicko ideas. Now stop squirming, or I might accidentally slip and end up inside you again." He arches his hips, the thick head of his cock sliding along my entrance.

I'm not sure I recognize the sound that comes out of my mouth. But before I can give myself over to another red-hot moment of debauchery, I hear Rook mumbling something to Draegan, and I know I've got mere seconds before they all burst in on the scene.

I'm trapped, nothing to do but sit back and enjoy the dirty, intoxicating warmth of the craziest gargoyle in the manor.

"Good girl," Jude whispers, nuzzling my ear as I relax into his hold. "Perhaps I'll reward you later with another thorough gargoyle dicking."

I lean my head back against his chest and sigh again, fairly certain I won't survive another one of *those*... yet counting down the hours until it happens again anyway.

"Look what the kitty cat dragged in," he says, his voice rumbling right through me as Draegan, Auggie, and Rook lope into the study. "About time you lot showed up. We were bored out of our skulls waiting for you."

CHAPTER THIRTY-SIX

ROOK

The entire room smells of fire and debauchery—Jude's signature scent.

"Bored?" Auggie laughs, taking in the full spectacle—furniture in disarray, a glass vase shattered on the floor, West sitting on Jude's lap with her hair a complete wreck and her cheeks bright pink, unable to make eye contact with the rest of us. "Is that what the kids are calling it now?"

"Well, what did you expect?" Jude presses a kiss to her neck, and the scent of her desire spikes. "We had to entertain ourselves *somehow*."

"Oh, for fuck's sake." Draegan heads for the bar and grabs a bottle, pouring himself a double. "I'm less interested in a report on your *entertainment* and more interested in what you learned from our recently deceased guest. So if you don't mind, kindly get on with it."

"Have a seat, gentleman," Jude replies. "And let me tell you a tale."

"Looks like Jude's songbird was telling the truth," I confirm, scrolling through the medical records I pulled up on my laptop after Jude filled us in about Hunter's alleged hospital visits. "Starting twenty-three years ago on October twenty-sixth, continuing all the way up until last month, Hunter was receiving regular in-patient treatments at New York's Garrison Medical Center."

"For what?" Draegan asks.

"It's hard to know for sure—they used a bunch of different codes to cover their tracks. Everything from kidney dialysis to collagen injections to bone grafts."

"Seems the old boy was falling apart," Jude says.

"No—that's what I mean. The codes are just random. Whatever treatments he was in for, I don't think they were sanctioned medical procedures."

"Then why do them in a hospital?" Auggie asks, setting another log on the dwindling fire. "What's the point?"

"Well, here's where it gets even more interesting." I tab over to another window. "I hacked into his health insurance records. The insurance company didn't pay for any of the treatments themselves, but they *did* cover localized anesthesia, blood transfusions, and prescriptions for painkillers, all of which were filled. So whatever the true reason for his hospital visits, he did seem to require some level of legit medical intervention."

"Every week for twenty-three years?" Draegan sips his drink, his brow furrowed. "And he never missed a treatment?"

"Not one. Not even when they fell on holidays—magical or mundane."

"Why would insurance cover the ancillaries but not the treatments themselves?" Auggie asks. "And even if it was some experimental or elective treatment, shouldn't there at least be a record of it on the claims, even if the insurance company ultimately denied coverage?"

"I've got copies of the original claims from the hospital here, as well as the EOB statements from the insurance breaking down all the costs. The hospital never even listed the treatment codes on the claims—they didn't even attempt to get coverage. My guess is they didn't want to submit fraudulent codes—it would raise too many red flags with the insurance company—but they wanted to submit *something* to legitimize the use of anesthesia and blood bags. Hospitals keep track of those sorts of things—they couldn't just steal them."

"Sounds like an awful lot of trouble to go to," Jude says. "What the fuck were they hiding?"

"A lot of trouble, sure," I say, closing the laptop. "But it worked. They had a good little scam going for more than twenty years."

"What about the doctors?" Drae asks. "Can we track them down?"

"Tried, but the trail went cold. None of the doctors or other personnel listed on the records and claims still work at Garrison. A few of them died, others retired or transferred. I'm trying to locate them, but no luck so far."

"What's got you so quiet all of a sudden, witchling?" Auggie takes a seat on the couch next to Jude and an unusually somber West, who hasn't said a word since I pulled up the records. Cupping her face, he says, "Seriously. You okay? Don't tell me you've got a hospital phobia."

She blinks at him, her eyes glassy and far away. "Garrison," she whispers.

"The hospital," I say. "That's the name of it. It's uptown, right off 96th Street."

"I know." She shivers in Jude's hold, and he tightens his wings around her. "I was born there, guys. Ask me what day."

Auggie cocks his head. "How old are you?"

"Twenty-two. I'll be twenty-three in a few weeks. On October twenty-fifth, to be exact."

"The day before Hunter's treatments began," I say.

"There's more." She closes her eyes. "Eloise used to work there. She was a pediatric nurse. Retired now, but she was there at that time. I only know that because she liked to rub it in my face that if she'd been on call the night I was born, she could've stopped me from killing my mother."

"What an *asshole*," Auggie says. "Seriously. What did your father see in her?"

West sighs. "I gave up trying to answer that question years ago."

"Her name wasn't in any of Hunter's files," I say. "Which makes sense—if she was in pediatrics, she'd have no reason to treat Hunter. He was nineteen when they started."

"But she *would* have access," West says. "We can't rule it out just because her name isn't on the file. It's too much of a coincidence."

"Yeah, I know." I've already got my laptop open again. "So now we've got your birth, your birthmother's death, a mage receiving mysterious treatments requiring blood transfusions, anesthesia, and painkillers who may or may not have already been harboring a demon by that time, and a pediatric nurse and shadow witch who—nearly twenty years later—went on to become your widowed father's second wife."

"If this was a TV show," she says, "I'd say here's where we've officially jumped the shark."

"So where do we go from here?" Draegan asks.

"Well, we're still working on cracking the Codex," I say. "Not much progress on that front yet. The good news is our wards are holding up—no signs of shadow mage attacks on the property or any of our networks."

Draegan swirls his drink and sighs. "Not sure how long we can count on that. The fire destroyed the Forsythes' library and most of the brownstone, but that doesn't mean

Lennon won't suspect the Codex was stolen. Once he puts two and two together—especially with Westlyn in the mix —I expect him to strike hard and fast."

"I'm not letting him anywhere *near* her," Jude says, resting his chin on the top of West's head. "Let him try, and then we'll see how well he can work his hocus-pocus with his own severed cock shoved up his arse."

"Aww! So romantic," West teases.

"If you think that's romantic," he says, that crazy gleam glazing his eyes, "wait till you see what I'm making for you out of Randall's kneecaps."

"Great," she deadpans. "I can't wait." She rolls her eyes and laughs again, but all too soon, her smile falters, a darkness gathering around her eyes. "All of this is connected—I'm sure of it."

"You and the hospital stuff?" Auggie asks.

"More than that. I'm talking about everything—you guys and the curse and the Codex too."

"What makes you say that?" Auggie asks.

"I don't know—just a gut feeling." She sits up a bit straighter and glances at each of us in turn. "The night of the wedding, when I saw Draegan and Auggie in the pews, I felt an immediate pull to them. Like a current, almost. It was the same thing I felt the first time I met Jude in Madison Square Park."

"I felt it too, scarecrow," Jude says. "We all did."

"Rook, the first night in the library, when we were trying

to connect the dots between Zorakkov and the artifacts in the Forsythes' collection? You said there could be links between their reasons for wanting the marriage, and your curse. You said I was brought into your lives for a reason, and we—"

"Owe it to ourselves to try and figure it out." I smile at her, remembering the conversation. Her too-big clothes. The birds. It was the night I vowed, in my own private way, to do everything in my power to protect her, just as the others promised.

"I don't know how Eloise, the Archmage, Hunter-slash-Zorakkov, and I all fit together yet," she continues, "but the fact that the Archmage bought the very Codex that holds the *one* spell you guys have been searching for your entire immortal lives... that can't be coincidence. That's simply another piece of the puzzle. We just don't know how all the pieces click together yet."

"We need more time," I say, glancing down at my laptop, still trying to make heads or tails of these odd records. "More data, more information, more demon lore, more... everything."

"Eloise," she says. "She's one of the missing links."

"As far as I know," I say, "she and your father are still on the west coast."

"I can call her," she says. "Get her talking. See if I can convince her to—"

The glass in Drae's hand shatters. "No. Absolutely out of the question."

West glances up at him, her eyes imploring. "It's just a phone call. No meetings this time, not even a video chat."

"Too risky." He shakes the glass and booze from his hand. "Phone calls can be traced."

"Not if Rook does his mojo with the re-router thing," she says. "Draegan, Eloise was there the night I was born. And the night Hunter started receiving treatments for some unknown—"

"Yes, Miss Avery, I was paying attention, thank you. I don't require a recap."

"But if you'll just let me—"

"The last time I quote-unquote just *let* you, you very nearly got yourself killed. So no, we will not be ringing up stepmum for a chat. End of discussion. Now if you'll excuse me, I've a call with the city planner's office to prepare for. Rook, keep digging into those hospital records. Augustine, check in with Mr. Teague and see if he's had a chance to review our proposal again—he may need a bit more encouragement."

"You got it," Auggie says.

Drae nods, already on his way out. "If anyone needs me, I'll be in my suite."

CHAPTER THIRTY-SEVEN

DRAEGAN

No matter how hard we work to break this curse, no matter what new avenues we explore, all roads seem to lead to the same disastrous outcome: Westlyn getting hurt.

Or worse.

I can't take another moment of standing here imagining what could've happened to her the other night had Jude and Augustine not gotten there in time. I *never* should've allowed her to meet with the Forsythes. It was an irresponsible and reckless mistake—*my* mistake—and she nearly paid for it with her life.

Leaving them to their work, I head into the kitchen to clear my head. We need a new game plan, and I can't bloody *think* when I'm around her.

I rummage through the pantry and unearth a vintage bottle of cognac I hid from the other heathens. Pouring a fresh glass, I take a deep breath, inhaling the sweet, pungent aroma.

But before I can even enjoy the first sip, the little mortal pads into the kitchen, refusing to give me a moment's peace.

"Um, Draegan?" Her sweet voice floats to my ears, chipping away at the wall I'm trying so desperately to keep in place. "Sorry to bug you, but... Got a sec?"

Fuck.

I take a single sip, then turn around to face her. Those bright, beautiful eyes. Black-and-silver hair hanging in long, messy waves that curl over her breasts. No wonder Jude had her all wrapped up—she's got nothing on but a hooded sweatshirt that scarcely even covers her thighs.

She's bare underneath it, the scent of her skin mingling with the scent of her desire—ample evidence of the trouble she and Jude got up to in our absence.

Bored out of their skulls, indeed.

Despite my best efforts, the thought has my cock stirring to life.

Stepping behind the counter to block her view, I bring the drink to my lips again and inhale deeply, hoping the pungent scent of the cognac will chase away the scent of this girl and all my *very* inappropriate, *very* depraved thoughts.

I wonder if she tastes as sweet as she smells...

"What is it, Miss Avery?" I ask, a little harsher than necessary.

"I wanted to talk to you about Eloise. If I could just—"

"It's a terrible idea and I've already said no. Please don't bring it up again."

She crosses her arms over her chest, disappointment and frustration swirling through her eyes. "You don't have to be so rude about it."

"If it's sugarcoating you're after, you'll have to seek it elsewhere."

"I'm not asking for sugarcoating. I'm just asking for you to give me a chance to share my ideas."

"I *did* give you a chance. Your suggestion wasn't sound, ergo, I rejected it."

"But you wouldn't even hear me out! You weren't listening to me, Draegan. You never do."

"Perhaps if you actually said something worth hearing once in a while, I *would* listen. Sadly, until that blessed event comes, here we are." It's a shit thing to say, but I need to shut this down before she gets any more ideas about putting herself in the line of fire. "Enjoy the rest of your evening, Miss Avery."

I turn and head for the stairs, but she's right on my heels again, relentless in her quest to *completely* fucking unravel me. I ignore her, swatting behind me with my tail as if she's a mosquito buzzing about, but she follows me up the stairs anyway. And down the long hallway. And all the way to the very last suite on the right.

My suite.

I grip the doorknob and turn to glance at her over my

shoulder. "This is my suite, Miss Avery. My *private* quarters."

"So?"

Unbelievable.

I rake my gaze down her bare legs, then back up. "So I appreciate the offer you're apparently making, but I don't need an escort tonight."

"An escort? Oh, you're hilarious, Draegan. Pure comedy gold right here, folks."

"Yes, well, as much as I'd love to stand here and regale you with my humor and wit, I really do have a call to prepare for, so if you don't mind—"

"By the *Morrigan*... What is your *deal?*"

I turn around and meet her indignant gaze full on.

"*Go. Away,*" I demand, but it's clear she's not backing down an inch. Turquoise eyes flashing up at me, hands propped on her hips, chest heaving... This five-and-a-half-foot sprite is seriously ready to go toe-to-toe with an immortal beast who could crush her in the time it takes to finish a sneeze.

I wonder how feisty she'd be if I put her on her hands and knees and made her crawl...

I'm damn near ready to grab her by the throat, throw her down on the bed, and teach her a *very* important lesson about trifling with a pissed-off gargoyle when she huffs out another indignant breath and says, "I'm not going *anywhere* until you tell me your deal."

"My *deal*, Miss Avery, is that the gargoyles in this house

—in this entire region—are my responsibility. It was difficult enough looking after them before you crashed into our lives and turned everything upside down, but now? Now I've got the added burden of keeping *you* safe and alive as well. A responsibility I gladly took on in service of our deal, yet you *insist* on making it harder for me by—"

"What? How is *that* fair? I'm—"

"At every turn, you're undermining me. Pushing boundaries, refusing to listen to reason, outright disobeying my orders and—"

"Orders?" She laughs. "I didn't realize I was signing up to live under a dictatorship."

"That's hardly what this is. I never said—"

"Oh, and you *love* it, don't you? Always being the one in charge, always in control like some kind of authoritarian king of old dominating his subjects and—"

"King of..." I scoff and close my eyes, desperately trying to rein in my temper. She's got me hanging on by a thread. "Sorry. I've got better things to do than serve as the proving ground for your authority issues and myriad psychological problems. Please find someone else to infuriate." I turn away and head into my bedroom, but the little mortal won't take no for an answer.

"Psychological problems? Are you kidding me?" She stalks across my room and follows me straight into the master bathroom, no sense of boundaries, no shame. "You know what? Just because you're the old man of the group doesn't mean you have to act like everyone's father."

"And just because you're the little girl doesn't mean *you* have to act like a petulant child."

"Whatever you say, *Daddy Drae*." She rolls her eyes, exactly proving my point, but...

Fuck.

A shock of desire shoots through my balls at her words. One word, in particular, and again I'm picturing her on her hands and knees, crawling for me. Crawling right into my lap, her ripe arse in my hands, her firm breasts brushing my chest as she slides her hands up around my horns and *begs* me...

Let me come, Daddy. Please...

"The sooner we can break this curse and I can get away from *you*," she snaps, "the better."

Anger flares in my chest, and I cling to it, grateful to have something to focus on other than what her smart little mouth is doing to my cock.

"*Believe* me," I grind out, "the feeling is mutual. *More* than mutual. More mutual than... than the sun, the moon, and the stars."

"What? That doesn't even make any sense! Rook would say you're undermining your communications by overcomplicating your similes and—"

"If my communications are too complicated for you to follow, allow me to simplify." I jab my finger in the direction of the exit. "*Leave*. Now."

She hops up on my bathroom vanity and folds her arms

across her chest, stopping just short of sticking out her tongue. "Make me."

Oh, I could very much make you...

I stalk toward her and grab the edge of the vanity, bracketing her small frame with my arms, shoving myself between her legs, my face so close to hers I can see every swirl of green and blue in her irises. The scent of her bare pussy has me damn near out of my mind with lust, my muscles trembling with the effort of holding back.

One more inch. One more inch and I could claim her so fast, she wouldn't even know what hit her...

"Behave like a brat," I whisper, "and perhaps you'll get spanked."

"Behave like a monster, and perhaps *you'll* get put in a cage."

"You think you know what a monster is?" My voice is low and dangerous, my wings rippling with barely contained fury. I don't know what she sees in my eyes, but it's clear she knows she's gone too far this time. Her mouth clamps shut, her eyes widening, pulse thrumming wildly beneath the pale skin of her neck.

I wrap a clawed hand around her throat and trace a delicate line up her neck with my thumb, making her tremble—a thing that's dangerously close to becoming one of my *favorite* new pastimes. "Be very, *very* mindful of how you speak to me, little mortal. My rope only extends so far, and once you reach the end of it, you will *not* like what you find there."

"I... I'm sorry," she whispers.

"No, not yet. But push me again, and you will be." I haul her off the vanity, throw her over my shoulder, and dump her unceremoniously in the hallway, slamming the bedroom door in her face.

Alone in the shower later, tail wrapped tight around my aching cock, it takes me a full hour to fuck the little brat out of my system.

CHAPTER THIRTY-EIGHT

WESTLYN

"I see we're still in hiding." Auggie takes a seat on the couch across from me in the library and smirks, his warm hazel eyes sparkling. "It won't help, you know. He can scent you. All of us can."

"Thanks for the hot tip." I roll my eyes and promptly return my attention to my current read—Gargoyles, Grotesques, and Chimeras: A Spiritual and Architectural History. "Anyway. If by *he* you're referring to the grump formerly known as Daddy Drae, then yes. I'm hiding from him."

"*Formerly* known? What's his current name?"

"*Dickhead* Drae. Alternately, he-who-kicked-me-out-of-his-room-last-night-and-dumped-me-on-my-ass-like-he-was-taking-out-the-trash Drae, but that one's more of a mouthful."

"You should know better than to push his buttons."

"But it's so fun."

"Yes, just like juggling knives. Fun... until it isn't." Auggie nods at my book. "Learn anything interesting?"

"Actually, I did! You're not really a gargoyle."

"No?" He laughs, his cute dimple flashing. "Well, that's a relief. When do I lose the wings and tail?"

"Real gargoyles," I continue, "have water spouts. Technically, you guys are called grotesques, which is fitting, don't you agree?"

"Are you seriously witch-splaining gargoyle anatomy to me?" He shakes his head. "Give a girl a book, and watch out, world."

Laughing, I shut the gargoyle book and set it aside. "I just needed a break from all the dark fae lore and that stupid Codex. Rook and I have been working on it for two nights straight, but it still won't open."

I stand and head to the library table behind me, where the cursed book has been sitting since Rook and Drae brought it home. With the barest brush, I trail my fingertips across the cover, unleashing a ripple of dark purple light that sends a jolt of pain shooting up my arm.

"Fuck," Auggie says. "Does that happen every time?"

I shake out my tingling hand. "Yep. Rook thinks he can build something to disarm it, so to speak, but we're not there yet. He's trying to find more info on the Cerridwen witches that translated the original dark fae work."

I return to my chair and close my eyes, the expected post-book-touching migraine pulling into the station right on schedule. I press my fingertips to my temples, trying not to wince.

"You okay, witchling?"

"Just another side effect of the book. The headache thing doesn't happen to Rook, thankfully, but... *Goddess*, it feels like... like someone's trying to split open my skull and dig through my thoughts."

"West, you don't have to do this," he says, his tone suddenly serious. Gentle, even. "You've already risked so much."

I open my eyes and shake my head, trying to ignore the jackhammering in my skull. "I can deal with a little zippety-zap and few lousy headaches if it means getting us closer to breaking the curse."

He holds my gaze for a long moment, the skin between his brows creased, his eyes full of a deep and endless ache whose origins I can only begin to guess at.

But then, just as quickly as it arrived, the vulnerability washes back out to sea, and his dazzling, teasing smile slides back into place. "Lucky for you, I've got *just* the thing for a migraine."

"Oh, I *bet* you do." I crack up. "Does that line actually work on people?"

"Come *here*, witchling." His voice is deep and commanding, those disarming hazel eyes glittering with mischief as he grabs a throw pillow and places it in his lap. Then, tapping it lightly, "Don't be difficult."

"I've told you a million times, that's like telling the sun

not to rise."

"Somehow, I think *that* would be an easier feat. Now stop fighting me for once and come here. Unless, of course, you *enjoy* that headache chipping away at your brain, in which case—"

"Oh, fine. Twist my arm." Powerless to resist his charms, I leave the safety of my cozy little chair and stretch out on the couch, resting my head on the pillow.

"That's it," he murmurs, gently running his fingers through my hair. "Close your eyes and relax, and your favorite, most handsome, most devoted gargoyle will take care of the rest."

I do as he asks, letting out a deep sigh as he continues his soft ministrations, alternating between stroking my hair and massaging my temples with light, tingling touches. It's not long before the pain melts away, leaving ripples of pure pleasure in its wake. There's no hiding his effect on me; my entire body erupts in goosebumps.

However, there's also no hiding my effect on him. Beneath my head, a hard bulge presses urgently against the pillow.

"Does that feel good, witchling?" he says, his voice like liquid honey. "Or am I being too hard on you?"

"No, it's... it's perfect."

"*You're* perfect," he whispers, so softly I'm not sure he even meant to say it at all.

His fingers stop their slow circling, and when I open my

eyes, I find him staring down at me, that ancient pain flooding his eyes once more.

I sit up beside him and take his hand into my lap, running my thumb across his dark palm.

"Auggie, will you tell me what happened?" I ask. "How you guys became gargoyles, I mean? If it's too personal, I get it. I just... I know you're in pain. All of you. And you've got this curse to contend with and I'm never quite sure if I should ask about it or just—"

"Westlyn..." My name is a heavy sigh on his lips, and he closes his eyes, his hand curling around mine. I'm starting to think maybe I shouldn't have brought it up, maybe I pushed it too far this time, but then he says, "It's not personal like a secret I don't want to share or don't *trust* you enough to share. It's more like..." He opens his eyes and looks at me again, releasing my hand to tuck a stray lock of hair behind my ear. With a sad smile, he says, "Stories are bridges, West. That's how I think of them, anyway. Once you know someone's stories—the deepest, darkest ones that rock us to the core and shape who we become—you're connected to that person in a way you can't undo. Even if you have a falling out, even if you never speak again after that moment, you'll always have that piece of them."

A tear slips down my cheek. I know exactly what he means, which is probably why I've never told my stories, either. Not the deepest, darkest ones. The ones that still burn a fresh path through my heart every time I remember them. Every time they haunt my nightmares.

"You don't have to say anything," I say, tracing my fingertips along his jaw. "I understand."

"No, you don't. I want you to, though—I truly do." Then, with another heartbreaking smile and a soft sigh, "but this isn't just my story to tell. It's all of ours. And I... I can't right now. I just can't."

"It's okay." I smile through the ache in my chest, because he needs to see that smile. He needs to know I'm on their side, no matter what. "Whenever you're ready—if that night ever comes—I'm here. And if not, that's okay too. It doesn't change the fact that I'm going to do everything in my power to help you break this curse."

He slides his hand around the back of my neck and draws me close, touching his forehead to mine. I breathe in his clean, masculine scent, like the air after a deep and cleansing rain, and a shiver snakes down my spine.

Kiss me, Augustine Lamont.

The thought tumbles through my mind—a wish unspoken, but nevertheless real. Memories of that all-too-brief maple syrup kiss in the kitchen bob to the surface, unleashing a flood of molten heat in my core. I realize it the moment he scents me; his nostrils flare, and he draws back to look at me, eyes darkening with desire.

Heat.

Need.

He still has the throw pillow in his lap, and now he tosses it aside, his hungry gaze never leaving mine.

"Come here," he rasps, and this time the command carries a sharp, desperate edge.

I climb into his lap, straddling him.

My yoga shorts are nearly as flimsy as the panties underneath, and he shoves them aside easily, his fingers sliding inside me with practiced ease.

"Fuck," he hisses, pumping me with slow, deliberate strokes. "You're already so wet for me, witchling. So eager."

I let out a soft moan. He feels so good. So amazing.

But it's not enough.

I want more.

I *need* more.

I slide my hands into his hair, raking my nails over his scalp, slowly making my way to his horns.

He shudders at my every touch, his thumb ghosting over my clit as his fingers curl inside me, but... no. I'm not ready to come for him yet.

For once, I want to take charge. I want to make the gargoyle come for *me*.

With a wicked grin, I wriggle out of his hold and drop to my knees in front of him, my hands gripping his muscular thighs and sliding upward, pushing aside his loincloth to reveal his stiff cock. It bobs invitingly before me, velvety gray like his skin, streaked with veins of darker gray running down the length, thick and heavy with a slight curve at the tip that already has me fantasizing about how it would feel buried inside me.

I wrap both hands around it, stroking him once, twice,

then dragging my tongue up along the underside, swirling over the tip. Auggie growls, sliding his hand into my hair and fisting it tight, his head lolling back against the couch. "You're... you're killing me, witchling. Fucking *killing* me."

Just like Jude's, Auggie's cock is impossibly large. There's no way I can take it all the way into my mouth, so I suck on the head, stroking his shaft with both hands, putting a gentle pressure on the underside as my thumbs run and up and down the length.

Goddess, he tastes so good. So rich and smooth. His hands tighten in my hair, and he guides my head into a slow rhythm as I continue to lick and suck and tease and stroke, coaxing deep groans of pleasure from my gargoyle until he's thrusting up from the couch, fucking me deeper, harder. I can't take all of him at once, but he doesn't seem to care that he's slipping in and out of my mouth, sliding across my lips, my chin, wet and sloppy and so fucking hot it's all I can do not to reach a hand down my pants and touch myself.

"Westlyn, *fuck*... That's it. Right there. *Right* fucking there..." He grips my hair so hard it makes my eyes water, and I give the head of his cock one more swirl with my tongue, then stretch my lips over it and suck, stroking him hard and fast with both hands, flicking him with the tip of my tongue, and then...

"Fucking *hell*!" He comes in a furious rush that hits the back of my throat and fills my mouth, and I swallow every red-hot pulse, every drop.

He finally releases his grip on my hair, and I rock back

on my heels, gazing up at him with wide eyes and what I'm sure are pink, puffy lips.

With a dimpled smile that melts my heart, he leans forward and runs his thumb along my lower lip. "You constantly surprise me, witchling."

"Honestly? I surprise myself too." I laugh. "I can't believe I just did that. I've never... was that... was it all right?"

A deep, rich laugh rumbles up through his chest, and he leans forward and gathers me into his arms, standing up and throwing me over his shoulder.

Before I can even utter a single protest, he says, "I can't even tell you how fucking amazing that felt, witchling. But I let you have *your* fun. Now it's my turn." He stalks across the library toward the barn door. "And *my* fun involves throwing you down and fucking you the way I've been *dreaming* about fucking you every goddamn night since I first saw you in that lacy black dress."

"You... You've wanted me since the wedding?" I breathe.

His laugh rumbles through me. "You're all I can think about, West."

"Where are we going?"

"Rook will be back from the city soon, ready to hit the books again. So unless you want him studying *us*, I'm taking you up to my suite."

CHAPTER THIRTY-NINE

JUDE

Apparently, Auggie and my little scarecrow were so eager to get to the good part, they didn't even bother undressing all the way. She's still got her sweatshirt on, but her thighs are bare, his talons gripping them tight as she rides him in a slow, seductive dance.

She's a fucking vision, her soft moans floating on the air, silver moonlight caressing the black hair spilling down her back, sheets half torn from the bed as her hips circle, drawing him deeper and deeper inside...

Rook and I just got home from a visit to the fire inspector with Drae—team effort, this one. Turns out the old guy's a real stickler for policy and procedure, and that simply won't do.

Cost the poor bastard a finger—my handiwork—and a live demo of one of his illegal offshore bank accounts being drained—Rook's—but we finally sorted out our differences about the Forsythe blaze.

Official cause? Faulty electrical. You've got to be careful with those old brownstones. And a library full of old books? Fucking tinderbox, that.

Anyway, that's all settled now. Drae's still in the city, and Rook's got his nose buried in the fae books again, and Lucinda and Huxley aren't that great at conversation, so here I am, stalking my scarecrow just like old times.

She's been with us a couple weeks now, and I've missed this. Missed watching her from the shadows. Fantasizing about her.

It's so fucking mesmerizing it's almost a shame to interrupt. If Rook were up here, that bastard wouldn't utter a sound. He'd just lurk in the darkness and keep watching, undoubtedly taking a few notes. Our resident spymaster never misses a beat.

Me? I've got no such restraint. Also, they're making me hard as fuck.

"I hope you're filming this," I call out, crossing my arms over my chest and leaning against the doorframe of Auggie's suite. "Be a shame to deprive the world of such a monumental artistic achievement."

Westlyn lets out a gasp and tries to reach for the sheet twisted up behind her, but there's no hiding from me now.

"Don't stop on my account," I say, heading into the room. "I rather enjoy a good plot twist. Although, I should've seen this particular twist coming. Kitchen countertop episode? Nice bit of foreshadowing, that."

Augustine sits up and hooks his hands around her shoulders, grinding hard into her sweet little cunt, drawing her attention back to him. I can't see his face from here, but I can imagine the look he's giving me.

"Join us or leave us, Jude," he finally growls. "This isn't a free show."

"Joining you sounds like a delight, but..." I approach the bed, my cock already growing harder at the idea. Westlyn looks up at me, her eyes bright, cheeks flushed with the same heat undoubtedly spreading between her thighs.

The scent of her... *Fuck*.

Gripping her chin, I tip her face toward me and claim her mouth in a bruising kiss. When I finally pull back, I whisper, "What does my little scarecrow have to say about that idea?"

She bites her lower lip, puffy and pink, just how I like it. Then, with a shy little smile, she nods. "But I've never... I don't know how to—"

"It's okay, witchling," Auggie cups her face and smiles. Hell, he's always been the charmer of the operation, but I don't think I've ever seen his eyes so full of sincerity. Of longing. "We've got you," he whispers, guiding her into another slow roll. "We've got you."

I catch his eye, and he nods.

That's all the confirmation I need.

Shedding my loincloth, I climb onto the bed behind West-lyn, kneeling between Auggie's outstretched legs and taking a moment to appreciate the view of our girl's perfect backside. The soft round curves of her arse swivel and dip as she finds her rhythm again, and I follow every movement, utterly entranced.

Gathering her hair in my fist, I run the tip of my tongue up the back of her neck, making her mewl and arch like a kitten.

With my free hand, I slide my middle finger across her lips, then shove it into her mouth. "Suck."

She does as I command, always so eager to please.

"So you've never been shared before?" I whisper, leaning in to nibble on her earlobe.

She mutters a "no" around my finger, and I shove it in deeper, fucking her wet little mouth while the tip of my tail slides between her cheeks, gently teasing her arsehole.

"And what about this?" I ask, pushing in the tip just enough to make her squirm. "Has anyone ever taken you here, scarecrow?"

She lets out a moan and shakes her head—another confirmation of the sweet innocence that radiates off her like a fucking beacon.

I remove my wet finger from her mouth and push it into her puckered hole, right up to the first knuckle. "Do you *want* to be taken here?"

A soft little gasp is all the answer I get.

"Tell me," I say. "Tell me what you want your gargoyles to do to you tonight."

"I... I want you inside me," she breathes, her hips rolling. Beneath her, Auggie grunts, his hands tightening around her thighs.

"How badly?" I whisper.

"I... I want it. I *need* it, Jude. Please."

"I just want to make sure you know what you're getting into, darling. Because if you want us both inside you—*really* inside you—here's how it's going to happen." I kiss her neck, then drag my mouth back to her ear, nipping the delicate lobe once more. Sliding my finger deeper into her arsehole, I whisper, "First, we're going to make you come on Augustine's cock. Then, before you've even caught your breath, I'm going to pound this tight little hole until you come all over again, *just* for me. Understand?"

"Goddess, yes," she pants. "Please. Please don't stop."

Leaning over her shoulder, I catch Auggie's gaze again. He knows exactly what I'm looking for.

"Nightstand," he says. "Second drawer, blue glass jar."

I lean over and open the drawer, revealing a variety of toys and the blue jar he mentioned.

Can't help the laugh that rumbles through me at the sight of it all.

"You're a real fucking boy scout, Augustine. Prepared for any occasion. Have I ever told you how much I appreciate that about you?"

"I'm not sure we've had an occasion quite like this before."

"No, now that you mention it." I twist off the lid and

scoop out a bit of the goopy stuff inside, letting it warm on my fingers. "We have not. But, as the saying goes, first time for everything."

I slide the lube between her cheeks and lean in close once more. "Do you remember your code phrase from the other night?"

"Hot waffles?" she whispers. "But that's—"

"Danger is danger, darling. So that's the thing you say if you need us to stop. Let me hear it again."

"Hot waffles," she says.

"Good girl." Slowly, I push one finger in—deeper than before—then another, giving her a few gentle strokes. She's tensing up, though. Scared.

"Relax," I say, easing back out, then in.

Auggie cups her face again, sitting up a bit so they're eye level. "Breathe, witchling. Just breathe."

She nods and lets out a breath.

"That's it," he says. "Deep breaths. Nice and slow."

She follows the cadence of his breathing, her body slowly relaxing around my fingers as I push in deeper, stretching her with each stroke as she rides Auggie's cock, losing herself to the pleasure once more.

Fuck, she's so fucking tight, and every time he rocks in deeper, her body constricts, pulsing hot around my fingers, and bloody hell... I need it to *not* be my fingers. I need it with a fiery desperation that has me damn near roaring inside.

"Are you ready for me, darling?" I remove my fingers and

stroke the lube over my cock, then press the tip to her entrance.

"Relax," Auggie says again, and she lets out a deep sigh, turning to look at me over her shoulder.

"I'm ready, Jude. Please."

I slide into her, doing my best to take it slow, but between the warm lube and her sweet, eager little moans, all I want to do is let loose and fucking *rail* this woman. I don't, though. Just continue to ease my way in, one intensely euphoric inch at a time.

She lets out a sharp gasp as I finally bury myself fully, and fucking *hell* she feels so good. So tight. So *perfect* with Auggie's cock stroking her from the other side, his tail curling up to brush against her clit, every wave of her pleasure reverberating through my balls.

"Do you need to use your words?" I whisper.

"No. I'm... I'm okay. Just... getting used to it."

I pull out a bit and give her another moment to adjust, then thrust in again, and again, and soon she's rocking back to meet my every stroke, her gasps turning into moans as her two gargoyles fuck her harder, deeper.

"You're such a good girl, darling," I whisper. "Taking us both at the same time like this."

"So fucking good," Auggie says, tightening his grip on her hips as he guides her to pick up the pace once more. "That's it, witchling. Just like... *fuck*. Just like that."

She leans forward and grips his horns, then takes

control, riding him harder. Taking him in deeper. Arching that sweet arse for more of my cock.

Our naughty little vixen.

I follow her lead, grinding into her from behind, deeper and harder with every thrust, and I know she's getting close.

We all are.

Her heartbeat kicks up, sweat trickling down the back of her neck, and soon she's right fucking there.

Sliding my tail around to join with Auggie's, I rub her clit, both of us teasing and stroking, bringing her to the very edge.

"Show us how much you love taking your gargoyles together," I command. "Come on Auggie's cock, just like I told you."

We increase the joint pressure on her clit, and she gasps again, then cries out, rocking against him, her body convulsing around us as she comes hard and fast.

I wait until the aftershocks fade, then start thrusting again, fucking her hard, driving her right back to the brink. Heat gathers in my balls, and I can sense Auggie's ready too, both of us panting and thrusting, hungry and desperate...

"Come for me," I growl, fisting her hair and gripping her hip and slamming into her once, twice, three more times. "Come with my cock in your arse, buried to the *fucking* hilt."

She shatters for me, trembling with the force of it, setting off a chain reaction that none of us can stop.

"*Fuuuuck.*" It's all I can manage as the pleasure finally grips me, and Auggie and I let loose at the same time, coming inside her in a hot, messy rush, wave after wave after wave, until all three of us are utterly spent.

We collapse on the bed in a tangle of arms and legs and wings and tails, the perfect little scarecrow sandwich, and Westlyn lets out a yawn that ends in an adorable squeak that sends my protective instincts into overdrive.

I brush a soft kiss to her cheek, and she turns toward me and smiles, and... fuck. My heart twists into a big old knot at the sight of her. She's fierce and soft and beautiful and too fucking perfect to be part of our world—this brutal, terrifying place of dark fae curses and demons and death.

She doesn't *belong* here.

Yet here is where she is. In our home. In our bed. In our arms.

Under our protection.

And I haven't felt this content in...

Ever.

I drape a wing over them both, silently renewing my vow to do whatever it fucking takes to keep her safe—to keep *all* of us safe—come what may.

"We should hit the shower," I finally say, stifling a yawn. "I'm starting to feel a bit sticky."

"I don't want to move," she says. "Besides, I like being dirty."

Auggie laughs. "And I'm sure I speak for everyone involved when I say we *love* you being dirty, but... Jude's right. You'll feel better with a bit of hot water and soap before you crash for the day. No one likes to wake up with their legs stuck together."

I smack her arse. "Or their—"

"Thank you, Jude," Auggie says. "We get the idea."

A tired laugh bubbles out of her, quickly turning into another squeaky yawn, and holy *fuck* she's wrapping me tighter around her finger with every passing hour.

"Fine, you win," she says. "But I'm going first, before you jerks use up all the hot water. And someone needs to carry me. My legs are Jell-O."

I rise from the bed and hold out my arms. "I've got you. Come here."

She gets to her knees and loops her arms around my neck, and I slide a hand beneath the hem of her sweatshirt, skimming my palm up across her lower back, but then—

"Hot waffles!" she practically shouts, jerking away from me and clutching the bottom of her sweatshirt as if my touch burned her. "I mean... sorry. I just... I'm a little... It's... personal. Please. I'm sorry."

The panic in her eyes sets my heart rate skyrocketing for all the wrong reasons.

Now, I want nothing more than to hit the rewind button and take back the last thirty seconds.

But it's too late.

I've already felt the scars.

"Come here," I say again, softer this time. "Please."

I wait for her to use her words again, but she doesn't. Just closes her eyes, then finally nods, turning around and grabbing the zipper.

With a shuddering breath, she unzips it, tooth by agonizing tooth, slowly revealing her bare shoulders to me, then the smooth skin of her middle back, and then she drops her arms to her sides and the sweatshirt falls away and I see it, gouged into her lower back in jagged, horrible slashes, pale as the moonlight against her skin.

WICKED

I brush my knuckles across the word, a soft touch that's at complete odds with the war raging inside me, and Westlyn—my fierce, beautiful scarecrow, flinches.

When I speak again, I barely recognize my own voice through the fury. "Who. The fuck. *Did this to you?*"

Thank you so much for reading Wicked Conjuring! Our fiercely protective gargoyles are just getting warmed up, and we've got plenty of twists, turns, and red hot nights to come as they work together to unravel the mystery of Westlyn's past and the tragedy of the gargoyle curse.

Westlyn and the boys are waiting for you in Wicked Awakening, book two of the Claimed by Gargoyles series.

But first... How would you like a little more of that hot, lovable psychopath otherwise known as Jude Hendrix?

Sign up for my newsletter and you'll receive A Gargoyle Obsessed, a free story that takes place the night Jude first meets his sweet little scarecrow in the park. This story is available in both ebook and audiobook formats (narrated by Shane East!) and can't be found anywhere else—it's an exclusive gift just for my subscribers.

Visit SarahPiperBooks.com/jude to claim your copy.

MORE BOOKS FROM SARAH PIPER!

In the mood for more Reverse Harem romance?

THE WITCH'S REBELS is a reverse harem series featuring five smoldering-hot guys and the kickass witch they'd kill to protect (yes, you may be sensing a theme here)! If you like dark magic, sexy, forbidden romance, and heart-pounding supernatural thrills, this witchy adventure will leave you spellbound!

TAROT ACADEMY is a university-aged reverse harem paranormal academy romance starring four seriously hot mages and one badass witch. Dark prophecies, unique Tarot mythology, steamy romance (of course!), and plenty of supernatural suspense make this series a must-read!

Craving some naughty vampires instead?

Get bitten by the
VAMPIRE ROYALS OF NEW YORK!

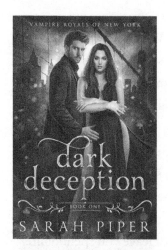

DARK DECEPTION kicks off Dorian and Charlotte's story, a scorching vampire romance trilogy featuring a dirty-talking vampire king reluctant to take the throne after his father's demise and the seductive thief who might just bring him to ruin... or become his eternal salvation.

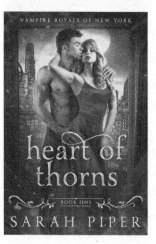

HEART OF THORNS is the first in Gabriel and Jacinda's series, a trilogy starring an ice-cold vampire prince and the witch he's captured from his enemy—the only person who can break his family's blood curse. Gabriel is Dorian's youngest brother, and his story picks up right where Dorian's ends.

ABOUT SARAH PIPER

Sarah Piper is a witchy, Tarot-card-slinging paranormal romance and urban fantasy author. Through her signature brew of dark magic, heart-pounding suspense, and steamy romance, Sarah promises a sexy, supernatural escape into a world where the magic is real, the monsters are sinfully hot, and the witches always get their magically-ever-afters.

Readers have dubbed her work "super sexy," "imaginative and original," "off-the-walls good," and "delightfully wicked in the best ways," a quote Sarah hopes will appear on her tombstone.

Originally from New York, Sarah now makes her home in northern Colorado with her husband (though that changes frequently) (the location, not the husband), where she spends her days sleeping like a vampire and her nights writing books, casting spells, gazing at the moon, playing with her ever-expanding collection of Tarot cards, binge-watching Supernatural (Team Dean!), and obsessing over the best way to brew a cup of tea.

You can find her online at SarahPiperBooks.com, on TikTok at @sarahpiperbooks, and in her Facebook readers group at Sarah Piper's Sassy Witches! If you're sassy, or if you need a little *more* sass in your life, or if you need more Dean Winchester gifs in your life (who doesn't?), come hang out!

Made in the USA
Monee, IL
25 June 2024

60460229R00194